# Strong Stuff

## A. F. Stone

*SRL Publishing Ltd*

SRL Publishing Ltd
Office 47396, PO Box 6945
London
W1A 6US

First published worldwide by SRL Publishing in 2021

ISBN: 978-191633738-1

*For Oliver*

# CHAPTER 1

Vvvvvvvv.

Ruby felt the phone vibrate and prayed the teacher hadn't heard it. She held her breath. *15:18*. Mrs. Henderson shot a knowing look in her direction. Ruby watched the crumpled bags around her eyes, the lipstick bleeding through the skin round her mouth. *Come on, we're both tired.* She willed her to let it drop. *I can't get detention today. Not today.*

The teacher looked at the clock. Ruby watched the hands. *Twenty seconds. Come on.* She gripped the edge of the plastic seat.

The bell rang out.

'Right, get off,' Mrs Henderson said, sighing. Ruby shut her eyes and exhaled.

Kids scrambled for the door. The Friday ritual of getting away from school as fast as possible began. The familiar end-of-the-week smell steamed off the crowd. Tatty blazers that smelt of damp cupboards, sweat from shirts and sports socks, mildewed rucksacks, body spray, aftershave, pencil sharpenings and sugar-sour breath.

*Go the back way. Takes longer, but it's quieter.* She read the text that nearly got her a detention.

**Mum:** *Did u get my tenna at lunchtime? Come home ASAP,*
*nurse coming 2night not 2moro x*

Ruby walked faster. *Shit. Tonight was my cleaning night!*

She thought about the pots stacked up in the sink,
the bin wedged open with ready-meal trays, the pile of
washing sat in the front room armchair. She imagined the
nurse raising her eyebrows and making notes.

*If I can just get there ten minutes before her, I can make it*
*look alright…but what if she wants to go upstairs?*

She turned the corner and slammed straight into
Katrina Wood.

'Why don't you look where you're going, twat?'
Katrina spat down at her, pushing her against the wall.
Ruby's rucksack fell to the floor. She tried to walk away
but Katrina caged her in, one hand planted on the wall at
each side of Ruby.

'I said, why don't you look where you're going,
shortarse spaz?' Katrina sneered, narrowing her eyes.
Ruby ducked under Katrina's arm and started to run, but
her stomach jolted and she stopped, turning back.

*Shit, she's got my bag!*

Katrina and her friends were already rifling through
the contents. Ruby made a grab for the rucksack, but it
was too late.

Katrina's eyes widened. Her mouth dropped open.
Kids walking past stopped to stare. They knew
something good was about to happen.

Everyone who passed by clocked the pantomime
horror and delight on Katrina's face. They knew it must
be worth hanging back for. All Ruby could do was stare.
Her stomach knotted. She felt her face flush and her
hands shake. *There's nothing you can do.*

'Katrina don't, please –' stammered Ruby.
She tried to control the pressure willing her to burst into

tears, rising behind her eyes, nose, up her throat. It was useless. The tears welled up. She tried to hold them back, blink them away.

'Oh. My. God. Now I know why she smells so bad...' Katrina announced to the grinning crowd. She reached inside the bag and pulled out the packet.

'She pisses herself all the time and has to use TENA LADY!!!'

Katrina brandished the blue and green plastic packet, shining under the corridor strip lights. Ruby watched the reaction of the faces in the crowd, gasping and shrieking with laughter.

Katrina began quoting from the packet.

'Tena Lady Extra Plus...'

Tears streaked Ruby's cheeks as she grabbed her rucksack back. Katrina let it go. She had what she needed. All Ruby wanted to do was to run home, but she knew her mum needed the pads. She couldn't leave anything to chance with the nurse coming to do her assessment.

'Superior absorption for peace of mind!' Katrina continued to read from the packet, holding it aloft so everyone could see. Ruby looked at them. They laughed in her face. She could hear snatches of what they were saying: *No way! Oh my god, that's so gross!*

She told herself, *this isn't happening. It's not real.* It was, though, and she knew she had to do something about it.

'They're not mine okay, just give them back!' Ruby managed to squeak. The crowd roared. Katrina looked down at her, smirking.

'Why? If they're not yours, then you don't need them back, do you?' Katrina's eyes were fierce.

Ruby felt the back of her head hit the wall as Katrina's hand gripped Ruby's shoulder and pinned her against it.

'Do you?' Katrina shouted.

'Careful Trina!' said one of the boys, 'you might catch the pissing disease!'

They were face to face now, so close Ruby could see flakes of mascara on Katrina's cheekbone.

'Say it,' Katrina hissed, 'say: I need my Tena Lady because I can't stop pissing myself like an old dog!'

It seemed to happen in slow motion. The fear in her stomach shot to her limbs, making her move. She felt her fist lunge into Katrina's stomach, harder than she had ever hit anything in her life. Katrina fell, like a puppet with its strings all cut at once. She dropped the pads. They spun across the lino floor. Ruby snatched them up and ran.

She glanced back to see Katrina staggering to her feet, holding her stomach, gasping. The crowd stared after her, stunned. Ruby turned and carried on running.

\*\*\*

Ruby ran all the way back. Fast. Faster than she ran in her dreams. Faster even than in her nightmares. She didn't look back.

The grey concrete treadmill pounded away under her feet until finally it stopped. She was home, the end terrace with the overgrown yard round the side. The one with the Japanese knotweed that annoyed the neighbours. Ruby caught sight of herself in the neighbour's car window.

*Jesus. Best go in the back way. Mum will be in the front room. Make a brew and straighten yourself up.*

'Hi mum!' she shouted through.

'Hi love,' her mum shouted, then coughed.

*I wish that cough would go away. It's been there ages.*

'Did you get my text?' her mum called through.

4

'Yep. Got them,' she said, leaning her forehead against the wall, adding, 'wasn't easy.'

'Oh I know. That pharmacy is bloody useless. You're a star.'

Ruby smiled to herself.

Her phone buzzed. *Three missed calls from Annabelle.* She swore under her breath. *You forgot about her.* She opened Snapchat.

*'WTF just happened?'* appeared over a selfie of Annabelle. She had masses of crimped brown hair, black thick-rimmed glasses and perfectly sprinkled freckles on each cheek. The photo was of her, stood at the school gates, with an exaggerated shoulder shrug and upturned hand. It disappeared.

Ruby closed her eyes, took a deep breath and called her back.

'Ruby?'

'I'm so sorry, I had to –'

'I heard what happened, are you okay?'

'I'm fine,' she lied, 'you're not still there, are you?'

'No, don't be daft. I saw you run up the road. I shouted but you were like some kind of possessed cheetah. I'm at home. Do you want me to come over?'

'No, the nurse is doing her home visit, but thank you. I'd better go. Got shitloads of cleaning to do.'

She made two cups of tea and carried them in to the living room. Her mum was struggling to change the channel, coughing.

Ruby liked to remember how her mum used to get dressed up for nights out. A little black dress, smoky eyes and her sleek bob. *So beautiful.*

Lisa was wearing what she always wore, now. Joggers and an old jumper. She couldn't blow-dry her hair or put make-up on any more. Her eyes always had dark shadows under them. She was so much thinner than before she got ill, yet her body seemed to weigh her down. *Skinny and slumped.*

Ruby wanted to ask her about the illness.

*What does it feel like? Are you scared? Are you angry? What will happen when -*

But she couldn't. She wouldn't.

Every time she started to ask, the change in her mum's face was unbearable. She looked as though the question had hurt her, physically, weakened her. As though it was a pain that was always there, dull and throbbing in the back of her head, the bottom of her stomach. Ruby's questions, even just when she sensed they were coming, gripped and twisted that pain. She couldn't do that to her.

'Ruby,' her mum coughed, patting her chest, then continued, 'what the hell has happened to you? You look awful!'

Lisa was staring at her sweat patches and half-loose ponytail.

'Oh, erm, it was P.E. last thing...forgot my kit. Had to play in this,' Ruby said, looking down at her shirt. Lisa rolled her eyes.

'Clean yourself up before the nurse comes.'

Ruby gave the downstairs of the house the best five-minute makeover she could manage and went upstairs to have a shower and find something presentable to wear.

Lingering in the doorway of her bedroom, she sighed and smiled. It was still the pink paradise it had been since she was seven years old. Most of the time she was frustrated that they couldn't afford to redecorate it, but sometimes, times like this, she loved it.

She lay on her back on the pink quilt and took in the security blanket surroundings, staring at the aertex ceiling. Ruby remembered choosing the pink daisy paper, candy floss colour curtains and fluffy rug with her mum. Her dad did the decorating. She remembered him up the ladder, singing *Sledgehammer* by Peter Gabriel, and trying to blow the smoke from his cigarette out of the window. That was her last memory of him before he left.

In the bathroom, she caught sight of her reflection in the mirror as she stepped into the shower and winced. She thought of Annabelle's D-cup boobs and looked at her own in dismay. Since Harv Macintyre called her an ironing board, she had wished every night to wake up in the morning with something more. It hadn't happened.

*No boobs. Mousey hair. Plain face.* She hated the way she looked. She tried not to think about it.

In the shower, she tried to imagine how she could face school on Monday. *Katrina is going to murder you. Actually murder you. Don't think about it now. You have to get through this visit. You can add it to the list. The massive list.*

Last time the nurse came, she told her to write down a list of the things that she was worried about. Then write down why they worried her. Work out the things she couldn't control, the things she could. Focus on the things she could control. The things she could do something about. The list was the same, still, except now she could add *being killed by Katrina.*

*I'm worried I've lost all my friends,* the list began, *except Annabelle. They've all stopped asking me to do things, because I can never do them. Sometimes I don't have the money, like for cinema or Meadowhall. Sometimes I can't leave mum, like for sleepovers. I can't control that. Annabelle is the only one who still puts up with it. Still hangs around with me at school. Still asks me over, when I can make it. But I worry it's just because she feels sorry for me. I don't want anyone to feel sorry for me. I don't want anyone to feel sorry for mum, either.*

*I worry about what will happen to mum. She doesn't talk to me about it, but I've Googled it. I know what will happen. She's going to get worse, then she's going to die. Mum doesn't want anyone feeling sorry for her, either, so she doesn't have any help, yet. She says she'll need it, soon, but for now we're okay. I don't want help. I help her in and out of bed. I help her with the stair-lift. The wheelchair. The shower. I don't want a stranger doing those things for her. But mum says soon, they'll have to. I can't control that. I worry about what will happen, after.*

Underneath, a new paragraph started *'I can control...'* but there was nothing she could think of. She told herself she would add to it, but the space was still blank.

She stepped out of the shower and looked at the mirror. It had clouded up with steam. On impulse, she walked over and drew with her fingertip in the steam: *You can control how you react. You are strong.*

Stepping back, she shook her head. *You can't. You're not.* Ruby stuffed a towel into her mouth and screamed, letting tears fall and melt into the fabric while she sobbed.

# CHAPTER 2

*A Place in the Sun* was on the TV. The nurse sat and politely drank the tea, even though she didn't take sugar and Ruby had put it in by mistake. She finished the last of her notes.

'I still don't like that cough. We'll try the different antibiotics. If that doesn't get on top of it, we might be looking at an admission,' the nurse said, clicking the top of her pen closed.

'Stay in hospital? No, don't be daft, Sarah. I've got the nebuliser here. I'm fine. Really, it doesn't bother me.' Lisa stifled her hacking.

'Only for a few days, Lisa. Just to get it gone, for good. Then you'll be back home. Anyway, like I say, we'll try these first.'

As she packed her kit away, she asked Ruby how things were.

'They're fine,' Lisa answered, 'we're great aren't we?' she said, smiling at Ruby.

'You're doing great, Lisa, but I just wanted to make sure things aren't getting on top of Ruby.'

*Crap. This place isn't tidy enough.*

She looked around the room, finding all the things that were out of place and berating herself for not noticing it. *Magazine on the floor. Curtains not tied back, coffee rings on the table.*

'I know you don't want to go to the young carers' group, Ruby, but I don't understand why. Please have a think about it. People have fought so hard to get the funding for it and we're being cut to the bone, we're so lucky to have it –'

'Sarah, it's not her fault that –' Lisa interrupted, but broke off, coughing.

'No, I'm sorry,' Sarah said, shaking her head, 'I didn't mean to come over like that. It's just been a long day. A long week. What I mean is,' she said, clasping her hands together, 'you're not alone, you know? You don't have to be. And it's not just the group. Between me and the social, there are a lot of things we can do to help you know, Ruby. We can send people to help you around the house. Or with shopping, bathing, anything,' she said.

Ruby felt herself blushing. *Even mum isn't clean enough. And she must have looked in the fridge.* She pictured its lonely contents – margarine and milk. She didn't want to go to the group because she was scared of hearing about how things were for other people like her, in case they were worse. She didn't want to know what was around the corner. *Besides, you're not one of them. You're fine.*

'Honestly, we don't need any help. Thanks, but we don't want it,' Ruby said.

'I know it will happen, Sarah,' Lisa said, 'but we're not there, just yet. Not yet.'

The three of them fell silent. On the TV, a couple paced around a villa and wandered out onto a sunny veranda, looking out over a hillside.

'Alright for some, isn't it!' Lisa said.

Sarah nodded, getting up to leave.

'It is. My sister lives out there. Always been jealous,' Sarah said, packing away her things. 'Mind you, they can't get baked beans. Funny, the things you miss. Anyway. I'll see you next week, okay?'

She gave a little wave then turned to Ruby, offering her one of the bags.

'Could you help me carry this out?'

Ruby followed her with the bag.

'I mean it,' the nurse said, quietly, at the front door, 'your mum is very ill and she might get much worse, very quickly. You'll need help soon. Honestly. There's no shame in it, Ruby, you're not superhuman. You can't do everything. You're still at school. You have exams. You do too much. That's what we're here for.'

The nurse looked at Ruby, searching her face. Ruby was about to speak, but knew she'd start crying if she did, so she nodded instead. Sarah rubbed Ruby's shoulder and spoke quietly, almost in a whisper:

'Think about it, won't you?'

\*\*\*

The bed was soaked with sweat. Ruby wiped the tears from her face with the duvet and turned on the lamp. The sweat cooled quickly, making her shiver. She huddled back into the dampness.

'It's just a dream,' she said out loud, under the cover, 'a dream.'

She had the same nightmare nearly every night:

They're on a ward at the Northern General. Ruby sits by her mum's bed. The doctors stand around them, discussing her miracle recovery. Lisa is better. She looks young again, happy, animated. The weakness is gone, she's sitting up, telling a story, pointing, throwing her head back in laughter, hugging her knees, excited.

Ruby beams. Somehow her mum is better, and she's coming home, and everything is back to normal. 'Go and get the kettle on, Ruby-Roo, I'll be back as soon as they've finished.'

Immediately Ruby is back at Marlborough Road, fumbling to find the lock on their front door in the dark.

*I'll make a brew. We can have a chippy tea to celebrate! Mum can go back to work at Gio's now, we can have a chippy tea every Friday, just like before!*

Just as she gets the key inside the lock she has a flashback. The doctors in the hospital weren't doctors. She could see them now, gathered round her mum's bed. They were just random people, evil people, who want to hurt her mum.

They start to close in, her mum screams *'Ruby! Help!'* and suddenly Ruby is running to the hospital, running over rooftops and through canals and on top of cars but the hospital never gets any closer. The cold air stings the back of her throat and her feet are bleeding. She keeps running towards the towering hospital but she never gets closer, every step she takes is replaced by the stretching horizon- 'RUBY!'

She wakes up, crying, drenched in sweat, every time. This time was like any other.

Ruby looked at the daisies on her walls and tried to think about something that would make her smile. Nothing came. She drew back the curtain and took in the black cold outside. The view was of endless roofs and backyards, all the same. Silhouetted two-up two-downs as far as she could see, narrow steep roads peppered with orange streetlights, sprawling down the hill into blackness. It all looked like it was being drawn down in a landslide, ready to wash away into the night. Ruby breathed a cloud on the window and drew a smiling face with her finger. She wiped it away.

Her head hurt. In the bathroom, she read the message on the mirror. She still didn't believe it, but she hoped maybe her mum would see it and believe it, of herself. Ruby looked in the cabinet for painkillers. *Can't have Mum's. Way too strong.*

On the landing, she heard Lisa's radio on. Her mum never seemed to sleep properly, day or night, but the nights were the worst. She struggled to breathe.

Ruby knocked on her door and opened it.

'Mum? Are you okay?'

'Ruby, you shouldn't be up at this time love, it's half three in the morning.'

'I couldn't sleep. Well, I had a bad dream. And – I just wanted to say, I would tell you if I needed help, I would. But I don't. Not yet.'

She saw tears begin to well in Lisa's eyes.

'Shit,' Ruby said, sitting on the bed, 'I'm sorry, I didn't mean to-'

'You do, Ruby,' she managed, between coughing and crying, 'I should've said yes. You shouldn't have to look after me. First thing tomorrow, I'm ringing her.'

'I don't do anything that you wouldn't do for me –'

'- that's the point, Ruby,' Lisa said, wiping the tears from her cheek, 'I'm supposed to do things for you. I'm your mum. And I know you'd do anything for me, but I don't want you to. Not anymore. It's gone on too long.'

Ruby knew when to argue, and when to let it go. She stayed quiet, biting her nails.

'I'm sorry, I didn't mean to snap,' Lisa said, 'look, I need to talk to you, love.' She managed to sit up, refusing Ruby's offer of help.

'We might get some help in the short term, but I'm going to be very ill very soon, and you won't be able to look after me.'

Lisa took a deep breath, then coughed. Ruby winced inside at the rasping. *It sounds so painful.*

'I don't want you to have to look after me. You already do too much as it is. It's no life for a fourteen-

13

year-old.'

The tears glimmering in her mum's eyes were too much for Ruby. She crawled up the bed and curled into her mum's side, sobbing.

She felt stupid, like a five-year-old crying after grazing a knee. She hadn't cried in front of her mum for a long time. They gripped each other, both trying to slow the sobs. They managed to calm the crying, both breathing slowly and carefully, between Lisa's coughs. They stayed silent for a while, until Lisa finally spoke again.

'We need to talk about what will happen to you when I'm gone, Ruby.'

Ruby didn't want to talk about it, but she listened.

'You know how I feel about your father. He wasn't cut out for being a dad. Or a husband, for that matter. But when I'm gone, he's all you'll have. And I know that deep down, he is a good man.'

*You don't believe that. I don't believe that.* She sat up, wiping her pyjama sleeve over her face.

'Mum, we don't even know where he is. He moves all the time. He won't want me around. Why can't I carry on living here? You know I can look after myself. You *know* I can.'

'It's not that simple, Ruby,' Lisa said, shaking her head.

'Couldn't I live with Auntie Carla? She likes me-'

'Listen, sweetheart. None of this has anything to do with people liking you. Everyone likes you. We love you. Your Auntie loves you to bits. But she's going through a really tough time at the moment. Besides, she doesn't have space. It's a two-bed flat, there's six of them.'

'Alright,' Ruby ventured, '...What about Cal?' As soon as the words left her mouth, she wished she could stuff them back in.

'It's late, Ruby, so I'm going to ignore that you said that. You know he's the last person on Earth who can look after you. Cal's still inside. He won't get out for another year.'

She fixed Ruby's eyes. 'And when he does come out, I don't want you going anywhere near him. He's your brother and I know you remember him as the kid he used to be, but he's a man now, with a lot of problems that I don't want you getting involved with. Understood?' She squeezed her hand. 'Promise me.'

'I promise. I'm sorry mum. I get it,' she said, but she didn't.

'Ruby, you can't live here alone. No-one except your Dad even comes close to being able to look after you. I don't know, maybe he can't… but I don't want you to go into care. Do you see what I'm saying, Ruby?'

*She looks exhausted. Tell her what she wants to hear.*

'I know mum, I'll do it, I promise, I'll do anything you want. I promise.'

'Thank you. I love you so much.'

Ruby shut her eyes and cuddled back into her mum's side. She wanted to stay like that for hours, just like she did when she was little. Ruby fell asleep in the damp patch of her tears, with a hint of a smile. She dreamed she was six years old again, sitting with her mum in the park, counting daisies.

\*\*\*

Ruby woke to the sound of a man, laughing. She jolted, looking around, then realised it was the radio. She looked at the time. 8:15.

'Mum?' she asked, wincing at the laboured sound of her breathing. Lisa shifted, but didn't open her eyes. Her hair was matted to her forehead and neck with sweat.

Ruby sat up.

'Mum, are you okay?'

Lisa murmured, flickering her eyes.

*Shit.*

'Mum,' she repeated, grabbing her shoulder and shaking it. Nothing. She put her hand on her forehead and snapped it back in reflex at the heat.

*Breathe* she told herself, *breathe. She needs you to keep calm.*

'999, what's your emergency?' the voice on the other end of the phone said.

'My mum,' Ruby faltered, watching Lisa's chest rise and fall, 'she's breathing but I think she's really ill – she's not moving or speaking or reacting – she has MND but she's got a chest infection and the nurse –'

'Okay, give me your address, sweetheart, you're doing really well…'

\*\*\*

*Her breathing sounds a bit better. Just a bit. Her eyes are open.*

Ruby was trying to comfort herself, sitting beside the bed, holding her mum's hand. She had an oxygen mask and lots of wires hooked up to her. Now and then she tried to talk, but couldn't.

'Don't, mum. It's fine. We're at the Northern. They're taking care of you. It's your chest, they said. They said you'll be fine,' she lied, squeezing her mum's hand. She hoped her mum hadn't been awake when the doctor said it was sepsis and they were doing everything they could. *They never said she'd be fine.*

Every time Lisa closed her eyes, Ruby's eyes tracked to the heart monitor, just in case. She watched it now, as her mum fell back to sleep. *Sleep. Delirium. Coma. Stop it.* The monitor kept beeping, at the same rate. She had no idea how long they'd been there for. Her phone was dead. There were no windows within sight. It could be any time, day or night.

'Ruby?' the nurse asked, gently.

'Hm?' she turned, still holding Lisa's hand.

'Your friend is here, Annabelle? She can't come on to the ward but you can go and see her in the area outside if you'd like?'

Ruby shook her head, looking back at Lisa.

'You're allowed to have a break, Ruby. I'll be here, with her.'

She hesitated.

'Go on. It's fine, honestly.'

She placed her mum's hand down and stood up, her vision swimming slightly. *Okay. Five minutes.* As soon as she saw Annabelle, she started crying. Annabelle ran over and hugged her. They didn't say anything at first. Ruby sobbed into her shoulder and Annabelle rubbed her back.

'Sorry,' Ruby said, pulling away, calming her breathing, 'I'm just so worried about her.'

'Don't apologise. Look, I brought you some stuff, here.'

Ruby took the carrier bag.

'Your phone charger. Well, not *your* phone charger but one that will work for your phone. Snacks. Juice. Sweets. I went a bit overboard with the sugar. Magazines. Puzzle book. I didn't know how long you'd be here, so…'

Ruby smiled and hugged her again, managing to thank her before the tears came back.

'Anyway,' said Annabelle, 'I can stay as long as you'd like, or I can go, it's up to you. I didn't know if you'd rather have company or not. Dad's just sat in the car but he's happy, listening to a podcast about chess, so there's no rush.'

'Thanks, Annabelle. I just want to get back to Mum, if that's okay – I don't like her being on her own. Thank you so much for this stuff. I'll message you.'

On her way back down the corridor, Ruby found herself running. As she turned the corner she saw the nurse, writing on a chart, and her mum, with the monitor still beeping. She exhaled. The nurse looked up.

'Did she bring you provisions?' she asked, pointing at the bag, smiling.

'Yeah. Is she…?' Ruby asked, looking at Lisa, not knowing how to finish the sentence.

'…the same,' the nurse offered, 'she's got a lot of work to do to fight the infection, but she's in the best place possible. Do you want a cup of tea?'

'Yes, please.'

Ruby took up her bedside position again, holding her mum's hand. She felt so tired. Her eyes were heavy. Sore. There was a sick feeling she couldn't shake, though, that made her edgy. It was the same feeling she had in her dream, when she realises her mum is in trouble and she has to save her. But this was real, and she was right next to her, and there was nothing she could do to help.

'Ruby, sweetheart?' the nurse appeared with her cup of tea and placed it on the bedside table.

'Thank you.'

'Ruby, there's a visitor, for you both, but if you're tired –'

'Who is it?'

'Your dad, I think. Gareth Morton?'

The sick feeling started to overwhelm her. She felt sweat start to dampen her top.

'No. I don't want to see him.'

'Okay, I'll –'

'How does he know we're here? We've not seen him for years, I don't understand why he's here…'

18

Ruby suddenly felt thirsty stood up to grab the plastic cup of tea. It was still too hot. Her face flushed. Pins and needles started in her arms and hands. Her breathing was too fast. *Don't let it get away from you.*

'He's listed as your mum's next of kin, sweet. We had to contact him. Are you okay? Ruby, sit back down,' the nurse coaxed her, gently getting her back to her seat, 'look, breathe with me, okay? In… out. In… out. In through your nose, out through your mouth.'

Ruby copied, resting her arms on the bedrail so she could lean her forehead on them. The nurse rubbed her back.

'Don't panic, okay? You don't have to see him. I can tell him she can't have visitors, alright?'

Ruby nodded, still focussing on her breathing.

# CHAPTER 3

Message from Annabelle:
*So I wasn't sure whether to tell you or not but I met your dad on the way out, he was asking at the ward reception where Lisa Morton was. I must have been staring at him because he asked me if I'd just been to see you. He gave me his number, to give to you. But then when I was getting in the car I saw him being escorted out by security. Don't know what happened. Did you see him? Xxx*

Ruby flicked off her phone screen. *Jesus Christ.*
     Another message.

*p.s. Jade and I are still doing Taron Egerton night tomorrow. I know it's a long shot but if you're back home or you need a break, it'd be lovely to have you with us xxx*

Ruby replied:
*I'm so sorry about my dad. I didn't see him. Thank you. I think I'll still be here, or I'll be looking after her at home, but thank you*
                                             *xxx*

'Why don't you try to get some sleep?' the nurse asked.
     'I don't want to leave her.'
     'Is there anyone who can come and be with her for a while, while you go home for a rest?'

*Home. It's not home without mum there.*

'No, not really. Her sister might want to come, but she's got four kids and two of them are young. Her neighbour sometimes watches them if her shifts clash with school. Maybe in the week, when they're not there. If we're still here by then?'

The nurse nodded, looking at Lisa. Ruby waited for an answer.

'Do you think we will be?' she asked.

'I can't say, my love. We just don't know. If it looks like she'll be in for a few nights, though, we'll have to get something sorted for you. You have to sleep, eat, see daylight, sometime.'

Ruby squeezed Lisa's hand, looking at her eyelashes, willing her eyes to open. They stayed closed.

'Tell you what,' the nurse said, 'I'll bring one of the big comfy chairs from the Day-Room and get some blankets. Put the curtain across and switch that light above her bed off. You can try to get a bit of rest then, but you're still here with her. How does that sound?'

Ruby nodded, smiling faintly. She didn't want to say thank you, because she knew if she spoke, she'd cry again.

\*\*\*

In the nest of blankets, Ruby closed her eyes and tried to think of nice things. *Gio's*. She missed Gio. She closed her eyes and went back there, two years ago, when she was twelve, nearly thirteen, and her mum still worked in the café.

'Buon giorno!'

'Hi Gio,' Ruby said, smiling at him as she put her school bag on the coffee counter. 'Where's mum?'

She peered behind him into the kitchen but all she

could see was the side of a stainless-steel fridge and the rota, with her mum's name down every day.

'Ah-ah,' he waved his finger, 'Italiano.'

Ruby squinted up to the ceiling. Gio raised his shaggy eyebrows in expectation, creating a concertina of deep grooves up to his wire-wool hairline.

'...duv... d-ov-ay...mamma?' Ruby searched his eyes for some hint of recognition. The whites of his eyes had a yellow tinge, like pages in an old book. The pupils were hard to distinguish from the irises, but she could just about see a ring of espresso splash surrounding the black.

'Si,' he replied, 'she's on her break. Hot chocolate, while you wait?' He began bustling behind the counter with milk and a silver foil bag of chocolate curls.

'Nah. Can I have an Americano?' she asked.

He stopped, looking at her sideways, frowning. 'Very strong. Intense. You sure?'

Ruby nodded. 'Si. Grazie.' She tossed her hand extravagantly. It always made him laugh.

He let out a wheezy chuckle and made the drink.

She sat down with her mug and watched the door. The café was quiet. She checked her notifications. *Nothing.*

'Ruby?' her mum said as she pushed the glass door into the café. 'I didn't realise you were meeting me here, I've still got two hours, you know?' Her eyes flicked to the clock, then back at Ruby.

'I know, I forgot my key. Anyway, I thought I'd do my homework while I'm waiting.'

Her mum paused.

'Is that an Americano? You're twelve. You'll be bouncing off the walls.' She sighed. 'Fine. Get your work done while you're on a high, then.'

She smiled and put her apron on as she headed

round the counter. Ruby heard her swear under her breath and she fiddled with the strings behind her back.

'Shit. Ruby, can you?' She backed up to her table, holding out the strings. Ruby tied the bow.

'Thanks love. Gio?'

He looked up from the biscotti basket he was carefully arranging.

Ruby watched her mum nod towards the kitchen and mouth '*can I have a word?*' then glanced back at her. She looked down at her phone.

'Ruby, keep an eye on things here ah? If anyone wants serving, shout me,' Gio said, following Lisa into the kitchen. Ruby nodded.

*What does she want to tell him?* She headed behind the counter, watching the only customer scroll down their iPad. She leaned towards the doorway. Ruby could hear her mum's voice, faintly.

'I just don't know how to tell her. She's so young. It's just her and me, y'know?'

She heard her mum's voice crack and a stifled sob.

'Shhhh. It's okay,' soothed Gio, 'it might not be that bad.'

'Gio, they can't tell me how long I have. Could be six years, could be six months. Not being able to tie my apron is one thing. Not being able to, to…'

Her voice descended into steady, quiet sobbing. It was muffled. Ruby knew she'd be hugging Gio. She grabbed the worktop to steady herself. Her stomach felt as though it was lurching up her throat.

'Excuse me?' A man standing in front of the till, looking at the menu behind her. She looked at him and loosened her grip on the side.

'A macchiato to go please,' the man said, answering his mobile.

Gio emerged from the kitchen, answering the man,

Sorry sir. We –' he turned and started. 'Ruby! How long have you been there?'

Nothing was ever the same again. *You were supposed to be thinking of happy things, Ruby.* Happy things. She opened her eyes and saw her mum shifting. Ruby sat up, leaning across to see her better.

'Mum?'

Lisa coughed, opening her eyes. She looked at Ruby and smiled.

'Are you okay?' Ruby asked.

Lisa shook her head, slowly, gripping Ruby's hand.

'Do you want me to call someone?'

She shook her head again, closing her eyes. Ruby watched the monitor. *No change.*

'They said you need to fight the infection. You need to rest, to do it. Try to sleep, okay?'

Lisa squeezed Ruby's hand again and dipped her head down, slightly, then back up, a slow nod of agreement.

'I'll sleep while you sleep, mum. We'll both get some rest, then we'll be back home soon.'

She left her hand holding Lisa's, her arm stretched across from the chair to the bed as she reclined back, pulling the blankets over herself with her free hand.

Ruby slept, but she didn't dream. She thought it was barely sleep, so light she was aware of everything going on around her, but she was wrong. She woke to see someone running to her mum's bed. Another person was already stood there. The monitor was beeping differently. Someone hit a button on the wall and an alarm started. Ruby turned to see the nurse, reaching for her hand.

'Ruby, sweetheart, we need you to come away for a bit, we have to treat your mum. Come on. I'll bring your stuff.'

She pulled her hand away. Ruby couldn't see her

mum's face, behind the people stood around the bedside. They were messing with wires, needles, tubes. Someone was reading numbers from the monitors.

'Mum?' Ruby asked, straining to see.

'Come on, Ruby, you need to leave,' the nurse said, pulling her away, 'let them do what they need to do.'

She followed, feeling as though she wasn't really there, as though she was watching herself in a nightmare.

***

They made her sit in *The Family Room*. She couldn't sit, though. She paced up and down, checked her phone, bit her nails, plaited and unplaited the laces from her hoodie. The door opened. She knew, instantly. The woman moved too slowly, too carefully. There was something in her eyes. *Fear.* Still, Ruby waited for her to speak.

'I'm Ange, the Family Liaison Officer,' the woman said, gesturing for Ruby to sit down. Ruby didn't move.

'I'm so sorry to tell you, Ruby, your mum has passed away. They did everything they could, but it wasn't enough.'

Ruby stared at her.

'Sit down, love. Come on,' the woman put her hand on Ruby's shoulder. She stumbled backwards and fell back into a chair. The woman was still holding her shoulder. She was talking, but Ruby couldn't hear her. She could see the woman was rubbing her arm, but she couldn't feel it. *This isn't real. It's not happening. It's a dream. It's just a different version of your dream. Wake up.*

She felt a stab of pain and looked down, realising she was pinching her own hand, digging her nails in. She swallowed. The tears were real. She felt them glide down.

'Can I see her?' she managed to ask. Her voice didn't sound right. Nothing sounded right. It all sounded as though she was underwater.

'Of course you can. I'm so sorry, Ruby.'

'I wasn't there,' she found herself saying, as she walked behind Ange, back to the ward, 'I wasn't there.'

Nobody heard her.

'I'll leave you with her. Take as long as you need. I'll be in the Family Room, okay? You just come find me when you're ready.'

*Ready for what?*

Ange drew back the curtain for her, then pulled it to, behind her.

Ruby made a sound, a strange sound she'd never heard before, when she saw her. She couldn't help it. She stifled her sobs with her hand, taking two steps towards the bed. Lisa's eyes were closed. She thought she'd just look as though she was asleep. She didn't. She wasn't her, any more, already. She'd lost her.

*You're alone.*

# CHAPTER 4

Ruby re-tuned in to what Ange was saying.

'Again, I'm here for you to talk to. Somebody from Social Services will be coming to see you, too, love. She's called Madge. I'm sorry you've had to wait. Is there anything you want to ask me?'

Ruby shook her head and looked at her phone.

'Well, I'll leave you to it, but Madge should be here any minute, okay?'

Ange left. Ruby checked her phone again. She still hadn't told Annabelle. She couldn't face it. *13:34.*

She could smell Anais Anais. *Carla.* She looked up.

Her auntie was there, arms outstretched, face crumpled, mascara streaked.

She felt her face smush into Carla's jumper and her ribcage shrink under the squeeze of the hug.

Carla was mumbling through sobs, but Ruby couldn't make out the words. She shut her eyes.

'Ruby?' The voice came from just behind them, soft and cautious.

Carla let her go. They turned. A woman with short, spiky hair and dangly earrings stood in the doorway, fiddling with the buttons on her cardigan.

'I'm Madge, your -' she paused, 'I'm from Social Services.'

Madge made a half-smile, half-sorry face.

Ruby didn't know what to say.

'She's living with me,' said Carla, stepping in front of Ruby, 'I want her to live with me. It's what Lisa would have wanted.'

'Well, let's sit down-'

'Why? Who the fuck are you to tell me what to do with *my family*? You people make me sick. My boyfriend can't see his own kids cos of you. Cos of some liar.'

'Carla, I don't think it's the right time to -'

'Do you know how long we've been waiting for a bigger place? If you're saying she can't live with me, then whose fault is that? We're like fucking sardines in that flat. I won't have my kids taken away, you know – I know that's what you want – keeping us cooped up, so we can't take it!'

Carla was right in Madge's face, pointing her finger.

'I need the toilet. I'm going to be sick,' Ruby said, feeling dizzy.

In the corridor, she heard them carry on arguing.

Ruby put her hand to her mouth. *No time*. She spun round, scanning the area. She ran to a pedal bin, opened it just in time and heaved out a jet of yellow bile. Coughing, she turned her head to see a few people sat, waiting for a clinic, staring at her. One of them started to get to his feet.

'Are you alright, sweetheart?' he asked.

Ruby nodded, putting her hand out to signal: *don't get up*.

There were no staff around. She walked quickly down the corridor, put her hood up and her head down.

\*\*\*

Ruby checked the time. *17:45*. The door knocked for the

28

second time. She stood, utterly still, on the landing.

Silence. She waited for a voice. Nothing.

*Are they going to break the door down?* She tensed her fists and feet.

More silence. After a few more minutes, she trod cautiously along to the front bedroom and peered through the net curtains. Madge was there, on her mobile.

'I don't think she's here,' Madge said, 'should I -' she looked up, right at her. Ruby stepped backwards, too late. *Shit*. Madge knocked on the door again.

Ruby stood at the top of the stairs, knowing she had to answer it.

The hall was long and thin. Ruby noticed her mum's coat hung on the line of hooks on the wall. The carpet looked like a layer of muddy water, flowing from the top of the steep, narrow stairs down to the doormat, swirling against the front door. The letter box opened.

'Ruby? It's Madge. I met you at the hospital. Look, I know this is hard for you. I'm here to help. Could you open the door?'

Ruby slowly descended the stairs, feeling the draft bristling in from around the door frame. The dark mahogany wood towered over her. It looked like a coffin lid.

She was trembling. She watched her hand shaking as she reached for the chain across the frame, but she struggled to focus. Everything shimmered. Tiny floating pinpricks of light danced across her eyes. Her body felt completely weightless. She opened the door.

Madge's face was the last thing she saw as she fell forwards, darkness descending over her eyes, the last of her energy evaporating.

She woke up on the sofa.

'Are you alright, love?' Madge was kneeling on the

floor in front of her. 'You gave me a fright there. Here, have a drink of water.' She handed her a glass.

Ruby sat up. For a few seconds, she thought that maybe the last 24 hours hadn't happened. Maybe it was just an extension of her nightmare. Maybe her mum was still alive. *No. It happened. It was real. She's gone.* Ruby wished she hadn't woken up.

*I should have made her do something about that cough, sooner. I should have known that first lot wasn't working. She needed something stronger, quicker. I should have been there. I wasn't there.*

'When was the last time you ate anything, hm?' Madge reached into her handbag and produced a Mars bar.

Ruby shook her head. She could still taste stale sick.

'Come on, you'd be doing me a favour - I need to get rid of this-' she grabbed a roll of fat above her hip, through the cardigan.

Ruby smiled faintly and accepted the chocolate. She hoped the gnawing emptiness in her stomach was hunger. Maybe she could make it stop. Madge stayed silent until she was on her last mouthful.

'I'm so sorry about your mother, sweetheart.'

Ruby felt sick again. She made an effort to swallow the sticky goop and stared at the floor. Madge carried on talking.

'We need to make sure you're taken care of. We're in touch with your father, but we don't know if he's quite in a position to look after you, at the moment.'

'You don't need to do that. I can look after myself,' she said, 'I've been looking after myself for the past two years. And mum. I don't need help.'

She thought of the conversation she'd had with her mum, about what would happen after. *I can't do it.*

'We don't need help,' Ruby carried on, 'I mean – I

30

don't. I don't need help.'

'I know you did everything for your mum, sweetheart, but you shouldn't have had to do that. We shouldn't have let that happen. You did an amazing job, but you're only 14. You should be going to school, going out with friends, having fun.'

It almost made her laugh. *Friends? Fun?*

'I'm nearly fifteen.'

'Okay. I need to tell you the plan, for now, and what we're going to look at for the short, medium and long term, okay?'

Ruby switched off. There was no point arguing. She was alone. She listened to her fate, staring blankly at Madge's face. She was to go to a place for kids who were 'between homes' until they could determine her dad's suitability, or find a foster family. She would pack a bag. She would go there now.

She packed enough for one night and made sure she had her keys.

*I'm coming back as soon as I can.*

On the way, it struck Ruby that she had got into a car with a complete stranger. She could be taking her anywhere.

*Should I have refused? Waited for the police to turn up?* She gripped her bag and eyed the car door. *Unlocked.* She thought about jumping out at the next set of lights. *Where would I go? Back to the house? Annabelle's? No. Her parents don't like me. Well, they don't like my family.* A memory of Carla, picking her up once, arguing with Annabelle's dad, made her shudder.

Madge was talking, trying to make her feel better. Ruby ignored her and stared at the grey outside. She had tears in her eyes. She wanted so much for it to be a bad dream. She wanted to wake up.

The place was called Denby House. Ruby had

31

distant memories of visiting her nana in a care home and this felt the same, like a cross between school and hospital. Laminated signs, notice boards, fire extinguishers. All the glass was like the glass in school – double-paned with wire grids in between. The place smelt of paint and boiled vegetables.

Ruby was introduced to staff members as a woman with pink hair showed her round. She felt like she was outside of her body, watching it all happen to someone else from a distance. Madge had gone.

There was a TV room. *Like nana's Day Room.* There was only one other room on the ground floor, which looked like a canteen. The second floor housed all the bedrooms.

Ruby guessed the kids in the TV room were around her age. Some of them stared at her. Most of them ignored her and carried on watching TV, playing pool, looking at their phones.

She zoned back in to what the woman was saying. Meals are at 8am, midday and 6pm. She could get a snack in between if she asked a carer. Except for going to school, she could only leave the premises with a carer to escort her.

*No swearing. No fighting. No drugs. No alcohol. No smoking. Respect others at all times.*

Ruby noticed that this A4 poster, with its six commandments, was on the wall somewhere in every room.

'You've got one of the single rooms. Just freed up this morning. Got a foster family,' the woman said. It made Ruby feel like a rescue dog, waiting in a shelter.

The woman carried on talking as they stood at the threshold of her new bedroom. Ruby waited for her to stop, then stepped inside and shut the door.

There was a bed, a wardrobe and a chair. The roof

sloped. An attic window loomed over her. It was so thick with grime that Ruby could barely tell the difference between the pane of glass and the gruel-coloured walls. There was no lock on the door. She grabbed the chair and lodged it under the handle.

Her phone buzzed. She looked at the messages, from Annabelle:

*How are you? How's your mum? We've started without you but you're more than welcome any time xxx*

She rubbed her eyes and shook her head. She replied:

*Sorry, I can't, I'm still at the hospital. I'll ring you when I can, tomorrow or next week sometime xxx*

Ruby didn't know why she lied, exactly. She just knew she wasn't up to telling the truth. She didn't want to see anyone, she didn't want to talk about it.

Annabelle:

*Oh no! That's rubbish, I hope she's okay. Tagged you on insta xxx*

Ruby tapped the app.

The photo was Annabelle and Jade, sat on the sofa in onesies, holding the *Kingsman* DVD, looking into the camera sticking out their bottom lips and arching their eyebrows up and inwards in exaggerated sad faces.

*Missing our lovely Ruby for Taron Egerton night* said the caption, with sad emojis. *#filmnight #girlsnightin #taronegerton #onesies #bffs #wishyouwerehere #missyou #notthesamewithoutyou*

Ruby thumbed away tears. *Don't be nice to me.*

The bed had the damp, musty odour of charity shops, but she was too tired to care. She pulled the duvet over her head and vowed never to emerge.

\*\*\*

*Christmas next week. Mum's funeral tomorrow.* She didn't

know who she was angry with, but she was angry. *Why me? What did I do? What did I not do?* She stopped her thoughts there, because she always had an answer for that. She had to work hard to silence the voice that told her it was her fault.

Someone knocked on her door. She didn't want to see anyone. *Not today.*

'Ruby?' the voice asked, as the door handle turned. It was Madge.

She watched her come through and sit on the end of the bed, making small talk about the weather. She pretended to listen.

'Ruby?' she said, after asking a question Ruby didn't register.

'Sorry, I was…' she trailed off.

'It's okay. They tell me that you haven't really spoken to anyone since you've been here, love,' Madge said, searching Ruby's face. Ruby looked down. 'It's been nearly a week. They just want to help you. We all do.'

*I know that. But you can't.*

'We've completed your dad's assessment. He's not there yet, sweetheart. I'm sorry.'

'Well, good. I'll go home then.'

'Home? You mean Marlborough Road? It's not your – look, as soon as they've sorted all that damp, there'll be a new family in there.'

'But I need my stuff, mum's stuff-'

'We'll go get that. Don't worry.'

'What about Carla? Can't I live with her? She wants me to, she told you herself.'

Ruby didn't really want to live with Carla and the kids in their tiny flat, but she'd rather be there than Denby House, or with strangers.

Madge shifted in her seat, fiddling with the collar of her shirt.

'Carla has gone into hospital for a while.'

'Really? What's wrong with her?'

'She's very down. She's...your mum's death hit her very hard. And with her boyfriend being sent down - she just couldn't cope.'

*This family is a mess.*

'What's happened to the kids?'

'Your cousins are living with his mum.'

Ruby put her face in her hands. 'Can we talk about this another time? I don't feel well. It's mum's funeral tomorrow, I can't –'

'Of course. You should know that we're looking into long-term fostering options for you, though, Ruby.'

Madge put her hand on her arm.

'I want to be alone,' Ruby said, flinching away.

\*\*\*

Sometimes, when she was alone at night, Ruby got scared. Lots of things scared her, real and not real. The lines blurred. She would lie awake, worrying that Denby House was a lie, a cover for a criminal gang. She'd read in her mum's *Mirror* about an international network who bought and sold children across the world, on the dark web. She couldn't get it out of her head. She'd stare at the door handle, waiting for it to turn. Listening out for footsteps thudding up the stairs, kids screaming, adults shouting. Men in balaclavas would come and bundle her into the back of a van.

Ruby didn't know if she believed in heaven, but she wanted to believe that her mum was watching her, and that somehow she would make everything okay. *Things will never be okay again though*. She felt like a different person, a new version of herself that she didn't like. This Ruby was always sad, always angry. This Ruby hated everyone and everything. This Ruby was alone.

On nights like this, she would take the door key from Marlborough Road out of her pocket and hold it tight. The metallic smell on her fingers reassured her. Sometimes she'd talk to her mum. The night before her mum's funeral, she asked her for help, just to get through the day.

It was a day of snow and ice. The registry office had organised everything. *It shows. They know nothing about mum. Why didn't they let me do it?*

Carla was there, with a support worker. Her hair was scraped back, she had no makeup on. Ruby couldn't remember ever seeing her without makeup. She smiled faintly at Ruby as she sat on the row across from her, but said nothing. She closed her eyes.

The support worker talked across Carla, to Ruby.

'She's on a lot of medication, flower. But she wanted to be here for you. And for Lisa.'

Ruby nodded, blinking back tears.

*Where is Cal? They'd give him escorted leave for this, surely.*

'Ruby?' said a familiar voice.

She turned to see an old, kind face.

'Gio!' Ruby said, struggling not to sob. She hadn't seen him since her mum had to give up work.

'Ruby,' he said again, grabbing her hands and holding them, letting his own tears fall, 'Ruby I'm so sorry. We miss her every day. She was a beautiful woman. On the inside, too.'

It was too much. Ruby sank into the seat underneath her, shaking, sobbing into her sleeve.

'I'm sorry,' he soothed, hugging her to his shoulder. 'You know you can come to me for anything, Ruby, don't you?'

She nodded. His smell took her right back to when she was twelve, waiting for her mum to finish work.

*Coffee. Almonds. Happiness.*

She straightened up off Gio's shoulder and out of her memory, wiping her face.

'Thanks, Gio,' she said trying to smile.

'I mean it. You need someone to talk to, you need money, come to me. Do you need a job?'

Ruby shook her head.

'Well if you do, my door is open. I remember you always made better cappuccino than I did. Hm?'

Ruby smiled, nodding, looking at her feet.

Halfway through the service, Ruby heard a hacking cough. She turned and saw him, for the first time in years. Her Dad smiled, hopefully. *He looks awful. How did he know about this?* She turned away and focussed on the fake flowers mounted on the wall. The colour of them made her feel sick. Nacho-cheese-orange carnations. *How could anyone think it was okay to use them? Ever? Why is Dad here? This is the shittest day.*

She didn't cry. Ruby had no more tears left, just anger. She frowned and chewed her nails.

She sneaked another look at him, when they were told to stand and pray.

There he was, in his same battered old leather jacket. *He's aged too much. Grey-yellow. Must be still drinking.* She hated him for turning up. *Mum wouldn't have wanted him here. How did he even find out about this?* She shot a look at Madge.

When she turned round to look at him again, he was gone.

*Good.*

\*\*\*

'Rubes, love, how are you?' She heard the gravelly broad voice from behind her as they walked out of the crematorium into the grey slush of the street. The cold hit her throat.

'Fine,' she said quietly, and carried on walking.

'You don't have to talk to him, Ruby,' Madge said, hurrying after her.

'I know,' she said, walking faster.

Madge was struggling to keep up. Her dad lagged behind them both. She did her best to ignore them and sped up, wishing they'd both disappear.

She could smell her dad's cigarettes. *Not the B&H Gold. The cheaper ones. Camel? Mayfair?* She couldn't remember the brand, but she knew the smell of those particular cigarettes. It was the smell of stress. He'd only smoke them when they were really struggling for money. It was the smell of fighting, too.

Her dad started his hacking cough again. He couldn't keep up.

'What do you *want*, dad?' she shouted at him, finally spinning round. She crossed her arms and glared at him as he caught his breath. Madge stood and stared.

'I just wanted to see what's going on with you love that's all, I- I'm sorry about Lisa.'

Ruby looked at the floor. Her pumps were wet through in the snow and she couldn't feel her toes any more.

'Our Cal wanted come you know... they wouldn't let him. You know how it is.'

Ruby didn't know how it was, at all, but she nodded.

'How is he?' she asked. She still couldn't look at him directly, but she could tell from his reply that he was smiling.

'Oh he's grand, Rubes. He's a new man, you know, a new man. They're great places these days you know, they give you training and that. He'll get a job when he's out. He's better for it. I don't know if he's off the gear, but –'

'– When does he get out?' Ruby interrupted. She didn't want to hear about gear.

She looked at him, properly. He looked so much older than he was, so exhausted and dishevelled. *His teeth. Where has he been living?*

'Could be as early as spring. He's been good you see, and it was only a minor offence really...'

'What did he do?' she was desperate to know anything he could tell her. It still felt strange, saying his name without being told off.

'Well, didn't your mother tell you?'

'No,' she lied.

*She told me something. It wasn't the truth. You don't get two years for shoplifting.*

One thing she knew about her dad is that he never lied, not even white lies or half-truths. He just wasn't capable. It made her wary about asking him questions when she didn't want to know the answers, like: *Why did you and mum split up? Are you still an alcoholic? When was the last time you had a shower?* But she wanted to know anything he could tell her about Cal. Cal, the brother who left her life completely, the day he got kicked out.

Her Dad hesitated. She could see he didn't want to tell her, but they both knew this was the only reason she was still stood there. Madge winced. She started to speak, but her dad continued.

'Him and Dale broke into an old lady's house up in Fulwood. They robbed the house. They didn't hurt her or anything, but she came down half way through... threatened to call the police. So they... look, he's never hurt anyone you know? But they were stupid and scared of getting caught, so they tied her up and left her there. Her neighbour found her the next day, but, she was so old, you know, it could have been a lot worse.'

There was a long pause. Ruby knew there was

something he wasn't telling her, something he didn't want to say, but it was going to come out. It always did. Sure enough, the words began again.

'When they found her... she had a black eye. And a couple of broken bones...'

'*Jesus!*' Ruby couldn't help exclaiming.

'Cal didn't do it. He's always said he didn't do it. He couldn't. He says she fell down the stairs. I don't know about that - I think it was his mate. He's off his head, that guy. Cal's just protecting him.'

'Christ...' Ruby said, leaning against the wall. She didn't know what to say. *Bloody hell. Not just in prison, he's robbed an old lady, maybe even beaten her up, left her for dead. And he's still doing drugs.*

She remembered when they were kids, she idolised him. Her older brother. She thought he knew everything and she trusted him, completely.

She liked to remember him before he went off the rails. He looked out for her. She remembered, when she was seven and he was eleven, they were out riding their bikes. She fell off on the high street and banged her head on the pavement, ripping a gash that bled down into her eyes. She remembered crying, and all she could see through one eye was red. Her favourite memory of Cal was in that moment. He stopped and ran to her. He took off his jumper and wiped away the blood with it, told her to hold it on the wound. He made her feel safe. He knew what to do.

'Stay here,' Cal said, and disappeared into the newsagents. Minutes later he came out, hands in his pockets, glancing into the shop through the window. He produced a bottle of water, which he used to wash the blood out of her eye. When her sobs had calmed down to sniffs, he put his hand in the other pocket and revealed a bag of Haribo. He handed them to her.

'For the shock,' he said, smiling. She loved that memory. She loved him, that memory of him.

*He always knew what to do, what to say. But now. Now, he's a ruthless junkie criminal.*

'…shit…' she said, out loud.

'Here you are love,' her dad offered her a cigarette, 'have a fag. It'll calm you down. I'm sorry I had to be the one to tell you. I thought you knew.'

'Excuse me,' Madge said, 'I can't let you do that. You shouldn't be offering her those,' she said, gesturing at the packet.

Ruby's dad looked at Madge for the first time.

'Well, I'm Gaz. Ruby's Dad. *Excuse me,*' he mimicked, 'but who *the fuck* are you?" he asked, frowning at her. Ruby laughed. She couldn't help it. It was the first time she'd laughed since her mum died.

'I'm Madge. Ruby's social worker. You know who I am. We've met before.'

She saw how pleased he was to have made her laugh, and her smile faded.

'Listen, Rubes,' he said, stepping towards her, 'you should be living with me. I'm your dad. I know I've been a twat all this time, but I'm changing. I've changed. Your mum - she made me see what I needed to do. Sort myself out. For you.'

Ruby felt like slapping him, but she clenched her teeth instead.

'No child of mine is living in care,' he carried on, 'I always said that. Messes you up. I was in care, look how I turned out!' He laughed, coughing. 'Seriously though, Rubes. It's not right. I don't want you-'

'I've got to go home,' she said, straightening up, 'I'm freezing. Bye.'

Before she knew it, Ruby was nearly running, with her dad trailing after her and Madge trying to stop him.

Her dad shouted after her.

'Wait, Rubes, love, I thought we could get some tea together? Warm up in the pub?'

She carried on walking.

'Ruby!' he shouted after her, 'I've not seen you for seven years!'

She turned and shouted back, her voice cracking.

'*And whose fault is that?*'

She let her tears fall, and carried on into the darkness.

# CHAPTER 5

Facetime with Annabelle.

'You have to let me come give you your Christmas present, Ruby. I've not seen you for so long. I know we speak like this but it's not the same! Also, it's Christmas in like, two days.'

Annabelle panned the camera to her right, where the huge Christmas tree in her huge living room stood.

'Look, it's this one,' she said, zooming in to a gold parcel with a purple bow. It said *Ruby* in fancy squiggly letters on the tag.

Everything about Christmas just made Ruby want to cry. But she smiled, for the camera.

'Aw. Annabelle, you didn't need to buy me anything. You know I can't have visitors here. I told you.'

*That's a lie.*

'I can't believe you're stuck in that place, it's like prison.'

Ruby nodded.

'Christmas is making everyone mental, too,' she said, 'yesterday the girl in the room next to me went to A&E cos she cut herself so bad. Then this lad's mum got arrested when she started on one of the staff…'

'I thought there were no visitors?'

'Except parents,' Ruby said quickly. She could see

Annabelle didn't believe her.

'You're looking really thin in your face, Ruby. Are you eating anything?' Annabelle frowned, examining Ruby on her screen.

Ruby felt her cheekbones. *Am I?*

'Yeah, I'm eating.'

*Another lie.*

'The food here is shit, though. I'm thinking of moving in with my dad, anyway.'

'*What?*' Annabelle looked horrified.

'I just-' she started, but Annabelle interrupted.

'Ruby you can't. He's a horrible man, you hate him - you said so yourself!'

'You don't know him. Yeah I do hate him, sometimes, but what's the alternative? Stay in care? Go to a foster home? You don't know what it's like here. Or how bad some kids get treated in foster care.' Ruby realised she was nearly shouting.

'Okay, yes, I get it,' said Annabelle, motioning *stop* with her hand. 'I get it. Why don't you come live with me?'

'Don't be stupid,' Ruby snapped, 'your parents look at me like something they found on the bottom of their shoe...' her voice wavered.

'That's really mean,' Annabelle said, quietly, 'they don't.'

'You just take things for granted, Annabelle. You don't know how lucky you are. You're so naïve. You have no idea how the real world works.'

Ruby knew she shouldn't carry on, but she couldn't stop.

'You have *everything*. And all you have to worry about is what shoes to wear. So don't be lecturing me about what to do with my life.'

'Fine, I won't,' Annabelle said, her voice trembling,

her face starting to crumple, 'I'll see you in the New Year then. If you ever come back to school. Have a nice Christmas on your own.'

She ended the video call.

\*\*\*

'Ruby? Come on sweetheart, we're having Christmas Dinner. You've been in there all day. You need to eat something.'

Ruby listened with one ear. One eye watched the door handle while the other stayed closed, buried with one side of her head in the duvet. She blinked to get rid of a lone teardrop, clinging to the edge of her eyelashes. It hit the side of her nose and stayed there, a cold pool settled on the horizontal shelf. *Dammit.*

'It's being served, love.'

She wrinkled her nose, but the pool was unmoved. *Fine. Fine.*

She rolled onto her front, closed her eyes and breathed deep as she lifted herself up and off the bed. Sparks swam around her peripheral vision as she opened the door.

'Good girl,' the care-worker smiled and patted Ruby on the shoulder as she walked past him, down the stairs.

The steam from boiled vegetables, sweat and breath hung in the air of the canteen. The heat of food, bodies and electric radiators forced Ruby to take off her jumper and sit in her T-shirt, holding her arms across her front, conscious of the old, baggy top she'd slept in and was still wearing.

Ruby tried to let it wash over her. She tried not to talk to anyone or look them in the eye. All she did with the food was push it around her plate.

'You eating that?' a voice next to her said. It was

Kay, the only other resident of Denby House she'd spoken to.

Ruby shook her head, sliding the plate towards her.

'Love sausages, can't waste them,' said Kay, stabbing one with her fork and lifting it, pointing it at Ruby before managing to fit half of it in her mouth. Kay carried on talking. 'You usually have a proper Christmas dinner? We did, sometimes.'

Ruby could see the grey-brown mulch churning round Kay's open mouth as it mashed away. She looked at the table instead.

'Mum didn't cook last year, she was too ill. We got an Indian.'

'On Christmas?'

'Yeah. She said I could have whatever I wanted.'

'I'd've got Chinese,' Kay said, shaking her head.

Ruby picked at her nails and tried to think of something to say.

'Is your...I mean, did you see anyone today?'

Kay nodded. 'Mum came. That bitch is hilarious,' Kay grinned, getting her phone out. 'Look,' she swiped across and tapped to show a video of a short, round woman in a velour tracksuit and a Santa hat, dancing through the foyer of Denby House, holding her phone that blared out *Merry Christmas* by Shakin' Stevens.

Ruby smiled.

'You look like her,' she said, quickly adding, 'I mean, round the eyes.'

'Fuck off!' Kay gave Ruby a shove, smiling.

A screwed up red crepe paper ball flew across Ruby's eye-line, hitting a boy's face who was sitting near them.

'Ben! Put your hat on, dickhead,' the thrower shouted.

'Jack! Don't throw things,' the care worker sat

opposite said, turning to Ben. 'You don't have to wear the hat. Let's hear your joke though, love. Come on, it's Christmas.'

Ben shifted in his seat, frowning. A few kids started chanting, *joke, joke, joke,* banging on the table in time, until he finally picked up the piece of paper. They all cheered.

'What-kind-of-mo-tor-bike-does-Father-Christmas-ride,' he read.

'I don't know!' said the care worker.

'A..Har-ley-Da-vid-son,' he said, looking up.

'What?' the care worker asked, ignoring the sniggers. 'Let me see,' he took the paper from him.

'A *Holly* Davidson. Holly. That's the joke. You know, Holly? Christmas Holly?'

The room roared. Ruby looked at the floor. She heard someone say *fucking retard.*

Ben looked round. She could see his breathing get heavier, faster, his face redder.

He stood up, picked up his plate and threw it across the room. It smashed against the wall, narrowly avoiding the head of Frank, the Home Manager. There was a sharp intake of breath across the room, then silence. Ruby watched the gravy bleed down the wall.

'What a load of fucking bollocks this is. You can all go fuck yourselves,' said Ben. He walked out, slamming the door. Ruby felt her heart swell. She wanted to applaud.

# CHAPTER 6

'When can I get my stuff?'

'Mm? You've got your stuff, haven't you?' Madge asked, looking at Ruby's wardrobe.

'I've got *some* of it. There's a whole house though, all mum's stuff.'

'Oh...I'm sorry, Ruby, I thought they'd told you...'

'Told me what?'

'The house has been cleared. I mean, it's a council house so-'

'*What?* Where's all her stuff? My stuff?' Ruby stood up.

'Don't worry, it will be safe somewhere-'

'*Somewhere?* Jesus Christ,' Ruby said, putting on her jacket and walking to the door.

'Don't, Ruby - I'll find your things,' Madge hurried after her, 'you can't go there, they're getting rid of all the asbestos and the damp, it's not safe.'

Ruby was already halfway down the stairs.

'Ruby!'

She turned back.

'Look,' Madge said, looking at her watch, 'I have to go pick up my dad from his hospital appointment now, but I'll take you on Monday, okay?'

Ruby folded her arms.

'Honestly. I promise. I just need to speak to someone to get access, but they won't be there now and it's New Year's Day tomorrow. Please don't go there on your own. Promise me.'

Madge fixed Ruby's drifting gaze.

'Okay,' Ruby said, looking at the floor.

*Screw you.*

As soon as she saw Madge's car disappeared round the corner, Ruby set off.

It was getting dark. She put up her hood and pulled her sleeves down over her hands. Her mum's voice said: *Why don't you wear your gloves? Where are they? It's freezing. Put your scarf on.*

She put her hand in her pocket and felt for the key. She held onto it. At the bus stop, then on the bus, she gripped it. Her phone buzzed.

Annabelle:

*I'm sorry, Ruby. I've been feeling really shitty about this. I shouldn't have tried to tell you what to do. It's only because I care about you. Christmas wasn't the same without our FaceTime! I hope ur doing something nice for New Year's Eve 2night. If not, do you want to come here? Xxx*

Ruby put the phone away and leaned her head on the bus window. Her phone buzzed again.

*Go away.*

Sighing, she took it out to look again and sat up, it was from Kay.

*Ruubz wer r u? goin offy 4 booze 4 park. want owt?*

Ruby smiled, but put the phone back in her pocket without replying. She got off at the stop near her house and turned the corner, heading up the hill. She could do it with her eyes closed.

Her breath made a white cloud between her and the green front door. It looked black, in the dark. She hadn't seen it since the day she fell through it, into Madge's arms.

The key worked. The air was just as cold inside. Colder, somehow. As she shut the door behind her, she closed her eyes and heard her mum's voice. *I love you. You have to be strong.*

Turning on the light, she stared at the empty space. *Everything's gone.* The stair-lift put in by the council was still there, but that was it. No coats on the hooks, no shoes under the radiator, no pictures on the wall. The smell of bleach hung in the air. The carpet was gone. Even the wallpaper was gone, stripped back to plaster. Ruby put her hand on the bare pink, mottled with black. *Damp.*

She walked into the living room. No furniture, except a single trestle table, holding a tin of magnolia paint. The curtains were gone. The net at the window was still there, hanging, lonely in the cold. Ruby swallowed and shivered.

Upstairs was stripped, too. The carpet had been taken up, the furniture removed. Blu-tak patterns on the walls were all that remained of her time there. In the bathroom, her message on the mirror was gone. *It was bullshit anyway.*

She looked at the doorway of her mum's room and stood still, taking in the cold, the smell, the bareness. Her limbs creaked. She stood, trying to swallow back tears, peering into the darkness between the frame and the door. She knew what should be in there. The jewellery, the mirrors, the trinket boxes, the hoists and handles and pill organisers. Her clothes. The dresses she went out in, the perfume Ruby used to borrow, the jacket she always wore for parents' evenings. Photos.

She pushed the door with her fingertips. Two squares of orange on the floor stared back at her, from the streetlight outside. In the shadows, she could see the fitted wardrobe doors open, empty. *Nothing.* She glanced at the spot where the headboard used to be, the outline still there in dust against the wall. She sniffed. *Tears. Again.*

'I miss you, mum,' she said, out loud, 'I miss you, so much.'

She backed up against the wall and sank down, holding her head, sobbing.

*You have to be strong.*

Ruby shook her head. *No. I can't be. I can't.*

Her phone vibrated.

Annabelle:

*Ruby, I don't care if you're still angry with me. That's fine, just let me know you're okay and I'll leave you alone xxx*

She looked at the ceiling and wiped her face with her sleeve. *I'm not okay. No, Annabelle, I'm not okay.*

*Get up,* she told herself. *Go downstairs.* Walking down, she remembered watching the door from the same place, that day. She turned at the bottom of the stairs, round to the middle room, through to the kitchen. A pile of cardboard and plastic boxes sat by the back door. She clicked the light switch and waited as the fluorescent strip-light flickered into life, finally settling on one beam, humming. Black marker pen capital letters stared back at her from the cardboard boxes.

*Care of: Madge Strachan, Floor 4, Pinstone House*

The corner of Ruby's mouth flickered, almost to a half smile.

She opened the top box.

A photo album. Ruby knew the shelf they'd taken it from. She took a deep breath and lifted the dusty cover. Her mum was there, as a child, on the balcony of the flat at Park Hill, where she'd grown up. The camera was behind her. From behind, it could easily be Ruby in that photo, staring out across the city and to the horizon, over the hillsides.

Ruby let the cover drop and opened the next box. She smiled, lifting out the black dress. She held it to her, then drew it to her face, burying her nose and breathing deep into the fabric. *Mum.*

She folded the dress and put it back, smoothing the creases.

The plastic crate underneath contained the contents of the drinks cupboard. Ruby dragged the heavy bulk out from under the other boxes, just enough to open the edge of the lid and stare in.

The bottles sat there. Amber brown, chocolate-cherry red, electric blue, glossy, holly green. Beautiful. Slender, fragile necks, solid fat sphere bodies, elaborate sculptured stoppers, textured lattice glass and old corks. She dropped the lid, pinned the other boxes against the wall and pushed the crate out from under them with her foot. She let the others down gently, juddering down the wall to the floor as she bent her knees to take the weight.

Ruby emptied the crate and looked at what she had.

*Bombay Sapphire Gin, Southern Comfort, Archers Schnapps, Hapsburg Absinthe, V.S. Cognac Courvoisier, Cointreau, Smirnoff Vodka.*

She unscrewed the Bombay Sapphire Gin cap. It smelt like lemon bleach. Ruby took a sip and immediately started coughing.

*It* tastes *like lemon bleach.*

Her throat burned and her mouth stung with sour, sharp prickles all over her tongue.

The word 'Comfort' called out to her from another bottle.

*Still smells like cleaning fluid, but it looks like... maple syrup. Or apple juice.* She swallowed this one holding her nose, just in case.

It didn't taste syrup or apple juice. It tasted like fire.

It went burning down her throat and into her stomach and up her nose. She could feel the heat rising from her guts up into her mouth and felt like retching. Ruby coughed, reading the bottle.

1L * 35% ALC BY VOL * 70 PROOF * LIQUEUR

*Snap-screeeeeeeech!*

Ruby spun round towards the sound, letting out a half-scream-half-shout.

'Argh!'

She put her hand to her mouth, stepping backwards, feeling her heart pound. It was a rat, snapped inside one of the traps the council had put down.

It was half the size of Ruby's foot. Its grey-brown fur was spiky with wetness from wherever it had come from but its long, pinkish tail was dry and hairless. Ruby stepped towards it, the small black eyes staring at nothing and everything all at once.

Its head was stretched out on the wooden board, the neck snapped flat, pinned down by the thin metal frame that caught it. Its limbs hung by the side of its plump body. Ruby could see its claws resting on the lino. One of its limb twitched, tapping the floor. Ruby screamed, jumping backwards.

She grabbed the bottle of gin and fumbled with the Yale catch on the back door, feeling her pulse throb in her neck and her fingers shake. She slammed the door behind her and inhaled the outside.

\*\*\*

Ruby:

> *Got gin. Where r u?*

Kay:

> *Park. Bring it!*

All Ruby wanted to do now was to forget. She didn't

want to feel anything. Her toes were numb. *That's a start.* It had been snowing, just enough to whiten up the grey slush from earlier that week. She cradled the bottle of gin under her jacket on the bus. *I'm going to drink as much of you as I can, then I'm going to forget it all.*

She walked through the park gates, trying to get the image of the rat out of her mind. There was a group of kids by the benches. Kay turned round and waved.

*Come on. Just drink, forget everything, feel better.*

'Expensive shit Ruby, where'd you lift that from?' Kay grinned, taking the bottle as Ruby passed it.

'Tesco,' she lied, and pointed to the WKD bottles by the wall, 'can I have one of them?'

'Go for it. You can have any of that. *This* is the good stuff.'

Kay took a swig from the gin and showed Ruby how to get the bottle cap off her WKD using a lighter.

'Don't need that,' a voice behind them said.

Ruby turned. A lanky boy, older than them, picked up one of the bottles. He was wearing an Adidas tracksuit and a Lonsdale baseball cap. Ruby watched the veins bulge in the tattoo on his neck as he clenched his jaw, biting the bottle-cap edge at the side of his mouth, twisting it off.

He offered it to her, but she was holding one already. Kay took it.

'Cheers Dean,' she said, holding it up. She nodded the bottle towards a group of boys on bikes by the underpass entrance, drinking cans of carling, 'they with you?'

He nodded, eyeing the gin in Kay's other hand.

'Want some?' Kay said, with a sly grin, 'you got any weed?'

He nodded, tilting his head and pointing back to the group of boys, turning and walking in that direction. Kay winked at Ruby and followed him, motioning for her to do the same.

*Right. Time to forget.* She looked at the group of boys, hoods up, smoking roll-ups, music blaring out of one of their phones, balancing on bikes that were too small for them. They were exactly the kind of boys her and Annabelle hated walking past. The kind of boys that shouted insults and threw things at you. The kind of boys that started fights.

Ruby downed the WKD in one go. She managed to silence a huge burp, then tossed the bottle behind her on the grass and blew her breath out, rounding her mouth. *Fuck it.*

\*\*\*

20, 40, 70, £1…

'Kay? You got 60p?' Ruby looked up, swaying slightly, 'Kay?'

She looked back at the contents of her purse. *Okay.* Ruby hauled herself away from the wall she was leaning back on and stumbled forward.

*Where is everyone?*

She frowned, shutting her eyes to scan back.

*We were in the park. Then there was all the gin. Kay with that guy. The boys hanging off the railings over the underpass. Did someone bring some vodka?* She could see the red label in her hand, upside down, in front of her face. Swigging.

'You alright love?' a man's voice snapped her eyes open. It was the guy from the takeaway. She stared at him, trying to focus on his face.

'You were just stood with your eyes shut, in the street outside my shop. You okay?'

Ruby nodded, shuffling through the slush towards him, rifling through her purse.

'Can you do chips?' she said, holding the stack of coins towards him, between her index finger and thumb. She stumbled and the pile burst out from between her fingers, clattering onto the pavement.

'Shit, sorry.' Ruby moved to pick up the coins.

'It's okay,' the man put his hand on her shoulder, 'they're free. Come in.'

The neon strip lights hurt the sockets of her eyes. Ruby realised the thudding she could hear was the sound of blood in her ears. The smell of meat grease caught the back of her throat and she gagged. She saw the guy behind the counter exchange a glance with the man that brought her in.

'Give her some chips, Sanj. And a coke. Think she's a bit worse for wear.'

He placed the tray in front of her.

'Where d'you live love? Shouldn't be out on your own at this time of night.'

She shook her head, concentrating on getting the chips in her mouth.

'I'm going home now,' she said, lifting the tray, turning to leave.

'Alright. You be careful. Take care.'

Ruby smiled and nodded. 'Thank you.'

She nodded the coke can in their direction as she stepped outside.

The cold barely touched her. She leaned against the wall and looked to her right. Laughing people. Smokers, outside the pub next door. They hadn't seen her. *Where did Kay go?* She drank the coke and ate the greasy handfuls of chips. Ruby burped loudly and looked around, but the smokers had gone back inside. She felt another burp coming, but it wasn't a burp. It was sick. She couldn't stop it.

It came with such a force that all she could do was

bend over and let it out. Her stomach felt like it was completely destroyed, like it was trying to come up her throat and escape out of her mouth in bits. All she could see was the green-yellow bile, mixed with mashed up chips and the brown cola, all over the snow and her shoes.

The alcohol burned her again on its way back up. Her throat strained with the volume and the pressure made tears spring from her eyes.

Suddenly, she wasn't looking at the sick from above anymore. She was at the side of it, on top of it, on the floor. She couldn't move.

Everything went black.

\*\*\*

'Rubes, oh god what's happened, *Ruby*!'

She could hear a voice. It was her Dad's. She still couldn't move.

'Dave, get us a pint of water mate.'

Ruby opened her eyes and tried to focus, but all she could make out were moving shapes and colours. She was being hauled up and propped against a wall. A wet cloth rubbed down the side of her face.

'It's all in her hair. Silly girl!' said a woman. She knew that voice too - it was Sharon, the landlady of the Fox and Hound.

'I can deal with it now,' her dad said, gruffly.

Ruby rubbed her eyes and the street spun into focus. She took the pint of water he offered and forced it down. Her head hurt. Half her body was numb with the cold and her clothes were wet through from the snow. The smell of sick cut through everything.

'What happened, Rubes? You been drinking?' he asked, searching her face, 'your friend rang me, said she couldn't find you. She was worried. I came looking round here, thought you'd be near your Mum's.'

'Kay?' Ruby croaked.

'What? No, Annabelle.'

Ruby closed her eyes. *Annabelle*. The countdown rang out from the pub.

'5…

4…

3…

2…

1…

Happy New Year!'

She looked at the cigarette in her dad's hand and the lines on his face.

'I just had too much. You know what it's like,' she said, quietly.

'You got that right!' he laughed. 'Come on, you can stay at mine tonight.'

He pulled her up and gave her his old leather jacket.

'Don't worry about me, love, I've got my beer jacket on.'

58

# CHAPTER 7

Ruby opened her eyes. *What the fuck?*

For a second, she thought her fear about being kidnapped in the night from Denby House had come true. She sat up, her heart loud in her ears.

It came back to her in pieces. She remembered the rat, the gin, the snow. Rubbing her eyes, she remembered the rest. *Chips, sick, dad.*

*Shit.*

Her head felt as though someone had tried to tear away her brain from the inside of her skull. Her mouth tasted like she hadn't brushed her teeth for weeks. She looked around the room - bare floorboards, no wallpaper, cracked plaster. No curtains. *So this is where he lives.*

She was lying on the only object in the room — a stained mattress in the corner. The room felt damp. It smelled stale.

Looking out of the grimy window, she realised where she was.

*Burnside Court.*

It was a development of flats, made up of four tower blocks surrounding a central courtyard that housed a children's play area. Kay had told Ruby about Burnside. None of the kids here went to Ruby's school, but a few of the kids at Denby House came from these flats.

She looked at the playground. The black tarmac floor was covered in fluorescent graffiti. Every spare inch of metal on the swings, the roundabout and the slide was filled with black marker pen scribbles and drawings. There were cans, polystyrene takeaway trays, and bottles scattered over the courtyard.

Looking at the tower across the way, Ruby guessed that the flat she was in must be about six floors up and it was right on the corner. The tower just across from them seemed so close. She thought if she sat on the edge of the balcony, she'd be able to climb over. She could even read the make of the bike outside the flat and a t-shirt hanging on a drying rack that said *Golddigga*.

They weren't really balconies like Ruby had always imagined balconies – little separate private areas, with pot-plants and deck chairs. There was just one big concrete strip, stretching across the front of all the flats, with no separation. Just a pavement in mid-air, with a chest-height barrier wall.

There was a knock. Her dad opened the door.

He stood there in socks, boxers and a Sheffield Wednesday t-shirt.

'Food, love, come and eat something.'

'I'm not hungry,' she lied.

'Yes you are. You threw up everything you ate yesterday. Come on.'

She followed him to the kitchen. The kitchen was a narrow room, with units on one side. There was barely enough space to get past them to the little camping table, stood at the end, by the window. The lino peeled away from the floor, the paper from the walls. Bacon, eggs and bread were all spitting away in lard on the hob.

Ruby didn't realise how hungry she was until she started to eat. She watched her dad trough through his fried sandwich. She did the same. When he finished, he lit up a cigarette.

'Rubes, you know you've got to live here now don't you?'

'What?'

She put down the last bite of her sandwich.

'You know it makes sense, love. Do you really want to go back to that place?'

'Well, no, but-'

'They can't take you anyway. I'm your dad.'

'They didn't want me to-'

'No they didn't, but that was just while I had my tag. It's off now.'

He lifted his trouser leg to expose his ankle.

'I did everything they asked. Moved out of the hostel, found a place. It's what your mum wanted, Rubes. That's why I sorted myself out. It's what I want, too. No kid of mine is growing up in care,' he shook his head.

He inhaled his cigarette, stared out of the window and then grinned at her.

'Proper family now, us. Fresh start.'

Ruby swallowed and lifted herself out of her chair, with shaking hands. She made it across to the counter just in time to spew up the remaining contents of her stomach into the sink.

*** 

It took two weeks for the letter to arrive. She sat on her bed and read it again. *Trial period. Living with paternal father. To be reviewed regularly. Meetings scheduled...*

She stopped. *That smell. What the hell is it?*

'Dad, what's that smell?' Ruby said, walking from her room to the living room. It smelled like wet dog. Urinals. She put her sleeve over her nose.

'Ruby, this is Tel,' her dad said, as she appeared in the doorway. *Tel is the smell.* A man with greasy grey hair and a stained T-shirt grinned at her. Two of his teeth were missing, the rest were brown. His jeans were too short, showing an inch of skin above his white sports socks and battered trainers.

'Can you get us some bits from the shop, Rubes?' Her dad held out a £20 note. 'Got nowt in.'

Ruby nodded, taking the money. She couldn't wait to leave the flat.

'Just get whatever. Tel and I are just talking business.'

'Sorry about the smell, sweetheart,' Tel said, 'I breed dogs. Smelly bastards they are. You want one just come see me. Just downstairs. 304.'

Outside Ruby breathed the clean air and shuddered. *Where are the shops round here?* She took out her phone and winced, seeing a missed call from Annabelle. She looked up the route to the nearest shop, then decided to call her back.

She took the stairs. *I can't show Annabelle this place. Not for a while, anyway.* Ruby tapped the green phone symbol, stepping over a hypodermic needle discarded in the doorway of the tower block.

*Please answer. Please. I'm sorry.*

'Hello?'

'I'm sorry, Annabelle, I should've let you know I was okay...and I shouldn't't've said those things. Before Christmas. I'm sorry.'

She could hear Annabelle laugh and sniff.

*Is she crying?*

'I'm sorry too. I was just, I don't know. It doesn't matter. So you're at your dad's now then? He said you were staying. What's it like? Is he okay?'

Ruby felt taller, as though she had been carrying

62

someone on her shoulders and they'd finally climbed down.

'It's alright. I mean, it's weird. His place is a bit gross. But it's been a couple of weeks now and it's better than Denby House. I don't have to be at this place by that time or whatever. I don't have to answer to anyone, really. But it is weird. He's different to how I remembered him. Which is good, but it's just... I don't know. He's trying really hard. His social worker thinks he's doing way better.'

Annabelle paused. '...Good. If he - I mean, if you ever feel like you need a break, you can always—'

'I know,' said Ruby, picturing Annabelle's parents, looking down at her, 'thank you. I think we're okay, though.'

'Okay. When are you coming back to school?'

'I don't know. Soon. It's too much right now. I just need to get used to things. Settle in. We're going to Meadowhall,' Ruby smiled, 'get some stuff for my room.'

'Ooh, go to Cath Kidston, their stuff is adorable! You have to let me come make it over, I'll transform it.'

Ruby nodded. 'Yep,' she managed.

*I missed you, Annabelle,* she thought, but didn't say it.

'Anyway,' she said instead, 'I have to go, I'm just buying some stuff. I'll text you.'

She put her phone in her pocket and looked at the shop front her phone had directed her to. *Polski Sklep. Oh, right. Google didn't tell me that.* Ruby looked round, but the only other shop nearby was a mobile phone repairs store. *Okay. I'll just guess.*

The shop smelled like cheese and earthy potatoes. Rows of neatly packed tins, jars, packets stared back at her, all brightly coloured and covered in writing she couldn't read.

*Masło orzechowe*

*Dżem malinowy*

*Almette z chrzanem*

*Filety śledziowe z olejem wiejskim beczka*

Ruby picked random jars and packets, throwing them into the basket.

*What are you doing? Where are you? You shouldn't be here, or there, at Burnside. With him. You should be at home, with mum. Mum would look after you. She wouldn't send you out while she sold weed to some horrible stinking stranger.*

*What's happened to you?*

Ruby swallowed and tried to breathe the tears in, back, inside. *Not here. Get a grip.*

'Dobry dzień,' the woman behind the counter greeted her.

'Um, hi,' Ruby said quietly, putting her basket on the counter.

'English?' The woman said, smiling.

Ruby nodded. The woman rung each item through and carefully stacked them in a carrier bag, then pointed at the digital display.

*£16.45*

Ruby handed over the note.

'Thank you,' the woman said, handing over the change, adding, 'Do widzenia.' She looked over Ruby's shoulder and her face fell.

'You,' the woman said, suddenly stern, 'I told you. You're not welcome.'

Ruby turned to see a boy, maybe a little older than her.

'My mum just wanted this,' he said, 'nowhere else sells it. Come on. I'm not causing any trouble.'

He was holding a box of something that looked like chocolates or sweets. He had a strong accent, similar to the woman behind the counter, but different, somehow. Ruby looked at his face. *He's beautiful. Actually beautiful.* He

64

looked at her.

She realised she was stood, staring at him. He blushed and looked back at the woman behind the counter. Ruby looked down at the floor. She knew she should go, but she didn't move.

'I told you,' the woman repeated.

The boy turned to leave. Before Ruby realised what she was doing, she found her hand reaching towards him, taking the box from him.

'Wait,' she said to the woman, putting it on the counter, 'I forgot this.'

The woman arched an eyebrow, sighed and pointed to the digital display again. Ruby handed over the money.

Turning, she held the box out, but he was gone.

Ruby picked up her bag and ran out of the door.

'Hey!' she called out on the street. He carried on walking, quickly.

'Hey, wait!'

He stopped and turned round. 'You didn't need to do that,' he said, looking at his shoes.

'It's fine, I...I don't know what her problem was,' said Ruby, holding out the box. *Ptasie Mleczko* it said, in swirly writing.

He took it and insisted she take the money back.

'She just doesn't like Ukrainians,' he said, looking her in the eye for the first time.

*Wow.* Ruby smiled.

'I do. I mean - I like everyone. Well, not everyone - but - what I meant is you shouldn't not like someone because of where they're from.'

*Oh god.* She cringed and wished she'd not opened her mouth.

He smiled and looked around.

'Well, I should go...'

'Me too,' she said, nodding.

They both walked in the same direction. *Shit.*

*Go on. Ask him.*

'D'you live near here?' she asked, watching the pavement disappear under her feet.

'Burnside Court.'

'Me too,' she said, feeling something skip inside.

He didn't say anything, his eyes still on the floor as he walked.

*He doesn't want to talk to you, Ruby. Just shut up.*

She glanced at him, sideways. *He looks like Nicholas Hoult. With lighter hair.*

*Ask him something.*

'Is… is it your mum's birthday, or…?' she said, pointing to the box.

He shook his head.

They walked under the *Burnside Court* sign. He started to separate from her, walking in the direction of the adjacent tower to hers.

She stood, feeling stupid.

'Bye,' she said, quietly.

He turned as he walked and, with his eyes still downcast, held the box up slightly.

'Thank you,' he said.

She smiled as she turned, then walked up the stairs, beaming.

# CHAPTER 8

'Pack it in, I mean it!' someone scolded a kid at the back of the queue, 'I've had it up to here now! Do you want to go home or what?'

*Primark. This was a bad idea.*

Ruby glanced across at her dad next to her. He was tensing and un-tensing his fist.

*Come on.* She eyed the cashiers, as though it would speed things up. A sign caught her eye on the wall opposite the entrance. Meadowhall: *Land of Shopportunity*

She wished she could be anywhere else. *Packed out Primark at peak time. Nobody can handle this. Dad is the* last person *who can handle this.*

The money was from her mum. She didn't know where, exactly, but Madge said it was hers. Ruby wanted to spend it on her bedroom and new clothes. The paint, curtains, a few sticks of second-hand furniture and a rug took up most of the money. She'd come to Meadowhall to spend the remainder on clothes and some speakers. Her dad didn't have a sound system or smart speaker. She was sick of always using headphones. She wanted sound in the room, not just in her ears.

She needed new clothes. The clothes she'd brought from Denby House felt tinged with the place. Besides, she had to fit in. She couldn't get away with the stuff she hung out at home with her mum in any more. *I don't want to be popular. I just don't want to be different.*

Ruby didn't like the flat, but she hated leaving it. She hated the groups of kids that hung round in the hallways, on the stairs, outside the entrance. She could never predict what they were going to do. Sometimes they did nothing, but mostly, they shouted things at her. Sometimes they threw things. They made her so nervous that she just carried on walking whenever they talked to her, even if they sounded nice. They could have been genuine, but she didn't dare take the chance.

*If I can just blend in, maybe they won't notice me.*

She thought carefully about what to buy. In the queue she clung to the items with hope, imagining walking through Burnside Court, blending in, looking like she belonged there. Gaz broke her reverie.

'I'm going to head off, Rubes. Can't be doing with this. You've got what you need, haven't you? Get something for tea while you're here. None of that Polish shite you brought home last time, though. You can get home alright on your own yeah? I need a fag. See you later.'

He pushed his way out of the queue and disappeared into the crowd.

Ruby took a deep breath and thought about the boy at the Polski Sklep. She decided to focus on him. *Make Primark disappear.*

She tried her best to stop the bulging paper bags from splitting on the tram, holding them between her feet as she gripped the handrail.

'The next stop by request will be: Burnside.' The speaker announced.

Getting off the tram, Ruby looked at the people who were staying on. They were travelling on to the nice side of town. They looked relieved. She didn't blame them.

*We make you feel uncomfortable.* She knew what they'd be thinking about her. She knew what they were thinking about the girl with all the kids. The group of boys who were shouting over each other. *You're so glad to see the back of us.*

Part of her wanted to swap places with them. *Get the tram back to a detached house with a big garden and silence whenever you wanted it. A car. Books. A laptop. A full fridge. Knowing when people come and go. Knowing the bills are paid.* She shook her head. *You didn't have that before. That's not what you miss. You miss living with mum in the damp end-terrace with the overgrown yard. It's not so different, here. It's just, not there.*

She knew it was gone, though, that life. Walking back to Burnside Court, she realised she had to try her best to make this trial period work. *Better the devil you know* was a phrase her mum used to say.

Back at the flat, she looked around her new room. *Cool.*

She smiled. It was still a novelty to see the room with curtains and painted walls, plus a proper bed instead of just a mattress shoved up against the wall. She'd gone for neutral, just like she'd wanted back at Marlborough Road but they could never afford. She put up her posters of Taylor Swift, The Arctic Monkeys, The Weeknd. It felt like company.

Ruby tried on her new outfits in front of her new mirror. She'd bought a push-up bra so she finally had a hint of cleavage in strappy tops. She'd got jeggings, leggings and some sweat pants with *Playboy* written on the backside. She also had a pink hoodie to go with the sweatpants and her fake leather jacket. Jewellery. She never wore jewellery. She smiled, thinking of how she drove her mum mad, nagging her to let her get her ears pierced, then after that summer never bothered to wear earrings. *Time to start again.* She had as many £2 pairs of earrings as she could afford, four rings, a bunch of bangles and necklaces.

Her dad was still out, so she decided to put her music on, loud.

*Fuck it. Fuck everyone.*

She put Lizzo on and tidied round the room while she sang along.

Ruby heard the neighbour upstairs get his *Trance Nation Megamix* going and laughed.

'Wanker!' she shouted.

She came across the book with her *Things I'm worried about/ things I can and can't control* lists in and tossed it across the room.

*Not now.*

*Mum died nearly three months ago. Every time I'm alone, I end up crying. Going over what happened. Asking whether I could have stopped it. Whether it was my fault. Stress about dad. About living here. You're allowed to enjoy some things. There have to be some good things.*

'My own space,' she said out loud, smiling, 'my own music. Nobody to look after except *me*. He doesn't care what you do. So you do what you want.'

She felt giddy. She danced around, singing along, breaking tags off clothes and hanging them up.

Ruby couldn't help the Polski Sklep boy drifting across her thoughts. *He lives here, on this estate. There's something weird about him. Like me.* She hoped she'd see him again.

She put Paramore on and gave up tidying, grabbing her body spray as a microphone.

*Sheffield Arena, welcome, Pa-ra-more! Pa-ra-more! Pa-ra-more!*

She sprang round the room, doing her best Hayley Williams impersonation.

She looked at her reflection in the mirror and

nodded, exaggerating all the moves for the audience. At her peak hair-tossing head-banging, pointing-at-the-mirror moment, she froze and stared. Her stomach flipped.

'Oh *shit*!'

The flat opposite was reflected in the mirror. She could see it, without turning round. The one that was so close she could almost read the labels in the clothes drying outside. There, stood on that balcony, was the boy from the Polski Sklep. Looking right at her.

*Shit shit shit shit!*

She turned, horrified, and looked directly at him. He quickly looked away, taking in washing off the rack and folding it. He kept folding, but she was sure she could see a hint of a smile on his face. Ruby wanted the block to just sink into the ground and bury her forever. She ran to the window and pulled the curtains together.

'Oh my god oh my god oh my god! Arrrggghhhh!' she shrieked, sinking to the floor with her head in her hands.

'You're such a dickhead!' she scolded herself. 'Such a knob. Jesus!' Her cheeks felt like they were on fire.

*Well done. Another thing to add to the list of reasons why no-one here will ever speak to you. Worse than that. Why did it have to be him? He already thinks I'm a loser. Oh god. How long was he there for? Shit.*

She got on her bed and buried her face in a pillow.

The front door slammed. She ran over to her phone and hit pause.

'Having fun?' her dad shouted through.

# CHAPTER 9

'This place isn't *that* bad,' said Annabelle. She was stood the living room, looking around. 'I mean, he's been living here for ages on his own, hasn't he? So it's just kind of, got a bit out of hand.'

She stepped over the takeaway trays on the floor to look out of the window.

'No, only a few months,' Ruby said, shaking her head.

'Oh. Well, that's just men, isn't it? I bet my dad would be the same if he lived on his own…'

'No he wouldn't,' Ruby laughed, 'it's okay Annabelle, I know it's a shithole. I was really nervous about you seeing it, but I've kind of gone past the point of caring, now. None of this is what I wanted. I've just got to keep my head down until I can get a place of my own.'

'That's a few years, yet, Ruby…'

'I know. If I can just get through without anything going wrong, I'll look back and laugh at this, one day.'

There was an awkward silence.

'Besides, he never goes in my room,' she said, turning and leading her down the hall. 'My room is my space.'

'Ah, Ruby it's really nice!' Annabelle looked around the bedroom.

Ruby knew Annabelle was humouring her, but she appreciated it. She told her about the Polski Sklep boy and the incident with the mirror. Annabelle held her face in her hands, eyes wide, mouth open.

'*Shut up*, no! That didn't really happen, did it?'

Ruby nodded.

'Oh god, Ruby!' Annabelle was laughing so much she was holding her stomach.

Ruby smiled, shaking her head.

'He's so… I don't know. Like, I've never made such a twat out of myself in front of anyone, let alone the fittest boy I've ever seen…'

'You have to do something about it, Ruby.' Annabelle sat cross-legged on the bed, fingers on her lips, suddenly deep in thought.

Ruby rolled her eyes. 'Annabelle, there's nothing I can do. Like what? Go round and tell him I have a twin who is a dick and that it was *her* that he saw?'

Annabelle held up her finger. 'Which one is his flat?'

Ruby pointed it out. Annabelle nodded. 'Okay. Here's what we do…'

\*\*\*

*Shit. What am I doing?*

The door in front of her started to look blurry. *Don't have a panic attack. Not now.* She looked down and saw her leg jigging up and down. Ruby turned to walk away, but Annabelle grabbed her shoulder.

'Go *on!*'

Ruby held her shaking fist to the door and knocked. *Oh. My. God.*

She suddenly felt the urge to vomit over the balcony but swallowed deep as the door opened. It was him. *Him. He's right there.* He looked at them both. He looked confused. She thought maybe even a bit panicked.

Ruby's mind emptied completely. Her mouth opened, but nothing came out. Annabelle's elbow dug into her side.

'*The T-shirt!*' Annabelle hissed.

'Oh, erm, is this yours?' Ruby thrust out her hand towards him, clinging to the damp white top, like a flag of surrender between them. He took it, frowning at it.

'It fell. Well, I think it did,' she corrected herself, praying that minutes before he hadn't seen Annabelle prodding it off his balcony with a broom handle, leaning out of Ruby's window.

'I found it on the floor...down-' she pointed over the side.

He turned the T-shirt inside out, still puzzled. Pink letters, in a font that reminded Ruby of Carla's tattoos, said: *Sexy Bitch: Hustler.*

He looked up at her. Annabelle stifled a snigger.

Ruby stammered, 'It's not mine. Well, obviously – I guess it's your mum's, I mean, or your sister. Or your...girlfriend...'

'It's my mum's,' he said, finally smiling.

'So do you have a girlfriend?' Annabelle blurted out.

Ruby screwed her eyes closed and willed the ground to swallow her up.

'No,' he said, looking down the walkway. A man was walking towards them, smiling, waving. The boy's smile fell.

'I have to go.' He stepped backwards to close the door.

'Hey, wait,' The man said as he drew closer to them, 'aren't you going to introduce me?'

The boy looked at the floor and stayed silent. The man stood next to them, looking between them all. He was dressed in a black overcoat, black jeans and a grey shirt. His dark hair was slicked back. He didn't talk like the boy. He was local. Ruby could smell smoke and aftershave.

'Well, who are they?' he man asked.

'I don't know,' the boy said, still not looking up.

The man pulled an exaggerated confused face.

'Really? Well that's weird isn't it. Mind you, he is weird,' he said, smirking, nodding towards the boy, but looking at Ruby, 'I'm Tony. Tony Hunter.' He held out his hand.

Ruby shook it. 'Ruby. I'm… a neighbour.'

'Ruby…?'

'Morton. Ruby Morton.'

'Morton…live over there?' He pointed at their flat. 'Gaz Morton's kid?'

Ruby nodded, catching sight of the boy behind him. He was still looking at the floor. She thought she saw a slight shake of his head, a brief closing of his eyes.

Tony grinned. 'I know your dad. From back in the day. Tell him I said hi.'

He reached into his inside pocket and passed her a card.

'Tell him I've got a job for him if he wants one. I'm a businessman. Now,' he said, turning to the boy, 'that wasn't so hard, was it? Your mum in?'

He nodded.

'Good lad,' Tony said, patting the boy's cheek, stepping inside the flat. The boy backed away, further into the hall.

Tony turned to Ruby and Annabelle.

'Ladies,' he grinned, 'lovely to meet you.'

As he closed the door, Ruby watched the boy behind him, clutching the T-shirt, his knuckles white.

# CHAPTER 10

'I'm just concerned, Ruby, that it's been quite a while now and you'll be falling behind. You have exams in the summer.'

Madge let the statement hang in the air, then looked at Gaz.

'Look, if she doesn't want to go, I can't make her,' he said, shrugging.

'You're aware that parents can be fined if their children persist in truanting, Mr Morton?'

Ruby knew Madge called him Mr Morton rather than Gaz when she was trying to get him to show some respect. *Good luck.*

Gaz looked at Ruby.

'I'm sorry,' Ruby said, 'I know I should go. I will. It's just so far away now, and…' she hesitated, fiddling with a loose thread of cotton on her sleeve.

'And?' asked Madge.

'Well, kids from Burnside don't go to that school. There's a couple, but everyone bullies them. I wouldn't fit in there, now. I mean I never did, but…it'd be even worse than before.'

'But you have friends there, don't you?'

'*A* friend. I have *one* friend. She's got loads of friends, but they don't like me.'

Madge sighed.

'Well,' she concluded, 'we have to sort something, Ruby, because I'm damned if you're failing your GCSE's on my watch.'

'Why don't you move schools?' Gaz asked. 'Go to Burnside High? Didn't do me any harm.'

Madge winced. Ruby paused. It had never occurred to her.

'And it's just round the corner,' he said, lighting a cigarette, 'all the kids on the estate go there.'

She thought about the Polski Sklep boy. *I bet he's there.*

'That might be a good idea,' Ruby said, looking at Madge, 'it might help me fit in.'

'Think about it, Ruby,' said Madge, 'it's a big decision.'

'I don't need to think about it,' Ruby said, 'this is where I belong now. I have to do whatever I can to make it work.'

Madge looked at her. Ruby couldn't figure out the expression on her face. Conflicted, somehow. Like she was arguing with herself. She took another deep breath then reached for her bag.

'Okay. If you're sure,' she said, standing up, 'I'll sort it out. But you tell me, if you change your mind, yeah?'

Ruby nodded.

'See you love,' Gaz smirked through a cloud of smoke, 'don't stress about that school. Builds character.'

'Mr Morton,' Madge said, turning round at the threshold, 'I let a lot of things go, because of what really matters. Right now, *this* doesn't matter. The state of the flat,' she gestured around the room, 'all that. Whatever it is you spend the child benefit on. I've not gone into it, because it's low on a long list of priorities. The most important thing is that you look after this girl. You love her, you care for her, you don't steer her wrong. If she's going to Burnside, it's a big change. She'll need your help. This whole situation is an enormous change. She needs you.'

Ruby watched him hesitate. A crack appeared, just for a second, before the front cemented again. He coughed and flicked the ash from the end of his cigarette, then grinned.

'Right you are, flower,' he said, putting his hand to his head in a salute motion. Ruby avoided eye contact as Madge left. The front door slammed shut.

She looked at her phone. *You have to tell Annabelle. You're moving schools. She's going to hate you.*

The door knocked.

'What does she want now?' Gaz said, 'Get a life, woman!'

He got to his feet, coughing.

Ruby stared at her phone screen, thumb hovering. She didn't know how to tell her.

'Alright Tel,' she heard her dad say in the hall.

*Oh god, not him.* Ruby jumped up to open the window.

'Hello again, sweetheart,' Tel said, appearing in the doorway.

She looked down. There was a dog, cowering next to his leg, on a chain lead. The dog was white and brown, a medium size staffie type. Its legs were shaking and its tail was firmly tucked underneath it. Ruby could see the dog was a female from the rows of swollen, drooping teats hanging underneath her.

'Just on our way to Asda,' Tel said, 'thought I'd stop in for a smoke.'

Gaz glanced at Ruby.

'Not right now Tel. I'll be in the Lion later.'

His smell had reached Ruby now. She backed

towards the window.

'How old is she?' Ruby asked, looking at the dog's grey muzzle.

'This one? I don't know. Too old. No use any more. Stopped having pups. That's why we're going Asda.'

Ruby frowned. 'What do you mean?'

'Well, if you tie them up outside a supermarket, sometimes someone takes them. You know like, someone that wants a dog. Or if nobody comes, staff tell the pound, then they come get them. Best thing for her.'

Ruby stared at him, then the dog. Her mouth opened to talk, but nothing came out. Her eyes started to fill with tears.

'Anyway, Tel, I'll see you later,' Gaz said, bundling him out of the door.

When he was gone, Gaz looked at Ruby as he put out one cigarette and lit another.

'None of our business, Rubes.'

Her face crumpled as she ran to her room, slamming the door shut.

'Ruby!' She heard from the living room.

She closed the blank message she'd opened to Annabelle and Googled *RSPCA Sheffield*.

\*\*\*

The next morning, her dad was still asleep when she heard them knocking on the downstairs flat. She was in the living room. She turned off the TV, listening. *Nothing.* She went to the window. Across the courtyard she could see the RSPCA van, parked. She opened the front door, listening again. Another knock. She stepped out onto the walkway, closing the door silently behind her. She paced. A loud bang-crash took her back.

*They've broken in. What if he finds out it's me that told*

*them?*

She peered over the ledge, but couldn't see anything beyond the ledge of the balcony below. Whining, though. She could hear whining. It was too much. She walked quickly, quietly, to the end of the walkway and then on down the first set of stairs, so she could lean around the pillar and see what they were doing. Someone emerged from the flat. He was in a blue uniform, unfolding a piece of paper with his free hand. His shoulder strap said *RSPCA*. Ruby stepped forwards, until he could see her.

'What's going on?' Ruby asked, looking at the cage.

'We're rescuing them, love. Got an anonymous tip-off last night. Breeding.' He carried on, telling her how it happens all the time, how much money there was to be made, how shelters are full of dogs like them.

'What happens if nobody wants them?' she asked, knowing she didn't want to hear the answer.

'It depends,' he started, then checked himself. 'I mean, most of them *will* find somewhere. Don't worry,' he said, then carried on down the stairs.

'They're not stopping you? Are they out?'

He turned back, nodding.

'We have a warrant.'

Another officer appeared with more cages. The puppies clamoured over one another, whining, tails wagging, sniffing.

They came back for a few older dogs, leading them down the stairs on leads. Ruby struggled to look at them. One looked like the dog she'd seen last night, but it was brindle. Another was white with black patches, the only one with a wagging tail. The rest were cowering, ears back, tails between their legs. They took small, hesitant steps. The sound of their claws skittering on the concrete was so dainty, for such sturdily-built animals. The white one barked and jumped when it passed her.

Ruby blinked back tears in her eyes as she watched them load up their van and close the doors. She wiped her eyes with her sleeve and shook her head briskly, trying to rid herself of the image of them terrified in the back of the van. *Tel's out.* She walked up to the door. Something compelled her to push it. It wasn't locked. She had to go inside. She didn't know why.

*The second you hear anything, run.*

The stench was overwhelming. *Piss. Shit. Something rotting.* She smothered her nose with her sleeve. The floor of the main room was covered in damp ripped-up cardboard. She had to tread carefully to avoid all the dog poo. There was one empty bowl in the corner of a room full of chewed-up rubbish and random furniture. Empty cages. She backed out into the hall and caught sight of the bedroom. A bed, buried under clothes and rubbish, sat behind piles of junk. Something made her enter the room. Morbid curiosity, maybe.

She heard a noise and stood still.

*Shit.*

She was ready to run past Tel. *Hit him if you have to.* But then the noise happened again, and she realised it was a rustling coming from the corner of the room.

'What the —'

She walked in its direction. A whimper came from the same spot.

'They've left one!' she said aloud.

*Is it under the pile of clothes?*

She held her breath and dug through it. *Nothing.*

She heard the small sound again and turned to look under the bed. Sure enough, cowering in the fluff and rubbish under the bed was a small dog. She could make out the eyes and nose, like a baby seal's, wet and black. There was definitely a wagging tail under there too, but it carried on whimpering and didn't come out when she

81

tried to coax it.

Her stomach fluttered. *If Tel comes back right now, you're fucked. But you can't leave it here. Think.*

She picked her way back through the junk to the kitchen. *This makes dad's look clean.* She scanned the stacks of pots, sticky surfaces and the sink, buzzing with flies. The hob was thick with something greasy. A pan sat on top of it. She frowned, trying to make out what it had once been *Beans?* They were hidden under a green-grey fur. *Come on. There!* Half a packet of biscuits. She grabbed it and ran back to the bedroom.

She took a few out and put them on the floor, at enough distance from the bed to make the dog emerge completely.

'Come on beautiful, come on out. Yum yum!'

The dog shot out, wolfing the biscuits in one impressive motion. Before it could scuttle back, Ruby scooped it up in her arms. It was only a puppy-dog, probably six or eight months, a black and tan brindle staffie.

She heard voices from outside from the stairwell. *Shit. Get out.*

Like a reflex, she pulled the bottom of her hoodie over the dog and held it to her stomach.

Ruby put her hood up and listened at the front door. Whoever it was, was on the stairs, seconds from the corridor. *It could be Tel.*

*Come on.*

One hand held the secret bundle, her other shut the door behind her. She kept her head down and walked on quickly, but not too fast. Someone walked past. She kept her head down and held the little body with both hands. *You know you have to be quiet and still.* She hoped that thinking it hard enough would somehow make the dog hear and understand.

She didn't look back to see if the person was Tel. If it was, he hadn't seen her. If it wasn't, she hoped whoever it was would think she was pregnant. *Not smuggling a dog.*

As soon as she'd turned the first corner she ran up the stairs, clinging to her warm hitchhiker. Ruby was convinced he was going to run up the stairs behind her, shouting, swearing. Her heart felt like it would beat through her chest and give her away.

'He won't get us, I promise,' she found herself saying out loud as she opened the door, looking either side of her. There was no one there. Inside, she shut the door and double locked it behind them.

Her dad was lying face down on the couch in front of the TV, snoring. She shut herself in her bedroom and exhaled.

Sitting on the bed, she slowly uncovered the bundle under her hoodie.

'You're a girl!' she said, smiling, 'I knew it.'

The little dog jumped off the bed and sniffed around all the corners of the room. Its tail was in the air, wagging.

*Now what?*

Ruby knew she should call the RSPCA, but she didn't want to let her out of her sight.

*Maybe I can keep her, without anyone knowing?*

The dog squatted down and let a stream of wee trickle all over the new rug.

\*\*\*

'What *the fuck* did you think you were doing, Ruby?' Her dad stood with his hands on his hips, looking down at her and the dog sat on her lap. The dog growled at him.

'I just - I couldn't let him- you should've seen what it

83

was like in there!'

'I *don't care*, Ruby. I told you, it's none of our business. I told you, and you did the *exact* opposite of what I said. Were you like this with your mum?'

She realised she was grinding her teeth. *Ignore him.*

'And since when did I say you could have a fucking dog?'

He jabbed a finger in the dog's direction. Her growl became a warning bark.

'Oh great, it's not just a dog, it's a vicious bastard too.' He shook his head. 'Unbelievable. This isn't what we agreed, Ruby. We agreed to start again. Part of starting again is *respect*. Respect for each other – that's what Madge said, isn't it? Respect for this flat, respect for this estate. Yeah?' He searched her face. She stared at her knees.

'*Yeah?*' he shouted in her face. The dog barked and Ruby stopped it lunging for him. She nodded.

'Good. Now, maybe it's my fault. I didn't spell it out to you because I thought it was obvious. But maybe it isn't. So I'm going to say it once and I'm not going to tell you again.'

He leaned over towards her and pointed both index fingers at her face.

'You. Don't. Grass. Okay?'

She nodded.

'Especially, *especially* on your mates. Yeah?'

*He's not my mate*, she wanted to say. But she knew the only way to calm him down was to say what he wanted to hear and keep quiet. She remembered her mum having to do the same.

'He knows it was you, Ruby. We'll be lucky if he doesn't come round and break my fucking legs when the fine comes in. Or the custodial. Or both!' He laughed, incredulous, 'un-fucking-believable.'

84

*Shit. Shit.* She hadn't thought that far ahead.

'I'm sorry,' Ruby said, quietly.

He stopped pacing and looked at her.

'Good.'

He looked at her face, then at the dog. He shook his head.

'Well...' he lit a cigarette and sucked deep, 'we'll need protection now, won't we? So I suppose the little bastard can stay.'

Ruby tried her best to look remorseful, meek and thankful all at the same time.

'Thank you,' she looked up at him, then down at the dog, 'I'll do everything for her.'

'Well yes you best fucking had do!' he snorted, raising his eyebrows.

In her room, she held her face in her hands, sat on the bed. She looked at the dog.

'What the hell am I doing?'

The dog cocked its head to one side, listening.

'Mum would've loved you, beautiful.' She stroked the dog's silky ears. 'Bella. Bella is what Gio would say. Bella for beautiful. That's your name.'

Ruby smiled at Bella, but then she thought about her dad and her face fell. *I don't want to go back to Denby House. He's on the edge. If something gets the better of him now... he needs a job. Some stability, something to get up for.* Ruby took out the card she'd kept for the last few days, from Tony.

There was no detail. No social media. Just his name and number. She thought of the boy's face, how angry he looked when Tony spoke. *How does he know him and his mum? He seemed kind of weird and mean. But then, Dad can be weird and mean.* She thought of how frustrated her dad got, applying for jobs and getting nowhere.

She ran her finger round the edge of the card. From the other room, she heard the crack-fizz of another can opening.

*Okay. I'm doing it.*

'Stay,' she said to Bella, shutting her in the bedroom. 'Dad?'

She stood in the doorway of the living room. He was on his phone. He looked up at her.

'Thanks. Take care,' he hung up and said, 'Rubes?'

'Rubes,' meant he'd forgiven her. Or was at least less angry with her than before.

'You know how you're looking for a job?'

He nodded.

'I bumped into someone the other day, they said they knew you. He gave me this,' Ruby said as she handed the card over, 'asked me to pass it on. He said he could give you a job.'

He stared at the card and smiled. 'Bloody hell, Tony. Been a long time. Where'd'you see him?'

'Just on the way in, to the estate,' she lied.

'That's really nice, thanks Ruby.'

He gave a half-smile and put the card in his pocket.

'Are you okay?' she asked. He was being too nice, too quiet. Something was wrong.

'Hm? Yeah. Yeah I'm fine. Just had some bad news, that's all.'

He drank. Kestrel Super Strength. He looked at the can, then downed the rest of it.

'Some bad news,' he repeated, then crushed the can in his fist and dropped it on the floor.

Ruby didn't know what to say. She stood, wondering whether to leave him alone and go back to her room, or ask him about it.

'It's okay,' he said, looking at her, 'nothing for you to worry about. I've just got to go to the police station tomorrow. Looks like someone has said something they shouldn't've.'

*Oh, shit.*

'Is it…to do with Tel?' Ruby asked, preparing herself for a bollocking.

'What? No,' he gave a short, flat laugh, 'nothing to do with that shit. Like I said, nothing for you to worry about.'

He got up and put his jacket on.

'Going to the pub. There's a tin of beans and some bread. I'll see you later.'

Ruby nodded and stepped out of his way.

She decided to push it to the back of her mind. She opened the bedroom door and smiled at the dog.

'Right,' she said to Bella, 'time for you to meet Auntie Annabelle!'

# CHAPTER 10

'Have you seen the fit Polish boy again?' Annabelle asked, after all her squealing and *oh my god oh my god oh my god!* at Bella was done with, and Bella had finally stopped licking Annabelle's face once Ruby dragged her away.

'He's not Polish, he's Ukrainian. I met him in the Polish shop, but he said the owners don't like Ukrainians. I think that might be bullshit though, I bet he's just been caught shoplifting there.'

'Right. And?'

'And no, I haven't seen him,' Ruby said, shrugging her shoulders.

'Damn. You need to figure out what school he goes to.'

*Oh god. You have to tell her.*

'Well, I think he goes to Burnside High. All the kids on the estate do.'

'Bloody hell Ruby, are you *sure* you fancy him? He's not, like, one of those kids that hangs out in the underpass is he?'

'They're alright, you know, they're not *evil*. They're just a bit loud. A bit…lairy. But they're fine once you get to know them. Fun. Dean can open bottle caps with his teeth. He's funny.'

'…Great… I'll remember that the next time one of

them slashes my dad's car tyres.'

Ruby laughed. *You're bullshitting,* her brain said, *trying to sound like you're friends with the bad boys. You're not. You spent a few hours with them on New Years' Eve, then they dumped you.*

'So he's one of that lot?' Annabelle asked, one eyebrow raised.

'No, no. He's different. An outsider. I don't think he has any friends.'

'Keeps himself to himself?'

'Yeah.'

'Like a serial killer?'

'Shut up,' Ruby shoved Annabelle, who threw her head back laughing.

'Well, don't come crying to me when you get cut up and put in bin bags. Actually, you wouldn't be able to, I suppose so there's no point me-'

Ruby jabbed Annabelle in her side.

'Don't, Annabelle. He's one of the good guys, I can tell.'

Annabelle smirked, but relented.

'Okay, okay. I'm sorry. I promise, I'll help you ask him out. Honest.'

Ruby laughed and put her head in her hands. 'Oh god, what a mess.'

'Your dad doesn't care then, about her?' Annabelle said, stroking Bella.

'Well, he did at first, but then I think he thought it might be nice having her round.'

'It *is!*' Annabelle said in a baby voice, kissing Bella on the forehead.

Ruby looked at Annabelle's pristine white room and realised Bella's hair was all over it.

'Your mum's going to go mental,' Ruby said, brushing the hair off the bedspread.

'Oh no it's fine, we have one of those pet hair Dyson things. She won't know, anyway, it's not her that hoovers.'

'Oh, is that how you get your allowance money?' Ruby always wondered why Annabelle had money for everything.

'What? No! God no, I'm shit at cleaning. No, Anka does it.'

'You have a cleaner?'

Annabelle shrugged.

'Yeah. All mum's friends do, I think she just felt left out. And she hates cleaning. Which is fair enough. I mean, so do I. I'll get one when I have my own place, even if it means buying less shoes.'

Ruby smiled and nodded. *Wow. Come on. Say it.*

'Listen, Annabelle, I'm moving schools.'

'What? Why?'

'I'm not in the catchment for King's any more,' she lied. *Coward.*

'No! Really? That's so shit, can't they just let you carry on coming, given what's happened? The bastards!'

Ruby shook her head. 'I'll be going to Burnside.'

Annabelle's face dropped. 'You're kidding?'

Ruby shook her head again.

'They can't do that, they just can't. I mean, aren't Social Services supposed to *look after* you? Listen, I'll have a word with my dad, he's always ranting on at the school and getting them to change things - I'm sure he'll be able to sort this out for you.'

'No, don't-' Ruby looked at her, 'I want to give it a go. I think... I don't know, maybe it'll help me fit in.'

'Is this because of that boy? Ruby, you don't even know his name! He could be a fucking psychopath!'

'It's *not* because of him,' Ruby snapped, 'I just- I don't know, I don't fit in on the estate, I still haven't made any friends…'

'You don't *need* any friends. You have me!'

'You don't know what it's like, Annabelle. You really, really don't.'

They sat in silence. Ruby's stomach started to knot itself. Finally, Annabelle spoke.

'Okay. I don't want to fall out with you again. It's not like I see you at school now anyway, I mean, you never really came back. But just remember, we can help,' she said, putting her hand on Ruby's shoulder.

Ruby looked at it. *I don't want your help, or your dad's. Or your pity.* She thought the words, but didn't say them. Instead, she just half-smiled and nodded.

'Thanks. Come on Bella, dad's expecting us back. He's making tea,' Ruby lied, thinking of the lonely tin of beans sat in their cold kitchen. She knew he'd be out all night, but she couldn't stand Annabelle feeling sorry for her any more.

They hugged goodbye. Ruby knew she wouldn't see her again any time soon.

\*\*\*

The flat was cold and empty. Bella ran round each room, sniffing.

In her room, Ruby lay on the bed and stared at the ceiling. Bella jumped up and curled up next to her, leaning her muzzle on Ruby's hip.

*What has dad done?* The thought kept scrolling through her mind, like a ticker tape.

Bella made a grizzling sound and sighed.

*Mum wanted me to live with him. She must've trusted he was better than a stranger. She must've loved him once. It's not what I wanted, but it's better than being in care. He's trying his best.*

She stroked Bella.

91

'What happens when he stops trying?' she asked her. Bella was asleep.

*You only have to stay here for another year. Then you can move out. Get your own place. Work part time while you do college. Or an apprenticeship. Get paid.*

*Tick*

Bella jerked awake and pricked her ears up

*Tick*

Ruby looked at her door.

'Dad?' she frowned, sitting up.

*Tick*

Bella barked. Ruby realised the sound was something hitting her window.

She walked over to the window and peered round the edge of the curtain. It was dark, but the orange streetlight lit up the path directly under her window. There was nobody there. *It's six floors down, Ruby. Nobody's throwing anything that high.*

'Ruby!'

She looked across. It was him. The Ukrainian boy.

*What the —?*

He motioned to her to open the window.

*He's there. He's there, he remembered my name and he wants to talk to me. Oh god.*

He was outside his flat, on the balcony. He could stand outside and see her, but outside her window there was no balcony, just a sheer wall. All she could do was open the sash. The night air rushed in.

He put a fistful of dried pasta on the wall next to him and brushed his hair out of his eyes.

'Hi,' she said, feeling her face start to burn.

'I didn't have anything else to throw that wouldn't break the window,' he said, pointing to the pasta.

She laughed. They stood silent, Ruby trying to think of something to say.

'Why-'

'I just wanted to let you know,' he interrupted her, 'the other day when you came round. That man,' he shook his head, 'don't give your dad his number. He's... a criminal.'

*So is my dad. And my brother.*

'Okay, thanks... for letting me know. I threw the card away anyway,' she lied, shrugging her shoulders.

'Oh,' he sighed, rubbing his eyes, 'thank god for that. You did the right thing. I'm sorry to have bothered you. I'm sorry he bothered you, too.'

'No, it's fine, don't apo-'

He turned to walk back inside, lifting his hand to indicate 'bye'.

'Wait!' Ruby shouted after him.

He turned and looked at her. Her mind went completely blank.

'What... what's your name?'

'Leo,' he stood waiting, as though he knew she wasn't done yet.

'Leo,' she repeated, nodding. *Quick. Think, quick!*

'Do you go to Burnside High?' she ventured. He nodded.

*Yes.*

'I'm starting there...soon. I - we -' she stammered, 'do you have any friends there?'

*Jesus Ruby, you're lame.*

'Not really,' he answered, shaking his head.

Something inside her leapt. *I knew it. He's like me.*

'Do you...live with your mum?' she asked. *Come on, he knows that you know he does.*

He nodded again, with a hint of a smile. She hoped he was at least starting to feel sorry for her, seeing as it was so obvious she was struggling.

'You?' he finally offered.

She smiled.

'My dad. Just moved here a few weeks ago. My mum died, so I had to move here…'

*Why did you say that? What is he supposed to say to that?*

'Oh, I'm sorry,' he said, looking at the floor.

'It's okay,' she said. She knew it wasn't, and never would be, but talking to him made her feel better.

She changed the subject. 'So you're from Ukraine then? Whereabouts?' *That's a ridiculous question. You don't even know where the country is, let alone where places in it are.*

'Odessa. You know it?'

It was a genuine question. Ruby felt flattered. *He thinks I might actually know.*

'Mm - yeah, I think so…' she said in a vague voice, trailing off.

He smiled.

'Does your mum have a job?' she was running out of questions.

'Cleaner.'

Ruby thought of Annabelle.

'Her name isn't 'Anka', is it?'

He looked bemused. 'No…'

'Doesn't matter. I just, know someone. Well, my friend does…'

He was about to speak, but heard a noise from inside the flat behind him and stopped.

'I've got to go,' he said, 'thanks, for opening the window. And… for asking my name.'

She felt butterflies.

He turned and walked inside, closing the door behind him, with a quick glance back to her and a smile.

The butterflies went crazy.

# CHAPTER 11

*So this is the worst school in Sheffield*, Ruby thought, watching Dan Brockway get manhandled out of the room by the Deputy Head, Mr Ogden. Mr. Haverbook cradled his face and struggled to stay upright at the front of the classroom. His hands were covered in the blood.

'Just, hang on there a minute. I need to deal with this,' he mumbled to the class, leaving the room.

Excitement rippled through the classroom.

'Did you see that?'

'He's mental!'

'He's broke Haverbrook's nose, what a legend!'

'Fucker deserves it.'

'Come on!'

The class turned to see Dan's friend climb onto the workbench that ran the perimeter of the classroom and start climbing out of the window.

'Do you want to join Dan in being expelled from the school, Lee?' Mr Haverbrook asked, walking back through the doorway. He held a paper towel to his nose.

'Because honestly, nothing would give me more pleasure,' he continued, 'please, I'm begging you. Give me the excuse I need. Do us all a favour and climb out of that window.'

He dabbed the paper towel to his nose one more

time then scrunched it up and folded his arms, watching Lee. The congealed blood glistened on his upper lip. The class was silent.

The boy looked at them, then at Mr Haverbrook. He climbed down, muttering under his breath, then sat back at his desk, heavily.

'You do surprise me, Lee. And for the record, my nose isn't broken. Now, if we've all finished fainting at the sight of blood, I'd like to get this over with and go home.'

*Me too.*

She hadn't seen Leo there yet. It had only been a week, but she was beyond disappointed. She hadn't seen him walking to or from school, in the corridors, the playground. He was nowhere. She struggled to think about anything else.

It helped, having Bella. She needed walking every morning, letting out every lunch time, walking at night. Bella meant she didn't have to face being alone for every dinner break.

After school, she hung around by the gates as she always did, hoping to see him walk out.

'Ruby?'

She turned around. It was Madge.

'Oh, hi. What are you doing here?'

'Our appointment. Remember? We said we'd meet after school?'

*Damn.*

'I can walk back with you — or we can go to a café if you don't want to talk back at the flat?'

*I'm not being honest with you. I don't want any drama.*

'I don't mind.'

'Okay, well, let's head back that way. There's a café nearby if we want a brew.'

They walked on. Ruby cringed, wondering if other

kids would know where Madge worked, why she was with her.

'Were you waiting for someone?' Madge asked.

'No… I was just… waiting.'

'…Okay…have you made any friends yet?'

Her impulse to lie was overridden by her exhaustion. It was too much work, making people up.

'Not yet.'

'But the kids from your estate are there, aren't they? Don't you talk to them?'

'They are, but…they've all been together for years, they have their groups set up already. I think that's why I've not really got to know anyone yet.' She shrugged. *That, and stalking Leo, and avoiding everyone else like the plague.*

'Are you sure having Bella is a good idea? Isn't it a bit too much responsibility? If you're going back to let her out every lunch time, you can't be doing much socialising… do you want me to get in touch with the local shelters –'

'No! No, please don't.'

*She's all I have,* she wanted to say. *I need her. She needs me.*

They stopped at the greasy spoon. Ruby didn't want her to see the state of the flat.

'Next time, I need to see your dad as well,' Madge said, bringing two cups of tea back from the counter. 'Now that he's back on tag, we need to make sure you're –'

'He's on tag? When did that happen?'

'Oh, I'm sorry, I thought he would've said. It's only for a month.'

*So that's what the phone call from the police was about. And why he disappeared for half of the next day.*

'It means he has to stay in, between certain times.'

'Okay.'

The drinking at home suddenly made sense. *He's not allowed to go to the pub.*

'How is he?'

*I think he's depressed. He doesn't really do anything except drink and sleep. Doesn't go anywhere, do anything, get dressed, showered.*

'Fine,' she lied, 'bit down, maybe. Think he wants a job. Well, needs one, anyway. It would be good for him, I think.'

'He has been trying. I'll see if there's anything more we can do to support him. It's hard, with no qualifications. But there are schemes – I'll look it up.'

'Thank you.'

'Is Bella the only friend you have, right now?'

Ruby didn't know what to say. It was true, but putting it like that was harsh.

'I know you're used to being quite isolated,' Madge said, 'and I can see you're sort of setting up a new version of your old life. Just you and her against the world. You have to look after her. She needs caring for...'

'Woah, woah woah. That's not what's going on,' Ruby said, shaking her head, 'I've only had her a few weeks. People have pets. It's normal.'

'Okay. I'm working with another girl, at the moment, who hasn't got many friends, either. She's at Burnside. Tia Williams, do you know her?'

'No.'

'I think you two would get on. Why don't you come to the youth club some time, I can introduce you?'

'It sounds like a blind date.'

'It'll get me off your back, okay?' Madge said, smiling.

'Fine.'

Back at the flat, Ruby almost wished Madge had seen the state of it, and the state of her dad. *Just to be worried*

98

*enough to bollock him, make him do something about it, but not enough take me into care.*

Gaz pushed himself up off the sofa and looked at her, bleary-eyed.

'Rubes, could you go to the shop for us?'

'For food?' she asked, hopefully.

'Yeah.' He rubbed his face, yawning. 'Get us some Skol while you're down there too will you love?'

'Dad, I don't want-'

'Look-' he pointed at his ankle, 'I'd go if I could, but it's past 7. You know the rules.'

'I know that, but I mean they won't serve me if I'm buying that, I'm fifteen.'

'Really? Already?'

He turned his head towards her, his bloodshot eyes struggling to focus on her face.

'When was your birthday?'

'Last week.'

'Shit, sorry love. Here,' he reached into his pocket and pulled out a £20 note, 'get something for yourself while you're there.'

'But-'

'Just take the fucking money, Ruby. Jesus. It'll be fine. They didn't ID you last time, did they? They don't care.'

On the way to the shop she passed the youth club. Bella waited patiently as she lingered near the entrance. A sign on the wall said: *Save Burnside YC!* She walked up and peered through the bars over the window. There were a few tables and chairs, a couple of sofas and a TV in the corner with a games console, both with bike chains attaching them to the wall. Beyond the seating area there was a pool table and a vending machine. Three girls and one boy were facing the other way, doing a dance routine in front of a phone that was balanced on a ledge.

*Save Burnside YC!*

She read the rest of the poster.

*We have lost our government funding. We are now 100% run by volunteers and paid for by local fundraising. Can you help? Have a bake sale, do a sponsored run, become a Friend of Burnside – every little helps to keep us open. We want local children and teenagers to have fun things to do, in a safe space. Help us stay open and help more kids to stay safe.*

'Ruby!'

She turned round. It was Kay.

'How you doing?' Kay asked, looking at Bella. 'She yours?'

'Yeah, only had her a few weeks.'

Kay gave Bella a fuss.

'She's gorgeous. You at Burnside now?' Kay asked, pointing at Ruby's uniform.

Ruby nodded.

'I used to go there. Shithole isn't it?'

'Where do you go now?'

For the first time since Ruby had met her, Kay looked shy. Awkward.

'Limegrove,' she said quietly, 'you heard of it?'

'No.'

Kay exhaled. 'It's only small. Anyway, you living with your dad now then?'

'Yeah.'

'I'm just off to Dean's, want to come with?'

She held up a plastic bag and the contents clinked.

'Got to get back,' Ruby said, then heard Madge's voice telling her to make friends. 'I'll message you, yeah? Do you live round here?'

'Just on Blackstock Rise,' she pointed up the hill.

'I'll message you.'

Her dad was right. She didn't get ID'd. The bag just about held up until she was at the front door, when it

100

split and the cans crashed all over the concrete floor.

'Fucks' sake,' she said, bending down to pick them up.

'Bad language, sis,' a voice behind her said. She turned round. Her brother stood there, smiling.

'Cal! What are you doing here? You look so different!'

He was taller, skinnier, sharper. She hugged him, awkwardly.

'Alright?' he asked, adding, 'old man in?'

Before she could answer, the door opened.

'Cal! Come here!' her dad exclaimed, throwing his arms open.

They hugged and Gaz laughed, which made him cough.

'You're looking well, son, how you been? Come in!'

Ruby walked in.

'You're clean, aren't you Cal?' Gaz said, as they walked through the hall into the front room. 'I can tell. Come here mate. Well done. Well done,' Gaz said, surveying the man in front of him.

Cal stood in the doorway of their flat. Bella jumped up at him, tail wagging, investigating the stranger.

'Come in, come in!'

Gaz stepped to one side, gesturing through to the living room with his Strongbow can.

'Nah, you're alright. Got to get to an interview. Just wanted to say hi, see you both.'

Cal smiled and looked at Ruby.

'How are you, Ruby?' he asked.

'Good. Yeah...' she trailed off. Ruby didn't know what to say. They had been so close when they were young and now it was like talking to a stranger. He looked at the floor and mumbled something about their mum.

'Did you try to come to the funeral?' Ruby asked the question before she thought about what it meant.

Cal looked hurt.

'Of course I did. They wouldn't let me.'

She wanted to believe him, but she had her mum's voice in her head, telling her not to trust him. She wondered if he was just a better liar than her dad was.

Cal looked uneasy. 'Right, well, I better get off anyway. See you round.'

He turned and disappeared off down the walkway.

'Don't be a stranger son!' Gaz called after him, 'always a can in the fridge round here for you!' Cal didn't turn round, but raised his hand in acknowledgement.

Ruby watched him stride down the concrete. He had a new swagger that she didn't like.

Gaz turned and glared at Ruby, slamming the door shut.

'What?' she asked.

'Why did you do that? *Why?*' he shouted.

Bella started barking and growling at him.

'Do what?' she said, 'I don't know what you're-' he slapped her, stopping her mid-sentence. She stood, holding her face, stunned.

Bella jumped and bit at his arm but caught his sleeve, hanging off it.

'Fucking hell!' He squirmed out of the jumper. Bella continued destroying it on the floor.

'You *know* what!' he continued, 'I *told* you he tried to come to the funeral. I told you on the day. Why did you have to ask that? Now he'll never come back here. *Never!*' he shouted, 'he's my son. My only son.' He shook his head. 'Fuck this tag, I'm going out.'

He opened the door and left, slamming it.

Ruby stood in the hall, her hand to her face. Bella looked up at her from the shreds of the jumper.

She didn't cry. She felt cold, somehow.

'You know what, Bella?' she asked the dog.

Bella sat down.

'He can go to hell. I'm done with him. I'm not cleaning up after him anymore. Not going to the shop for him. Not reminding him about his appointments. He can go fuck himself.'

# CHAPTER 13

A few days later, the mark on her face had faded. The police cautioned her dad about breaking his curfew, but nothing more. She hadn't spoken to him since. It was Saturday afternoon, so he was in the pub, watching football. She was alone again in the flat.

She'd spent the whole day trying not to think about Leo, which of course meant he was the only thought in her mind. She'd walked Bella, gone to the shop, checked her notifications – none – walked Bella again, watched TV, scrolled through Instagram, tidied the kitchen. She was running out of things to take her mind off him.

She wandered into her room and looked out of the window, avoiding looking straight across at his flat. Instead, she looked down at the playground.

All the chip papers and polystyrene takeaway boxes were being soaked to mulch by the drizzle. Some guys were smoking on the swings.

*Why don't they hang out somewhere else? They're old enough to be in the pub.*

A girl with a toddler started arguing with them. Ruby guessed that she wanted them to let her kid use the swings, but the boys weren't moving. They were shouting at each other, but she couldn't make out the detail. They all looked as though they were in their late teens.

Suddenly, the girl put her little boy down and pushed one of the guys in the shoulder. The boys both immediately stood up. Before the girl could step back, one of them grabbed the girl in a headlock. The other boy was shouting at her.

*Shit.* Ruby looked round the room, helpless. *Should I do something?* The toddler started screaming. She made a snap decision to leave Bella in the flat, worried she might get hurt, or hurt someone else. She ran down the stairwell, not entirely sure why or what she was going to do when she got down there.

Outside, she finally heard what they were shouting.

'Say you're sorry you fat fucking bitch!' the boy snarled. His mate laughed.

'Get off me! Get off me!' the girl screamed, frantic. She tried to bite the boy's arm but it was wrapped too tightly round her neck. The toddler, still bawling, stumbled towards his mum and fell over. Ruby ran over and picked him up.

'Who the fuck are you?' said the boy.

*Shit. What am I doing?*

'Just - just let her go, her kid's crying,' Ruby said, suddenly feeling sick. She was in too deep.

The boy loosened his grip but kept the girl close. He sneered at Ruby, eyeing her as though he didn't know whether to laugh at her or spit at her. Her legs started to feel hollow. She struggled to bear the weight of the toddler on her hip.

The girl managed to free herself and made a dash towards Ruby and the kid. But just as fast as he'd got her in the headlock, the boy grabbed her by the hair and held her face close to his. Ruby held her breath.

The girl's makeup ran down her face in the rain, black down her cheeks and tan foundation down her pale neck. Her eyes were fixed on his. Veins throbbed in the

105

boy's forehead. He bared his yellow teeth, hissing, 'say it!' and spat in her face.

'I'm sorry! I'm sorry okay, Jesus Christ!' shouted the girl, wincing at the phlegm sliding down her cheek.

He loosened his grip on her hair, but didn't let go.

'Good.'

She strained to get away. 'Now you can go.' he said, smiling. Ruby exhaled.

But as the girl tried to walk towards Ruby, he whipped her head back in his hand and threw it forwards, smashing her head-first into the metal frame of the swings. Ruby screamed.

She watched the girl sink to the floor, bleeding from her scalp. The boys laughed and turned to face her.

'Do you want some?' they asked Ruby.

They smirked, walking towards her and the toddler.

Ruby stood, unable to make her limbs move. The toddler gripped her tightly, its tiny fingernails digging into her side.

She scanned around her for a route to run away.

*None. Fuck...what the hell?*

She looked again at the figure behind them. It was Leo, silently making his way from the block to the playground.

Her heart was beating so hard her jumper started to pulse in and out over her chest.

*What is he going to do? Oh my god. Is that a baseball bat?*

'I think this one needs teaching a lesson, don't you?' said the boy. The girl was still unconscious on the floor. Ruby's stomach tied itself in knots. She stood firm, gripping the toddler, shaking on the inside.

Leo ran towards the boys, controlled, quiet. Ruby tried not to look and give him away. Suddenly, he was right behind them. Ruby swallowed and breathed deeply. One of the boys turned round just in time to see the bat as it swung towards the side of his head. The *crack* sound as it hit his skull made her heave.

She clung to the toddler and stared at the boy's body, writhing on the floor. Her pulsing blood felt as though it would burst through her neck.

She looked up. The other boy grabbed Leo. The bat fell to the floor.

'Shit, Leo!' Ruby screamed.

'Call an ambulance!' he shouted. Ruby got her phone out and tried to dial, her hand shaking uncontrollably.

The girl opened her eyes and struggled to get to her feet, swaying.

Leo and the boy were each trying to wrestle the other into the railings. The boy aimed a clumsy fist at Leo's face, stunning him. He shook his head, blinking. The boy lunged at him again, but this time Leo managed to knee him in his stomach. He crumpled, staggering backwards.

'And police!' Leo shouted. He ran to the bat and picked it up, holding it ready.

The boy was winded, gasping for air, holding onto the railings. He looked up at Leo, scowling.

'You're fucking mental, you are, you Polish fucking scrounger!' he managed to spit.

Leo stepped towards him, gripping the bat.

'Alright, I'm going, fucking hell,' he relented. The boy walked away, glancing back at his friend on the floor who was still coughing, trying to get to his feet.

'There's no signal!' Ruby shouted.

'Don't call the police,' said the girl. She had managed to walk over to Ruby. 'I don't need an ambulance either. I'm fine. Thanks,' she said, taking the toddler back.

'You're not okay, you're covered in blood!'

'No I'm not.' said the girl, quietly. She dipped her coat sleeve in the puddle of water by her feet and rubbed at her forehead and cheeks. The blood seeped into her sleeve and smeared around her face with the traces of make-up. She swapped arms, balancing the toddler on her other hip. She repeated the process with her clean sleeve. Ruby and Leo just stared at her.

The boy got to his feet too, blinking and rubbing his scalp.

'There's no need for the police.' he said, looking at the girl, 'is there?'

'No,' she said, holding his gaze, 'we're sound, aren't we Gav?' she said to him, her voice wavering.

'Oh yeah. Sound,' he said, glaring at her.

The girl stroked her kid's hair.

'Come on, sweet, let's go home,' she said, and kissed his forehead.

She walked away and didn't look back.

The boy turned to face Leo.

'Do yourself a favour and don't ever fucking show your foreign face round here again. I know people. And we've got more than a shitty baseball bat. I swear, we will kill you. Alright? You best watch your fucking back.'

Leo nodded, gripping the bat till his knuckles were white.

The boy walked off, lighting a cigarette. Ruby and Leo stood, watching him walk away.

The evening had drawn in. The rain was heavier, falling hard and straight in rods, lit orange by the streetlights. The sound of the rain hitting concrete filled the silence.

'Crazy,' said Leo, finally. 'Are you okay?'

'I'm fine. Are you?'

He nodded. She knew her clothes were soaked and she should feel the freezing cold but she didn't, she was too pumped full of adrenaline to notice.

'Thank you,' she said, 'I don't know what just

happened, but thank you so much.' The words spilled out quickly, she couldn't slow them down. 'I - I mean, I don't know what would've happened if you weren't here. If you hadn't-'

'Just lucky,' he said. She was grateful for the interruption. 'You shouldn't be thanking me, though,' he carried on. 'I'm not the one who saved the day, you are. You saw what was going on and stepped in, on your own. That's brave. I'm not the hero.' It was the most he'd ever said to her. The most she'd heard him say, even. 'My mum keeps the bat by her bed,' he continued, 'sometimes you need it.' He smiled. 'That girl must be mad, don't you think? And the boys. *Polish*. Ha!' he shook his head.

'Yeah.'

She nodded, feeling the rain drip from her nose. Her toes were numb. She didn't care. All she wanted was for him to grab her and kiss her.

'Come on, you need warm,' he said. She nodded.

*Is this really happening?*

Up the stairs, at his front door, she glanced over at her flat. Her bedroom was in full view. She could see Bella, asleep on her bed.

*God, you can see everything.*

'I liked your dance, by the way,' he said, smirking.

'Shut up!' she laughed, and gave him a little push. The thrill of touching him rippled through her. A pang of regret hit her as she felt the need to message Annabelle about this.

When he was through the door, he turned round. She was hesitating outside.

'Don't worry, that man isn't here,' he said, and motioned her through.

A female voice came from inside the kitchen. She was speaking another language. *Ukrainian*. Leo replied.

Ruby wished she could understand what they were saying.

The woman came through to the hall. *Wow, she's so young!* But she was his mum, there was no mistaking it. Her eyes were just like Leo's, but her hair was platinum blonde. She was wearing a 'Golddigga' grey tracksuit. As soon as she saw them, she exclaimed something in reaction to the state of their appearance.

Leo said something to his mum, mentioning the word 'Ruby'.

'Ruby, my goodness look at you!' she said, with the same accent as Leo, 'you must get warm. What have you been doing, you two?'

She ushered them into the kitchen and filled up the kettle. She was talking in their language again to Leo. Ruby gathered that he was telling her what had happened, but she had no idea if he was telling the truth. His mum seemed to be scalding him, but then she hugged him.

'My boy does stupid things,' she said to Ruby, 'are you the girl over there?' she said, pointing out of the window with one hand, and giving her a towel with the other.

'Erm, yep, that's me,' Ruby said, awkwardly dabbing her hair with the towel.

'Oh! So here you are. He talks about you a lot you know.'

Ruby's heart skipped. Leo blushed.

*I'm in his flat. I've met his mum, he's talking to me. He talks about me. Jesus Christ.* She pinched the back of her hand, behind her back. Yep, it's real.

'Aren't you going to work?' he said.

'Of course, of course. I'll leave you alone,' she winked at Ruby, 'he'll look after you.'

Leo smiled and shook his head as she left, closing

110

the front door behind her.

'She's mad,' he said, and put a glass with a metal handle in front of Ruby.

She had no idea what it was. It was hot. She'd never had a hot drink in a glass before. It was very dark brown, almost black. The only thing she could think of was cola. But it also smelt like vodka. *Hot vodka and coke?*

Leo could see she was confused. 'It's black tea,' he explained, 'we have it black in Ukraine. Sometimes, if mum's had a bad day, or if it's a special day, she puts vodka in,' he drank some of his own.

'Oh right, I get it,' Ruby said, distracted by his mouth, which was glistening with the tea, or the rain, she wasn't sure which.

*Get a hold of yourself.*

She took a sip and tried not to cough. The first taste was fiery hot vodka. The heat made the burn stronger. Then she got the bitter-sweet herbs of the tea. *Not too bad.*

'My mum is so embarrassing. Is your Dad the same?' Leo asked. He was already halfway down his glass.

'He's definitely embarrassing, but not in a funny way,' Ruby said, already disarmed by the drink.

'How do you mean?' said Leo, leaning his head on his hand.

'Well,' Ruby hesitated. She wasn't sure what to say. She couldn't think of anything except the truth. 'He just drinks. When I moved here he seemed okay, but he just started drinking more and more. He's a dickhead.'

She felt guilty for saying it out loud. He was the first person she'd talked to about it.

He nodded. 'This is a problem in my country too. Men drink. Some of my family were the same.'

He finished his drink.

Ruby drank the rest of hers. Her limbs felt warm and

111

loose.

'I wanted to say sorry…' he said, looking in the bottom of his glass.

'What for?'

'Not talking to you. Well, not much, I mean. I just… we came here under, kind of strange circumstances. We don't know who we can trust. My mum is nice to everyone, because that's just what she's like, but I'm more… careful. You've been really nice to me,' he smiled, 'but it's hard to know who is on your side.'

'I'm on your side,' she put her hand on her chest and patted it, 'Team Leo,' she said, laughing.

*God Ruby. That was really cringe. Change the subject.* She shivered, deliberately.

'You want a jumper?' he said.

'If you've got one, that would be great.'

Her hoodie was saturated with water. Leo came back in.

'I'll put it on the bed, you can put that one on the radiator…I'll stay here,' he said, looking at the floor. She followed his direction and found his bedroom.

*Here it is.* The bedroom she already knew from watching him in it. *I'm not a stalker*, she told herself, over and over.

His room was exactly the same size as hers. He had a bookcase full of books, all in different languages. *He's got a whole library*. He had novels, books on history, geography, politics – Ruby suddenly felt very small and stupid.

*It doesn't mean he's read them all.*

She took off her top and put it over the radiator. His jumper was far too big for her, but it was warm and smelt like him. She breathed it in.

Ruby looked at his desk. It was covered in sketches. They were landscapes, windswept moorlands and craggy hillsides. *They're beautiful.*

She called through to the kitchen, 'are these your drawings?'

He came through and leaned against the doorway.

'Yes they're mine. I'm not an artist...'

'No they're really good, are they of Odessa?' she said, pleased with herself for remembering where he was from, but suddenly embarrassed that he'd know how long she'd remembered that for.

Leo laughed. 'Odessa does not look like this. Don't you know where it is?'

She took a guess. 'Um, Scotland?'

'No, Peak District.'

'Oh, yeah, of course, sorry!'

'You just get the train, don't you?' he said.

'I've never actually been.' she said, fiddling with her sleeve, feeling inadequate again. He looked stunned. Ruby searched for an excuse.

'My mum wasn't well for a long time, so I didn't really go anywhere.'

She felt guilty for saying that. *That's not the reason. You didn't go* before *mum got ill.* She didn't want to tell him they'd never had a car, or that none of her family were the kind of people who would get public transport to a place where all they could do was walk up hills.

Suddenly he reached out and grabbed her hand.

'We will go. You must see it,' he said.

'Okay' she managed to squeak. She held his gaze. She wanted to kiss him, but instead she just stayed frozen, unable to move.

He took a step towards her. *This is it.*

The sound of a key in the front door ruined the moment.

Leo dropped her hand and they both turned round to see his mother, taking off her shoes.

'Bloody bus man. He took my pass and said it's out of date. *He's* out of date!' she said, and laughed. 'I'm not walking at this time. I'll call in sick. Bloody bus bloody man, don't you think, Ruby!' she said, smiling at her.

'I'm just going. Thanks for having me round,' she said, looking at the floor.

'Oh, erm, your jumper-' she turned to Leo but still couldn't look at him directly.

'You need it now Ruby,' said Leo's mum, patting her arm. 'I'll wash yours, don't worry.'

'Oh, thank you.'

Leo's mum grabbed Ruby and kissed her cheek.

'Isn't she lovely?' she said to Leo.

'Mum, you're embarrassing her!'

'Well she is. Bye, Ruby, come back soon!' she waved. Ruby waved at his mum and looked past her to Leo, who put his hand up and said 'bye'.

His half-smile was there again, just like it was when he'd seen her dancing.

Outside, Ruby faced the darkness and breathed in the night.

*Wow.*

# CHAPTER 14

Ruby would do whatever Madge wanted, now. She was so happy about Leo, all the things she'd been reluctant to do didn't seem scary any more. *Fine, I'll go to the youth club. Make friends. Go to school. Do normal things that normal kids do. It's not going to kill me. Ignore dad, leave him to it. Doesn't matter.* If she let the rest of her life wash over her in a meaningless blur, she could focus on Leo without any aggravation.

'Ruby, this is Tia,' said Madge, beaming at them both.

Tia smiled, awkwardly. Ruby did the same and wondered if she was supposed to shake hands. The three of them stood in silence.

'Anyway,' said Madge, 'come sit down.'

She led the way to the sofas. There were a couple of kids playing pool and one watching TV. A volunteer came through from the kitchen with a box of biscuits and opened them up, placing them on a table.

'He's lovely, Mick,' Madge said, nodding towards the volunteer. 'So anyway I wanted to introduce you two, because you've got a bit in common. Ruby, your mum sadly passed away, didn't she, and you live with your dad.'

*This is the most awkward thing I've ever been through.* She remembered the dancing-in-the-mirror-incident. *Okay, second most awkward.*

'Tia, your father sadly passed away, and you're living with your auntie, now. She's very different to how your dad was, though, isn't she, Tia? So you're finding it a bit hard.'

Tia looked mortified.

'You're finding it hard with your dad, aren't you Ruby?'

'Sometimes,' she said quietly, desperate for the conversation to end.

'I know I'm deeply uncool,' said Madge, 'and this is all a bit awkward, but it does help to talk to other people who are in situations like yourself, you know? You both live on the estate, you both go to the same school. I'm not saying you have to be best friends, I'm just saying it might be nice to have a chat now and then.'

Ruby cringed. *I have a best friend. Or I used to, anyway.* Tia didn't say anything.

'I can tell you both wish the ground would swallow you up now. Or me, maybe. So I'll leave you to it. Just humour me, okay?'

Madge got up and said bye to Mick, taking one of the biscuits on her way out.

Ruby and Tia sat in silence. Tia was the first to speak.

'Well that was horrendous,' she said, with a slight laugh.

Ruby was so relieved.

'Yep. I'm sorry, I think it's my fault, she's worried I won't make friends now I've moved here.'

'How long have you been here?'

'Just a couple of months. Only started at Burnside High a couple of weeks ago.'

Tia nodded.

Awkward silence, again.

'Eyup, losers, how do you know each other?'

*Kay.*

She stood in the doorway for a second then saw the box of biscuits and wandered over to them. She picked out a few and came over to them both, sitting between them.

'We don't,' said Tia, 'we have the same social worker. She introduced us just now.'

'Oh. Jammy Dodger?'

'So, how do *you* know each other?' Tia asked, shaking her head at the biscuit.

'Denby House,' said Kay, holding the biscuit out to Ruby, who took it.

'Oh, I see,' Tia said, looking at Ruby differently.

'So you know Tia from...?' Ruby asked Kay.

'School. Well, Dean and Jack know each other, don't they?' Kay said, turning to Tia. Tia nodded.

'Tia's boyfriend,' Kay explained to Ruby.

'You still seeing Dean?' Tia asked.

Kay nodded.

'You guys want to see the new Avengers movie? I mean, I've not seen any of the others, but I'm bored, and I know a guy who works there and he'll get us in for free. Plus,' she reached inside her jacket and pulled out a hipflask, 'I've got rum, so if we just get a coke, we're all set.'

'Where did you get that?' Tia asked, taking the silver bottle. 'It's engraved: *My one and only* – did Dean give you this?'

'Did he bollocks,' Kay laughed, 'lifted it from someone in Rev de Cuba last Friday. They were wasted. They won't miss it.'

\*\*\*

Ruby shrieked with laughter. She couldn't remember the

last time she'd laughed like that. They were running down the alley at the back of the cinema.

'As if! I can't believe you did that, Kay!' Tia screamed.

'The man was a twat! He's lucky it was just a drink in his face, I should have lamped him,' Kay shouted back.

They slowed at the entrance of the canal path.

'Well done, Kay,' Tia said, 'I've never been kicked out of the emergency exit of a cinema before. First time for everything.'

'Me neither,' added Ruby.

The evening was still warm. The sun was still just about over the horizon. Other than that one Ukrainian tea, Ruby hadn't drunk anything alcoholic since New Years' Eve. *Fair enough, Dad. I can see the appeal.* She felt weightless, but full of energy, as though she could run for miles.

They carried on, along the towpath. Ruby assumed they knew where they were going. She had no idea.

'Dad hit me, the other day,' Ruby said, out of nowhere. 'He's never done it before.'

'That's shit, Rubes,' said Kay, 'he's a fucker. Just hit him back next time. Take a fucking bottle to his face, I would. Mind you, when Mum hit me with the iron, I didn't do anything, so... you never know how you'll react.'

Kay lit a cigarette and offered one to each of them. Tia took one. Ruby did the same, pretending she'd done it before. *Don't cough. Don't be a cliché. Don't cough.*

Kay held her lighter and Ruby held the end of the cigarette to it, watching it glow. She sucked, and Kay took away the flame.

She coughed.

*For Fucks' sake.*

'Sorry,' she said, 'went down the wrong way.'

'What?!' Kay asked, laughing.

'I don't know,' Ruby said, shaking her head, giggling.

'Do the social know he's drinking again?' Kay asked.

'He never stopped drinking, really. It's just got worse.'

'Don't let them know if it's got worse,' Kay said, 'they'll move you.'

'No,' Ruby said, 'I won't. I don't want to go back to Denby House.'

'Oh, that place was fine. It's foster care you need to worry about.'

'I don't know,' said Tia, 'my cousin and his wife are foster carers, they're really nice.'

'Oh yeah? They your auntie's kids?'

'Yeah.'

'So are they religious nutters too?'

'It's not a religion, it's a cult.'

Ruby laughed.

'No, seriously, it is,' said Tia. 'They own the flat. But no, my cousin isn't in it. My aunt only converted a couple of years ago, after he'd grown up and left. Someone caught her just at the wrong time. One of those people with the signs that everyone avoids on Fargate.'

'My point exactly,' Kay said, turning to Ruby, taking a drag on her cigarette, 'you just don't know what you're getting into.'

'She's manageable,' Tia said, 'as long as she has absolutely no idea about my life,' she added, laughing.

'She still making you go to that weird centre every Sunday morning?' Kay asked.

Tia nodded.

'Let's carry on drinking, then, see how hungover we can get you for the service tomorrow. Come on, if we get the tram up to town, I know one of the doormen on West Street.'

119

\*\*\*

In the toilets of the bar, Ruby hurled her guts up. Tia did the same. They shared the toilet bowl.

'You okay?' Tia asked, eyeing Ruby over the rim.

Ruby nodded.

She'd never been out on West Street before. She'd never been out in town before.

'I'm fine. I can still see. Just needed to get that out. Come on,' she said, staggering to her feet, shaking her head, 'let's dance.'

\*\*\*

*Fucking hell.*

Ruby kept her eyes closed, knowing she would struggle with the light when she opened them. *Bang, bang, bang.* Her blood thudded in her ears.

*Bang, bang, bang.* It was faster this time. She opened her eyes. It was the door.

*How did I get home?* She couldn't remember. *Shit. Answer the door.*

She hauled herself up, feeling the room spin.

'Package to sign for,' the guy said, handing over a gadget with a screen for her to scribble on.

She struggled to focus on the screen and make her mark. The fresh air was welcome, though.

'Sunday delivery costs a bomb - they must really want you to have this.'

Ruby signed. She had no idea what it could be. She checked the typed label: *Ruby Morton. Weird.* It was quite a big parcel, probably half her size. It wasn't heavy, just bulky.

Her dad was asleep on the sofa. There was a bottle of Vladivar lying on its side under his hand, which was hanging over the edge of the couch.

*I bet I feel worse than he does. He's used to it.*

She opened the parcel in her room. Tearing the brown paper, she caught sight of an envelope taped to the clear plastic bag underneath. The bag looked like it contained fabric, maybe clothes.

She ripped the envelope off the bag and turned it over.

*Ruby*

She knew the handwriting. *Annabelle.* Ruby smiled.

*Happy belated birthday Rubester! Sorry I've been rubbish at keeping in touch recently. I've been in London at my auntie's office over Easter, doing work experience, it's SO COOL! She has like a million samples through every day that she has to check over. She took me on a few buying expeditions to Paris and Berlin. I DEFINITELY want to work in fashion.*
*Anyway, here are a bunch of samples that I picked out for you. You'd look amazing in them.*
*Miss you Ruby. Message me when you get chance, it'd be great to catch up when I'm back in Sheff.*
*XOXOX*

Ruby felt like crying. *I haven't replied to her messages. All this time. She's the nicest person.*

Ruby tore the plastic open and emptied the samples on to her bed. *Jeez, Annabelle!*

*Topshop. Forever 21. H&M. Brandy Melville. Marc Jacobs. Zara.*

She unfolded each beautiful item. Tops, skirts, dresses. She didn't own any dresses. Or skirts. Ruby lived in jeans, leggings, jeggings. *This is all so stylish. Grown up. Wow.*

She took out her phone and drafted a message. Then she cancelled it. *Hang on.*

121

She tried on each garment and looked in the mirror. It only showed to her waist, but it was enough to get a good idea of how each one looked. She smiled and ruffled her hair. *You look like an actual woman. They're so fancy.* A wraparound cut-on-the-bias dress instantly became her favourite. *I wish Leo could see me in this.* She took a photo, getting as much of her reflection as possible in the shot.

Instagram: #bestie #marcjacobs #dress #fashion #thankyou #friends #smile #style

She posted the photo, tagging Annabelle.

Ruby messaged her.

*I love my present! Thank you so much. When are you back in Sheff? We have loads to catch up on Xxxx*

She opened her curtains and let the sun in. *Get over it. Get over the hangover. You'll be fine.*

She sat on the bed and sighed, looking out of the window. *There he is. Reading again.* He looked up, out of the window, but not at her.

*Shit, he'll see me. It looks like I'm watching him…* it was too late to move, he'd seen her. She smiled, self-conscious. He waved, and signalled for her to wait while he got something. She could see he was writing something in big letters on his notepad. He returned and held it up to the window.

*07830167132 - MY NUMBER* it said. Ruby smiled. She put it in her phone and texted him:

*Got it x*

Leo:

*Got to go out now. Let me know when you're free for our walk ☺ x*

He waved at the window and disappeared.

*Our walk? The Peak District! Yes. Yes yes yes.* She sat

back on the bed, hugging her phone. She hadn't dreamed it. *Going to his flat a couple of nights ago really happened. He meant what he said. He didn't regret it. Plus, he just saw me in this dress.*

'Now that's how to recover from a hangover, Bella,' she said to the patient dog, waiting at the bottom of her bed.

Bella ran to the corner of the room, retrieved her lead and dropped it on Ruby's knee.

*\*\*\**

Ruby put her alarm on snooze for the fifth time and rolled over.

*School. No. Please, no.*

She'd spent the last hour snoozing the alarm in ten minute bursts. *Alright.* She sat up, stretched and stroked Bella, who sprung off the bed.

'Let's get you out, then.'

Ruby hated leaving her while she was at school. Bella stayed in Ruby's room while she was out. She didn't go back at lunchtime to take her for a wee any more. She managed to hold it.

Ruby started to get dressed when she heard a voice and stood still.

*What?*

It was a woman's voice, coming from the next room, laughing. Ruby finished putting her clothes on and walked into the hallway slowly, listening. Bella jumped up at her, whining to go out.

'Shh, Bella!' she whispered. The voice stopped. Ruby started for the front door, hoping to get away before whoever was in there emerged. The door of her dad's bedroom opened. *Too late.*

'Rubes, are you off already?' her dad said, 'I want

123

you to meet someone.'

He sounded rough, but excited, like he'd had a winning night at the dogs maybe, she thought.

Ruby was freaked out. He hadn't said more than two words to her since Cal came round. He'd barely been conscious. Now he wasn't sober, exactly, but he was awake and talking to her, as though they were on good terms.

A woman emerged from behind him, smiling. She had a lined, thin face that looked like it had been in the sun too much. Her eyeliner and mascara was smudged down her cheeks, but some still clung where it should be. She had a mass of strawberry blonde permed hair.

'Hiya love. I'm Kaz,' she said.

Her voice was warm and gravelly. She was wearing tight jeans, black stiletto boots and a white vest top. Gaz was in his dressing gown. They smelled of smoke, cider and sweat.

'Hi,' Ruby said. *This is too awkward.* Bella sniffed at Kaz's boots. Kaz bent down to stroke her.

'Aren't you gorgeous?' said Kaz.

Bella licked her hand.

'Get out of it!' Gaz said, laughing. Bella immediately backed away.

*He's pretending to like the dog. This is pathetic.*

'Come on Bella, we need to go,' she said.

'Don't be rude Ruby,' her Dad said, 'this is Kaz. She's my girlfriend.'

He put his arm round her. Kaz grinned.

*Her teeth are as bad as his.*

'Okay,' Ruby said, nodding.

'Me and Kaz go way back, don't we babe?'

He looked at her and kissed her neck. Kaz giggled. *Eurgh.*

'We do,' said Kaz, 'I'm going to whip him into shape

124

Ruby - sort this shithole out ey?' she cackled, pointing round the flat. Gaz slapped her back-side in fake protest and pulled her towards him, kissing her again. *Oh god.* Ruby tried to hide her reflex to gag.

'I have to go. I'll be late for school.'

They weren't listening. Ruby shut the door behind her and took a deep breath of the fresh air.

*Jesus.* She shuddered. *Okay. School's fine.*

# CHAPTER 15

*Two weeks. You had to wait two weeks, but tomorrow, it's finally happening. You're going out for the day with him. Oh dear god. I need help.*

She messaged Annabelle:

*I'm going out with Leo tomorrow. He asked me to go for a walk in the Peak District weeks ago but the weather's been shit but tomorrow it looks like it's okay so we're going and oh god I'm just so nervous I just want to vom. What do I wear? What do I do with my hair? HELP ME xxx*

Annabelle replied straight away:

*OMG this is a BIG DEAL Ruby! I wish I was around tonight to help you go through options but it's my grandparents' wedding anniversary thing, I can't miss it. Send me photos of options tho! You're going to look HOT I promise xxxxx*

'*Ruby!* Put the phone *away*, I won't tell you again!' Mr Haverbrook shouted.

She thrust it back in her rucksack and looked down at her notebook.

After 15 more minutes of pretending to work, it was finally home-time. *Friday.* Ruby remembered what Friday home-time used to mean - going back to her mum and spending two whole days with her. *It's okay. You have Leo now.*

Suddenly she felt guilty. She walked out of school, in

her own world, trying to reason with herself. *Nobody can replace her. But she's gone. We've been through this. You cried for weeks. Months. And it didn't bring her back, did it?*

Her eyes were fixed on the ground, trying not to cry. She felt a body bump into her and stopped. It was Kay.

'Sorry,' said Ruby, stepping backwards, 'you alright?'

'Alright,' Kay muttered, looking straight past her, carrying on walking.

*Weird.*

Ruby looked around her on the way back to Burnside Court. Everything was covered in grey autumn drizzle and mist. She felt as though she was breathing in the grey and it was slowly becoming part of her. She shuddered. *You should be happy. Things are good. You're not in care. Dad has a new distraction. You're friends with Annabelle again. You're going on a sort-of date with Leo. You can't let feeling bad about mum ruin every time you feel happy.*

Ruby carried on walking through the mist, past disembodied voices and outlines, drifting in and out of her vision like tadpoles in muddy pond water. Finally she looked up. There was Burnside Court, hanging over it all like a man swinging from a noose.

*It's not just mum. It's this place. You'll get out, you know. One day. Just keep your head down.* Her mum's voice was in her head, now. *I want you to do better than I did, Ruby. Work hard at school. I don't want you worrying about bills. I'm not saying money makes you happy, but I don't want you struggling like I have. Work hard, get a job that pays enough. Not three jobs on zero hours. Something with security. You need qualifications, for that.* She thought of the empty exercise books from this week. *Is it too late to suddenly start caring about school?*

She stood at the entrance of the estate, eyes glazed, picking at the peeling paint on the railing. *It's not too late to start sorting yourself out. You have to try.* She thought of Annabelle and her work experience at her auntie's

127

glamorous office. *She got her Saturday job at Topshop off the back of that. She doesn't even* need *a job.*

Ruby turned and walked away from Burnside, nodding to herself.

*You have to do something. You don't have an auntie that can get you a placement at a swanky fashion house. But you have someone who offered you a job once.*

She looked at the time on her phone. 16:10. *There's time.*

\*\*\*

Ruby felt ten foot tall. She waved back at Gio as she walked out of the café door.

*I have a job. I can pay for myself. I can even move out in a year. Gio said I could get part time hours to fit round college.*

She walked back to Burnside, which seemed totally different now. The mist had cleared and made way for golden rays to glint off the windows of the tower blocks. Kids ran through the playground, laughing. She wanted to tell someone about the job. *Annabelle. Leo.* She got her phone out and started drafting a message as she put her key in the door.

The flat was empty. *They'll be at the pub.* She thought about Friday nights with her mum, snuggled in front of the TV in a clean, warm house. *Stop dwelling on mum. You have things to look forward to. She would be proud.*

In the kitchen Ruby eyed the pile of bills under the toaster. *You won't be like him. You'll pay your bills.* Ruby imagined living in a flat, on her own, or maybe with Annabelle. *Nah. She won't move out till she goes to uni. But she can come round all the time. She'll help me decorate. I'll buy whatever food I want and keep it all so clean and tidy. I'll have a little desk and proper work space for all my college stuff.* She imagined the neat row of box files, the coffee mug on a coaster, next to a proper laptop. *Leo can come round and stay. He could move in! Alright. Calm down.*

After searching for anything edible left in the kitchen, she scraped the last of the jam from the sticky jar and spread it across the one piece of bread that wasn't stale.

*It will be so good.* She smiled and ate her tea.

*Right. You need to sort an outfit.*

Her phone jingled. It was a number she didn't recognise.

*Hey Ruby, it's Tia. I hope you don't mind, Kay gave me your number. Can u come over? Need sum1 2 talk 2 x*

She hesitated.

*It's okay. You can pick out clothes when you get back.*

She replied:

*Sure, where are you? I just have to walk my dog, then I'll be over xx*

Ruby felt guilty about Bella. She decided tomorrow she'd give her a really long walk, with lots of throw and fetch. Tia was right at the top of the tower and the lift was out of order, so Ruby had a lot of stairs to climb. She wasn't sure what to expect. *I hope her auntie's out. She sounds weird.*

By the time she reached Tia's floor, she was out of breath. She felt good, though, leaning on the balcony, looking out over the streets and the city ahead.

She turned and knocked on the door. Tia answered. She'd been crying.

'Hey, are you okay?' Ruby asked.

'I'm sorry. I messaged Kay but Dean is being a dick, not letting her see anyone. I didn't know who else I could talk to,' Tia said, starting to sob.

'Hey, hey what's wrong, what's happened?' Ruby asked, offering an awkward hug. Tia held her briefly, then pulled away, stepping back to let her into the flat.

'I've fucked up,' she said, closing the door.

'Is your auntie in?'

Tia shook her head. Ruby followed her through to her bedroom.

'Is it Jack?' she asked.

Tia sat on the bed, rubbing her eyes.

'My life is over,' she said, and looked at Ruby.

'Oh… you mean?' Ruby glanced, involuntarily, at Tia's stomach.

'I am. I'm pregnant. And I've got to have the baby. She found the test,' she said, lying down on her side.

Ruby didn't know what to say. She barely knew her.

She stared around the room while Tia cried into the pillows. It didn't look how she'd expected. No posters, no clothes on the floor, no photos, no piles of make-up, hair accessories, no books, no posters, no trace of teenage girl - just floorboards, a wooden chest of drawers, plain walls and a portrait of a man in a suit, above the bed.

'How far along are you?' Ruby asked, simply to break the silence.

'I'm already past twelve weeks. My cycle is so messed up anyway, I had no idea. I'd been feeling ill, but...what am I going to do Ruby?'

Tia sat up and looked at her for an answer. Ruby had nothing.

'She'd murder me if I had an abortion, I swear,' she continued, 'she's talking about sending me to the commune, to have it there. She wants me to have the baby there and leave it with them. Then just come back here like nothing has happened.'

'Shit,' Ruby couldn't process what Tia was saying.

'I just don't want it, at all. But I'm too scared to go on my own. I don't even know if I can – can you get an abortion without parental consent at our age?' Tia looked at Ruby, her eyes desperate.

'I – I don't know but… you must be able to, surely? I'll come with you,' she said, putting her hand on Tia's shoulder.

'Thank you, Ruby,' said Tia, wiping her eyes with her sleeve. 'I'm so sorry. This is so messed up. You don't even know me.'

'Don't apologise,' Ruby said, 'I would want someone to talk to if it happened to me. I'd want someone to be with me.'

'The thing is,' Tia said, putting her hand on her belly, 'I don't even know if that's what I really want. I don't know if I can do it. But if I don't… even if I managed to do it alone, get a flat… all that stuff. I had plans, you know? I wanted to go to college. Go to uni. I wanted to be a nurse. Or,' she shook her head, laughing, 'or a midwife. Ironic, isn't it?'

'Have you told Madge?'

Tia shook her head. 'Not yet.'

'Does Jack know?'

'He doesn't want anything to do with it. He says it's not his. Fucking dick.'

'You…' Ruby started, trailing off. She didn't know how to finish the sentence. 'You have to do what you want, not what anyone else wants. Do what you think is right. If you have it, though, it's yours, not theirs.'

'That's so easy for you to say Ruby. So easy.'

*She's right.* It made her feel so childish. Inadequate. Useless. *You know nothing about sex. Relationships. Life.*

'I don't know what to say, Tia, I have no right to tell you what to do. It's never happened to me, it's never happened to anyone I know… all I can say is I'll come with you, if that's what you want to do. And if it's not what you want, and you need a friend to help you if you're out on your own… I'm here. I mean, I'm not like

131

Kay. I'm like a child, compared to her. I don't know
bouncers on West Street or who to get weed off round
here... I've not even... you know... well, it's no wonder
I've never been in your position, if you get what I mean.
But...I'm good at looking after people. That's one thing I
can do.'

\*\*\*

Kaz's leather boots were sat in the hallway when she got
back.

'Ruby! Where do you keep the pans?'

Ruby sighed and made her way to the kitchen.
Before she could say anything, Kaz carried on.

'And the sponges. Honestly, Ruby, this place is a
state.'

She was going through every cupboard, pulling
things out and rooting around. She was wearing a short
pink satin dressing gown and had rollers in her hair.

*When did she move her stuff in?*

'How have you let it get like this?'

Kaz turned to Ruby, with her hand on her hip.

'Nothing is where it should be. Everything is filthy.
When's the last time you cleaned out the fridge? Bleached
the sink?' Her voice was getting louder, sharper.

'Are you having a go at me for the state of *Dad's*
kitchen?' Ruby asked.

'Not just the kitchen - the bathroom is disgusting.
I'd never let my dad live like this,' Kaz said, staring at her.

'Are you serious?'

'It's not funny Ruby. If the social came round here
what do you think they'd say? You need to get your act
together, sweetheart, because this just isn't good enough,'
she said, gesturing around the room.

'It's not my flat, it's dad's! Why is it *my*

responsibility? He does *nothing!* I'm the only one that does anything - we'd have rats if it weren't for me!' Ruby could feel herself getting angrier with every second.

*Who does she think she is?*

'You can't expect your dad to do anything. He has an illness. He's an alcoholic, in case you hadn't noticed.'

'Really? I thought he was teetotal,' Ruby said, folding her arms.

'If you were my kid I'd slap you for that. It's not something to joke about. You're a woman. You need to learn how to keep a house. How to look after a man. And you should be helping him out. He's been good enough to take you in. He didn't have to. You'd be on the streets without him. He pays for the food you eat and the clothes you wear, he's battling his demons and you can't even keep the place clean. It makes me sick.'

She stepped closer to Ruby, pointing in her face as she spoke. Ruby held her gaze.

'It makes you sick? Does it?' Ruby asked. 'Well you know what you can do don't you? *Fuck off out of here and don't come back!*'

Ruby turned and marched up the hall to her room, slamming her door. Kaz shouted after her but she couldn't hear her. She was concentrating on resisting the urge to punch her in the face.

'Jesus Bella. That woman is evil. I swear to god. Unbelievable.'

She punched her pillow, shouting, and threw it at the wall. It made her feel slightly better.

Her phone buzzed.

Message from Annabelle:

*Outfits please! Dad's got the Monopoly board out and mum's 'tipsy'. This is torture. Choosing clothes would be a welcome distraction xxx*

She opened her wardrobe. *Okay. Think.*

Message from Leo:
*Can't wait for you to see how beautiful it is. You'll love it. See you tomorrow. xx*

She gripped the phone. *This is a date. It's totally a date.*

There was a knock on the door.

*Oh god. Fuck off.*

'Come have a drink with me Ruby,' Kaz shouted through, 'I'm sorry. I want us to be friends.'

Ruby frowned at the door and willed her to go away.

'Please,' Kaz continued, 'I just want what's best for you. And your dad. Yeah?'

Ruby reluctantly opened the door. Kaz stood there, smiling.

'I feel like we haven't got to know each other properly. Come on love, come sit down.'

Ruby followed her through to the living room and sat down, bracing herself. Kaz lit another cigarette.

'What d'you drink?'

*Ukrainian tea.*

'Erm... vodka and coke?'

'Ruby, I'm not daft. You're fifteen. You can have a WKD.'

Kaz disappeared into the kitchen and came back with the neon blue glass bottle.

'Thanks.'

The taste took her back to the start of New Years' Eve. *Before it all went wrong.* Fizzy bubble-gum with a hint of vodka.

'What do you think of me, Ruby?' asked Kaz, taking a drag. Ruby could tell she'd been to the sunbed salon that day. Her face had a red-orange glow and the lines round her eyes and mouth were a little sharper than they were the day before. Her rusty-blonde perm looked a little frazzled, too.

'I don't know...we haven't known each other that

long.'

*This is either going to make me cringe, or hit her. Or both.*
*It's not going to end well. Come on. Think of something.*

'Bella likes you,' she ventured.

Kaz smiled.

'Yes she does. And I like her. I like you too Ruby, I hope you know that.'

'Right.'

Ruby looked at the floor.

'We have to put our differences aside for the sake of your dad. I think we're doing okay, don't you?'

Ruby nodded and swigged her WKD, wishing she had something stronger.

*Can I leave now?*

'Do you know where your dad is, Ruby?'

'No.'

'He's out looking for work.'

'What? It's half ten... the job centre isn't open.'

'What have I told you about being sarcastic, Ruby?' Kaz pointed her finger in mock disapproval, 'he's not at the job centre. He's meeting someone that might have work for him. Some guy called Tony, friend of a friend. Warehouse or something like that, I don't know. Anyway, the point is, he's doing this for us. For you. He's really come on since I moved in, hasn't he?'

Ruby nodded. *Shit. Tony.* Her stomach fluttered as she pictured the card with his number on it, in her dad's hand.

'I think I've been a good influence,' Kaz continued, 'he's cut way back on the booze.'

*That's right, you've won. Saint Kaz has sorted us all out. I wasn't enough to motivate him to stop drinking, but you are. Well done.*

'He was a heroin addict, you know, back in the day,' said Kaz, 'when I first knew him, before your mum did.

135

In and out of prison. Just like Cal.'

Ruby hated the way she spoke about her family, as though she knew them all better than Ruby did.

*You were there before me and you know everything about everyone. Fine. Now please shut up.*

'Why did you think his teeth were so bad?' Kaz asked Ruby.

*Why are you still pushing? I don't care.*

'I don't know, they were always bad, I suppose.'

'Well, he stopped the smack before you were born, but still got into trouble. He still drank,' she said.

*How does she know all this? Were they having an affair?*

'You kept in touch with him then? Even after you broke up the first time?' Ruby asked. She wanted to imply they would break up again.

'I never said we were going out back then, Ruby. We were friends. I knew we'd be together one day, but it took a while. Your mum came along and turned his head. He fell for her, but anyone could see it wasn't going to work. Fair enough, he got clean, but not for long,' Kaz sucked her cigarette before continuing, 'he could've turned things around a lot earlier if he'd had the right people round him. She was no good for him, your mum. Thought she was better than him. Above it all, you know?'

Ruby felt the rage rising in her, like it did before, but punching a pillow wouldn't help this time.

*She's not getting away with that.*

Ruby stood up.

'She *was* better than him. She was *always* better than him. I'm not going to sit here and listen to you slag her off!'

'You need to know the truth Ruby. You can't put your mum on a pedestal just because she's dead.'

Ruby immediately smacked Kaz right across the

face, before she realised what she was doing.

Kaz held her face, staring at her. Ruby stood, shaking with anger, wanting to hit her again.

'Don't ever hit me again,' Kaz said, 'I don't let anyone hit me. Not you, not him, not anyone, you hear?'

Ruby took a deep breath.

'I'm sorry. But she's my mum. You can't say things like that.'

Kaz didn't accept the apology. Her eyes glinted.

'It was your mum's fault that he fell off the wagon. Her fault for chucking him out. She was never a real wife to him. It was her fault he hit rock bottom. A homeless alcoholic. She didn't love him enough,' Kaz spat the words.

That was it. In that moment, she wanted to stab Kaz. To suffocate her with a pillow, hit her over the head with a cricket bat, anything. But she couldn't move, the rage had paralysed her.

Kaz continued.

'You know what else?'

She stepped close to Ruby, so she was right in her face.

'The way your mum made you look after her? Despicable. To make your own child wash you and wipe your arse...' Kaz shook her head and wrinkled her nose, 'disgusting.'

Ruby couldn't control her body. It seemed to act independently of her mind. She grabbed Kaz by the neck with both hands and screamed at her.

'*Shut up!* Shut your mouth you fucking bitch! You know *nothing!*

Kaz pushed and grabbed at Ruby but she held tight, squeezing her neck. The rage had taken over, she'd snapped, and nothing could reset it. A voice in Ruby's head was telling her to stop, but she couldn't. Kaz gasped

137

and pushed Ruby as hard as she could, but she was locked on to her neck. It felt so hot and full, as though it was about to burst out over her fingers.

'Ruby - stop it! *Get off her*!'

Her dad's voice was shouting behind her. Neither of them had heard him get back. He grabbed the pair of them and pulled them apart. Kaz coughed and gasped. Ruby sobbed.

'What the *hell* were you *doing*?' he shouted in Ruby's face. His face was red, his veins pulsating.

'She tried to kill me!' Kaz cried, 'she tried to kill me Gaz. I didn't do anything. She just lunged at me!'

Ruby opened her mouth but was cut off.

'Get out,' said Gaz. 'Get out of my flat.'

'But, she-'

'*Out!*' he screamed in her face.

Ruby ran to her room, grabbed a bag and shoved a few things in it. She put Bella on her lead, struggling to breathe through the sobs.

Gaz shouted something after her as she shut the front door, but she didn't hear.

She started to run. Into the night, in no particular direction, she ran.

# CHAPTER 16

*Think, Ruby, think.* She stopped at the end of the high street. *I can't see Leo like this.*

She didn't want him to know how messed up things were for her. She wanted him to think she was normal.

*Annabelle is with her family at her nan's huge house, ages away.*

Ruby searched her mind for anyone who might take her in, just for the night. *Tia.* She turned and made her way back to Burnside.

On her way up the stairs, she rehearsed what she would say. *I'm so sorry. I wouldn't ask unless I was absolutely desperate. I know you've got enough on, at the moment. I've been kicked out and need somewhere to stay just for tonight. I swear I'll be gone first thing. You won't know I'm here.*

A man answered the door.

'Yes?' he said, looking confused.

'Is Tia in?' Ruby asked, peering past him, down the hall. It was dark.

'No, it's Friday night,' he said, squinting his eyes slightly, searching for recognition.

'Sorry, who are you?' Ruby asked, her patience gone.

'I'm Paul. Geraldine's brother. Who are you?' he looked down at Bella, then back at Ruby.

'I'm Tia's friend.'

'Right... well, it's Friday night so she's out doing the outreach with Geraldine – sorry, I thought you'd have known, that's all. Are you okay? Do you want me to call her for you? You look upset. Come in, you can stay here until they get back. Have a cup of tea.'

Something felt wrong.

'No, it's okay, but thank you.'

'You can't be out and about at this time on your own, come in.' He reached and put his hand on her arm. She flinched.

'I'm not, I'm going home,' she lied, backing away.

'Okay, well, if you change your mind, do just pop back,' he called after her.

She shuddered, hurrying down the stairs.

*Gio? No. He lives on the other side of town. Besides... you don't want him knowing what things are like. I could call Annabelle. Ask her if her dad could come pick me up...*

She thought of his face, drawing up in the car. Stern, disgusted. *What the hell have you gotten yourself into* he'd say. *Why are you dragging my daughter into it? Don't you have any family?*

*No, I don't.*

It was cold. *Some spring*, she thought. It felt Baltic. She shuddered and looked at Bella, who stared up at her as if to say, *now what?*

*I used to have family, though. Just one person, but she was all I needed.*

Suddenly Ruby was overwhelmed with a wave of sadness, missing her mum.

*She'd sort all this out.*

She just wanted to be with her for five minutes. Just enough for her mum to hug her, tell her everything would be okay, and that she loved her. *That'd be enough. That's all I want.*

'It can't happen though, can it Bella?' she said, finally

140

letting the tears roll.

'We can go see her bench though, can't we? Come on. Let's go.'

Lisa's ashes were scattered near the place that had meant most to her, where she grew up, in Park Hill. Just near the huge complex of flats, there was a park with an amphitheatre, a rolling green slope with sweeping rows of stone steps, overlooking the city. She heard her mum's voice: *The best view of Sheffield that there is.* There was a bench there, where Lisa would sit and watch the city. *One day,* Ruby promised herself, *I'll put a memorial bench there.*

Ruby knew how to get there. Even at midnight on a Friday.

She caught the bus into town with Bella. It dropped them off at Castle Market. It wasn't a part of town she wanted to be late on a Friday, but she had Bella with her. She kept her head down and her hood up. The partygoers were all up at West Street, Division Street, Barkers Pool. It meant that this side of town was eerily empty, but the odd few people hanging around were ones she wanted to avoid.

Ruby followed the tram tracks round to the back of the train station. The wind chilled down to her bones. Her hands, feet, nose and ears were numb. The route wasn't lit in some places. A lot of it was deserted. She reached in her pocket for the key to Marlborough Road and gripped it, like a talisman.

It took longer than she'd expected. The flats had been redeveloped, since her mum lived there. *The streets in the sky,* her mum called them. The new design was bold, but warm. Yellow, orange and red strips and squares added splashes of glowing colour in neat intervals throughout the sheer cliff-face of windows. It was an impressive sight, all across the hillside, waiting for her to reach them. She finally hiked up the wet grassy hillside to the top, to her mum's bench, lit by the orange streetlight above.

She sat down. Bella jumped on her knee.

'We're spending the night with mum, Bella,' she said. Ruby was shattered. The cold wasn't her priority any more. She just wanted to rest her body. It was nearly 3am.

*At least this way, I'm close to her.*

She pulled a jumper from her bag, wrapped it around Bella and held her close. Ruby looked out over the city.

*Mum was right. It is beautiful.*

She could see the whole city, lighting the night like glowing embers in a grate. She picked out the different landmarks and wondered what the people inside would be doing.

There were a few lights on in the Arts Tower.

'Big university building, that,' she said to Bella, 'used to be the tallest in the city, until that one got built.'

She pointed to St Paul's tower. It was close enough that Ruby thought she could just about pick out the people in their penthouse apartments - all chrome and glass, cutting edge design and chic furniture. At least, that's how she imagined them.

'Me and Leo could have a flat like that. You never know.'

Suddenly she heard a noise - something in the bushes behind her. Bella growled. Ruby turned around, her eyes wide in the dark. She couldn't see anything. She held her breath. A car drove past.

Her eyes scanned the floor. There was a smashed bottle at the foot of the bench. Slowly, she picked up the biggest shard of glass she could see. Still nothing from the bushes. *It was probably a rat. Or a fox. Get some sleep.*

Eventually, she lay down on the bench, cradling

Bella to her side, and tried to close her eyes. It was impossible. Her body was completely spent, screaming at her to sleep, but she couldn't. She lay awake with her eyes open, staring at the sky. It was inky blue with an orange hue from the city lights. Her whole body was numb from the cold now. She couldn't get any colder, and somehow stopped feeling it.

'Alright love?' a man's voice broke the silence.

'Fuck!' she sat up and spun round. Bella barked at the man, straining on her lead.

'Leave me alone!' she shouted at him, shaking.

'Alright, okay. Calm down. Just wondered if you wanted summat take the edge off, that's all,' he said, smirking. He was wearing a hooded top and tracksuit bottoms. He had his hood up, so she could hardly see his face.

'I don't. Get away from me,' Ruby said, trying to sound calm and assertive.

'Young girl like you shouldn't be out here alone. Dangerous,' he said, stepping closer, 'you need some money?' he said, coming closer still.

'*Fuck off!*' she shouted at him. She knew he wasn't going anywhere. She gripped the glass shard and pointed it at him, her hand shaking.

'Alright, no need to get nasty,' he grinned, 'mind you, I like my girls nasty.'

He lunged towards her. Bella leapt up and bit his leg, hanging off his thigh. He screamed. He hit her again and again but she held fast.

'Get it off, get it off!' he kicked and thrashed but Bella held tight, growling the whole time. Ruby wanted to run but couldn't get Bella to release her grip and she couldn't leave her.

'Off, Bella, off!'

She dragged at her collar. There was blood

143

everywhere, black under the streetlight. Bella's jaws were locked. The man screamed. He gave up punching Bella, it did nothing. Ruby was trying not to be sick. Her limbs were shaking, a cold sweat started to dampen her hair.

'I said off! Get off! Leave it, Bella!'

Bella finally loosened her grip, immediately lunging at him again as soon as Ruby yanked her away, barking and howling. He struggled to get to his feet, the blood everywhere, black in the dark. By the time he managed to stand, Ruby and Bella were in the distance, running as fast as they could.

*\*\*\**

Ruby opened her eyes. She was aching all over, still freezing cold. She had no idea where she was.

The room spun into focus. It looked like the inside of a shed. Bella licked her face.

*What the…*

It came back to her. She was in the old shed, at Marlborough Road. *Oh god.*

Ruby remembered catching the first bus to Hillsborough, at about 5am. She used up her last reserve of energy to walk up Marlborough Road. The key didn't work. She remembered hitting the door, slumping to the floor.

*Shit. Someone came to the door. A woman, in a dressing gown. I woke them up.*

She remembered scrabbling to her feet and apologising. *The woman looked scared. No wonder.* She couldn't remember how she got in the yard. *Did I crawl through the gap under the gate?* Her front was covered in dirt and her hood was torn.

Ruby's stomach roared. She felt nauseous, weak and thirsty. She knew Bella must feel the same. A wave of

144

guilt washed over her as she looked into the dog's big brown eyes, Bella's tail wagging now that Ruby had finally woken up.

*What time is it?* She looked at her phone. It was nearly out of battery. She had three messages and one missed call from Annabelle. Three missed calls and two messages from Leo. It was 2pm.

'Shit. Leo!' she said aloud. *Today. I was supposed to see him today...*

10am: *Just called round at your flat but your dad said you've gone - are you okay? X*

11:30am: *Call me if you need anything. Just want to make sure you're alright x*

1:22pm: Missed call from Leo

1:54 pm: Missed call from Leo.

Ruby had no cash left for the bus. Even if she knew the way, walking three miles was impossible. She was too thirsty, too hungry, and too exhausted. *Call him. Just call him.*

# CHAPTER 17

'You stay with us for as long as you need, Ruby,' Leo's
mum said, enveloping her in a warm, vanilla-scented hug.

'Thank you...'

'Natalya.' she smiled.

'Natalya. Thank you. I'll be fine, I just need a shower
really. And Bella needs something to eat.'

'No no no. You need food. Banquet, bath, bed!
Welcome to Hotel Kovalenko.'

She hugged Ruby again and stroked her hair. It made
her cry. She missed this.

'Oh, shhh. It's okay.' Natalya soothed, Ruby's sobs
muffled in her shoulder.

Ruby couldn't help it. She stayed buried in the
shoulder, enjoying the warmth radiating through her,
savouring all the forgotten feelings it stirred up -
reassurance, comfort, safety.

'Come on,' Natalya said, 'you stay in my bed tonight.
I'll have the couch.'

She hated the look on Leo's face. *Pity. He feels sorry for
me.* Of all the things she wanted him to feel for her, that
was very low on the list.

She went to have a shower, wishing she understood
Ukrainian. As soon as she shut the bathroom door, they
started a heated debate. Ruby had no idea what they were

saying but she heard 'Ruby' a few times.

*This is not how I wanted things to start for us. Today was meant to be special.*

She turned on the shower and stood under it, trying to imagine the hot water stripping away the last 24 hours.

Finally clean, dry, and wearing Natalya's tracksuit, Ruby wandered into the kitchen and watched her cook. She didn't know what was being prepared, but it smelled like pure comfort. It looked boring – some kind of stew in a pot, but the smell of the seasoning made her mouth water. She hadn't eaten anything like that since before her mum got ill.

Ruby finally mustered the courage to speak to him.

'I'm sorry, Leo,' Ruby said, sitting down in the chair next to the sofa.

'What?' he said, frowning.

'I'm sorry. For dragging you out and ruining everything...'

'You have nothing to apologise for. Don't worry. It was just a walk.'

She looked at her knees. *Just a walk.*

'I mean,' he corrected himself, 'it's nothing that won't wait. We'll go sometime soon. I was excited for you to see it, but I still am.'

'I was excited, too,' she said. *Go on. Say it.* 'But... kind of, more excited about the fact it was with *you*.'

He smiled. They both looked away, laughing.

He moved closer, to the edge of the sofa arm next to her. His eyes were staring right into hers. Ruby could smell him, his skin. She breathed him in.

He lowered his voice, glancing over at Natalya, then back to Ruby.

'People are bastards. My mum's boyfriend is a bastard, too. We should do something. They can't keep treating people this way.'

'Like what?' Ruby asked, willing him to say *run away together*.

'Dinner's ready!' Natalya announced.

He stood up and walked over, glancing back at her. They said nothing more about it.

\*\*\*

Ruby sat up in bed, suddenly awake and breathless in the dark. The nightmare was back. It hadn't troubled her for so long.

*Breathe. It's just a dream.* She turned over and tried to sleep. She felt as though Natalya's room was closing in on her, as though every time she opened her eyes, the walls were a little closer, the ceiling a little lower. She finally fell into fitful sleep, tormented by the face of Kaz, gasping for air.

Bella's low growl woke her, hours later. It was light.

'Shh, Bell,' Ruby whispered, sitting up.

Bella was growling at the sound of arguing, coming from the next room. Ruby went to the door and listened. It was Natalya and a man. *Not Leo.* They were speaking English. His voice sounded familiar.

Quietly, Ruby placed her hand on the door handle and gripped it tight. She turned it, as slowly as possible, until the bolt was out of the frame and in the door. She pulled it towards her, just a fraction, to reveal a shaft of light and a sliver of the hallway and living room. The man paced past her line of sight. *Tony.*

'You'll be there,' he said, in a low tone, looking down at Natalya, sitting on the sofa with her head in her hands. She made a noise.

'Hm?' he said, 'what was that?'

She shook her head.

'I said, no,' she repeated.

She looked up at him and held his gaze, despite her eyelids flickering, sending two teardrops sliding down her cheek.

He turned away from her, put his hand to his mouth and rubbed his muzzle. She exhaled and started to wipe her eyes. He turned back and grabbed her face with one hand, so that her mouth was clenched between his fingers. Ruby held her breath.

'You. Are. Going,' he growled, 'Hm?'

Natalya struggled to nod her head.

He released her. She watched him leave. As he slammed the door behind him, she put her hands to her face and hunched over, sobbing.

*Where is Leo?* Ruby didn't know what to do. Her urge was to help, to go and hug her, to do what Natalya had done for her the night before. It didn't feel right, though. She wasn't supposed to see it. *Maybe she wouldn't want me to know. Maybe I don't want to know.* She held the handle still, the metal hot in her hand. Finally, she pulled the door open and shouted through. She didn't want to catch her off guard.

'Natalya?' she called.

Natalya immediately straightened up, wiped her eyes and smoothed her clothes, standing up. She walked towards the hall.

'Ruby, you're up!' she said, bright and breezy, 'let me get you something to eat. You slept so long! Leo is out. I asked him to do some shopping. We have nothing in the fridge. Very embarrassing.' she laughed.

'Are you okay?' Ruby asked.

*Does she really think I didn't hear all that?*

'Of course, why would I not be?' Natalya asked, 'The sofa is not the best bed. But I'm only in my 30s, Ruby, not an old lady yet!'

'You're really young, to –' she started, then

149

stumbled.

'I was young, when I had him,' Natalya saved her. 'Your age, maybe.'

She was beautiful, just like him - the same eyes, the same smile.

'Where is he?' Ruby asked.

'Shop. We have nothing in. I think he got bored, waiting for you to wake up.'

'Oh, I'm sorry, I shouldn't have slept so long…'

'Don't be daft. You needed it. Do you want tea? Coffee?'

'Coffee, please,' said Ruby.

'Leo is very fond of you,' Natalya said, walking to the kitchen area.

Ruby smiled and looked at the floor.

'You will be good for him,' Natalya continued, 'he has no friends, you know? It's hard for him. He left everything behind. We thought things would be different here, better.'

Natalya handed Ruby a mug of black coffee. She usually had milk but was too polite to ask for any.

'Are you going to stay?' Ruby asked, suddenly panicked by the thought that they might not.

'It's complicated. Our visas are temporary. We thought we'd be able to extend them, but it hasn't worked out…'

'You can't go! I mean,' Ruby checked herself, 'if you want to stay, I'm sure there's a way around it.'

Natalya looked at her for a second, as though she wanted to tell her something, but stopped.

'We'll see. I have a plan.' She smiled. 'Anyway. Let's talk about you,' she said, patting Ruby's knee, 'you stay as long as you need. But whatever happened yesterday, family is important. I know this.'

Ruby shifted uncomfortably. *Family.* The word made

her feel ill.

'I got kicked out when I was your age, Ruby. This is life. Things happen, people argue. It hurts, because you love each other.'

Ruby shuddered inside. *Do I love Dad? No. Maybe. I don't know.*

'But they took me back,' Natalya continued, 'I was lucky.'

'I don't think they ever want to see me again,' said Ruby. *I don't want to see them, either. But what's the alternative? Care.*

'You have to try. Swallow your pride. That's what I had to do when I was your age. Otherwise...' she trailed off in order to compose herself, to stop the urge to cry. She took a deep breath.

'Otherwise, one day you may find yourself alone. You may do something they can't forgive, and cut your ties forever. Then you can never go back. Do you understand?' Natalya looked at her, her eyes glistening.

Ruby nodded. 'I'm sorry, I didn't mean to upset you.' she said, quietly. Natalya shook her head.

The front door opened. It was Leo. Ruby's system shot adrenaline through her body.

Just as before, Natalya flicked a switch. She turned away from him, dabbed her eyes and turned back cheerful, light.

'Leo!' Natalya got up and gave him a hug, 'Ruby finally woke up,' she beamed at them both. Leo smiled at Ruby and put down his bags.

'How are you?' he said, sitting down.

'Better. Thanks.'

Ruby had butterflies. The news that he might leave at any random point in the future was making her nauseous, nervous. She didn't think it was possible, but suddenly she loved him even more.

*I love him.* She said to herself as she watched him, talking to Natalya who was unpacking the bags in the kitchen.

*I do. This is bad.*

He turned back to Ruby and walked over to where she sat.

'Ruby, when I went over yesterday to try to find you, your dad was really worried about you. I wasn't going to say anything, because I know he's a bastard,' he said, with a slight laugh, 'but it's been getting to me – he was a bit of a mess.'

'He's always a mess,' Ruby said, snapping more than she meant to.

'He asked me to tell you to come home,' Leo said, looking at the floor, 'I don't know if you should. I wasn't going to say anything… but it's not my place to keep things from you. They don't deserve you, Ruby,' he struggled to get the words out, but she could tell he meant them.

'Dad said that?' she asked.

Leo nodded.

Ruby thought about Cal, and how devastated her dad was when he didn't stay. She thought about all the times he'd talked about starting again, about being a proper family, making it work. That night in December, after the funeral. *He really wanted to see me.* His jacket around her shoulders as they walked to Burnside, after he found her in the snow. *Maybe he does want me to come home. But what about Kaz?* Her face, gasping for breath, her neck, bulging against Ruby's hands, flashed through her mind again.

'Maybe Dad does. But Kaz… she hates me.'

Leo looked at her.

'She made you do what you did, it was her fault. If someone said those things about my mother, I'd want to

152

kill them too.'

He hesitated, then took her hand and held it with both of his.

'I'm just telling you what he said. It's up to you. Whatever you decide to do, I'm here. We're here. You stay here. I-' he stopped himself, and let go of her hand, 'I'm sorry. I'm not telling you what to do. It's not my place.'

She looked at her hand. *That's not how I wanted the first time he held my hand to go, either.*

He smiled, looking over to the kitchen. 'Do you want anything to eat?'

She shook her head.

'No, but thanks,' she took a deep breath, 'I'm going to see them. I have to apologise. See if they'll take me back. Otherwise, if they won't have me, I'll be back out on my own again. Care. Foster parents. If I can just stick it out for another year… that's all I need.'

She didn't want to admit that she was worried about her dad, too, or that she was touched he actually cared.

'Don't apologise – it should be them apologising to you,' he said. 'But at least this way, you give them the chance.'

Natalya looked on from the kitchen and smiled.

'You're a good girl, Ruby.' she said.

Leo turned back to Ruby and rolled his eyes. She smothered a laugh.

\*\*\*

Ruby paced up and down the walkway with Bella. Every time she thought she had gathered the courage to walk up and knock on the door, something stopped her.

*They'll slam it in my face, straight away. Or let me say my piece, then hurl a load of abuse at me, chuck the rest of my stuff out*

153

*and then slam it. Kaz might go for me. Dad might let her. Oh god.
I can't do this.*

Bella sat down and sighed.

'You're right, Bella,' Ruby said to her, 'come on.'

She took a deep breath, walked up to the door and
knocked. She felt the fight-or-flight adrenaline kick in as
she heard the lock. Her dad appeared. She braced herself.

'Ruby!' he grabbed her in a hug. She froze. It was the
first hug she could remember getting from him, ever. He
felt like a cellophane bag of warm water. She resisted the
urge to recoil. He smelled of Camel cigarettes and old
sweat. She couldn't hug him back.

'Where have you been? Why didn't you come back?'
he asked, letting her go. His bloodshot eyes had the same
intense focus that they had when Cal came over after
getting out of prison - as though he didn't want to let her
out of his sight. Ruby shifted awkwardly.

'You kicked me out,' she said, quietly.

'I didn't *kick you out*, Rubes,' he shook his head,
thumbed a tear away from his eye and sniffed, 'just
wanted you away from the situation, you know? Didn't
want you getting hurt.'

He motioned her inside.

She hesitated.

'Is Kaz-?' she started.

'She's alright, Ruby. Calmed down,' he said, holding
his hand out in the direction of the front room. Kaz
grabbed it and stepped out into the hall, looking at the
floor. Ruby quickly scanned her neck. A couple of faint
bruises stared back at her.

'I'm sorry, Kaz,' Ruby said, bracing herself in case
she needed to duck, or run.

'Yeah, me too. I'd had a lot to drink. Let's forget
about it.' Kaz shrugged, finally looking her in the eye. 'I
used to fight like that with my mum sometimes. Nothing

new. Shit happens.' She sucked her cigarette.

'Come on love, sit down,' her dad said, ushering them both into the front room.

*Something's wrong. This isn't normal.* She wondered if, maybe, it was normal for them. *Arguing, screaming, fighting all the time. It's not the end of the world. Some people just live like that.* She remembered when her dad lived at home. *Blazing rows, constantly. Doors being slammed, plates being smashed.* She remembered her mum throwing all of his clothes out of the top window of the house once, watching them fall like leaves. *You used to row with mum, before she got ill. Before the guilt became unbearable. You're out of the habit.*

'Rubes, we're celebrating,' he pointed to the can of Skol and the bottle of Magners on the coffee table. 'We have something to tell you,' her dad said, reaching across the sofa for Kaz's hand. She shuffled up next to him and smiled.

*Oh my god. They're getting married.*

'We're having a baby!' said Kaz, grinning.

'Shit!' Ruby blurted out. 'I mean...wow,' *Fuuuuuuuck....* 'when did you find out?'

'Went for the first scan this morning,' said Kaz, grinning, 'I mean, I was a bit worried after what happened last night, but... no harm done.'

Ruby couldn't process the information. She had strangled a pregnant woman, endangering her unborn sibling.

'We're going to be a proper family now Rubes,' her dad said, 'you, me, Kaz and the baby,' he grinned, 'I'm going to have a son. Another son.'

'It's a boy!' Kaz shouted.

'Really?' Ruby asked.

'Well, they can't tell yet. Even at this private place we went to. Annoying really, when it costs so much. But *I* can. I'm never wrong.'

'How… I mean… I didn't realise you'd been together that long…'

'On and off for six months, Rubes. Just took me a while to introduce you,' Gaz said.

'Can you afford a baby?' Ruby asked, before she thought about what she was saying.

'Like I told you before you went mental, Ruby, your dad's got a job now,' Kaz said, through her teeth.

'That's right,' Gaz jumped in, 'bits and pieces for that bloke, Tony. You know from that card you gave me? Deliveries. Driving.'

'I didn't even know you could drive,' she said, shaking her head. 'That's not the point, though…Dad, I don't know if it's a good idea to work for him.'

Gaz looked ruffled. 'Of course I can bloody drive. Just not done it in a few years, that's all. Tony's a good bloke. You're the one that gave me his bloody card-'

'Anyway,' said Kaz, staring at Ruby, 'You'll be gone in a year, so that'll help, won't it?'

*Damn right.*

'You should really think about getting a little job in the meantime though, Ruby. Evenings, weekends. Pay your way. I started work when I was younger than you.'

Ruby stared back at her. *She knows exactly how to wind me up.*

'I do have a job actually. Just got one this week.'

'Great,' Kaz smiled through clenched teeth, 'we'll work out what you owe then.'

'Anyway, we don't need to talk about that yet,' said Gaz, standing up and raising his can.

'To our new family!' he announced. Kaz lifted her bottle and cheered.

Ruby took a deep breath and did her best to fake a smile.

# CHAPTER 18

Once her phone was charged, she could see a list of missed calls and texts from Annabelle. *Shit. You never replied to her. Should I tell her what happened?*

She slid her thumb over the phone screen, making patterns. *No. It's too embarrassing. And complicated. And...she wouldn't understand. Just make something up.*

Message to Annabelle:

*I'm SO SORRY! My phone died last night, couldn't find my charger. We ended up not going for our walk because the train out there was cancelled. But I went over to his flat for something to eat instead, met his mum, she's so nice. How's your nana's weekend? Xxx*

She decided to text Leo to let him know what had happened.

*They took me back. Like nothing had happened. So weird. Kaz is pregnant - that's even weirder xx*

Ruby lay on her bed and stared at the ceiling, holding her phone to her chest.

Message from Leo:

*Wow - that's big. Do you want to walk to school with me next week? You can tell me all about it xxx*

Ruby smiled.

Her phone rang. Annabelle.

'*Ruby* you scared me! Don't do that again. I thought

he'd kidnapped you and buried you in the woods!'

Ruby laughed.

'Anyway so you went round to his house? What did you wear?'

*A hoodie and jeans, covered in dirt, with a few tears. Stinking of sweat and dog and damp shed.*

'One of the dresses you gave me,' Ruby said.

Annabelle squealed. 'Ahhh! You will have looked smokin!' I bet he was annoyed his mum gate-crashed. I bet you were too! Why was she there? Is he a mummy's boy?'

'No... she just, well, we were supposed to be out, weren't we? So if anything we kind of gate-crashed her.'

'Hm. Spose so. Did you kiss him?'

'No! His mum was there the whole time!'

'Oh yeah. Well, next time, get in there.'

Ruby squirmed. Even over the phone this was embarrassing. She changed the subject.

'What have you been doing this weekend, then?'

'Oh god. It's so lame. Don't even get me started. I wish I'd smuggled you with me. Last night was the seventh circle of Monopoly hell. This afternoon we went for afternoon tea, which was alright because I got a prosecco out of it. But tonight we're going for this big meal at this restaurant which my parents love but it's *awful*. Everything is tiny and tastes like fennel.'

'I don't know what fennel tastes like,' Ruby said, laughing.

'Anyway stop changing the subject,' Annabelle continued, 'when are you seeing him again?'

'We're walking to school together next week-'

Another squeal. Ruby held the phone away from her ear.

'I have to wait until Tuesday, because the teachers are on strike Monday. But that means I can work my first shift at Gio's, so –'

'Oh god,' said Annabelle, 'I'm sorry, I've got to go, they're hassling me. I have to help blow up 100 balloons. 100! I mean, honestly. I love them, but this is like some sort of *three-day grandparent festival.* Jesus. Anyway, I'll see you next week sometime. Yeah? And don't drop out on me like that again. I want to know how the walk to school goes!'

Ruby smiled as she hung up the phone. Hearing about Annabelle's family always fascinated her. It was so different from hers.

The front door slammed. From her window, she saw Kaz disappearing down the walkway. Ruby crept into the hall and listened. *Nothing.* She walked into the front room.

'Dad? Are you okay?'

Gaz looked up from *The Star.*

'Yeah. Why?'

'Kaz just left...'

'She's just gone to see her mum. Tell her the news.'

He smiled.

'Oh, right.'

Ruby turned to leave.

'Ruby,' he said.

She turned back, holding the door.

'We've been through some stuff, you and I,' he folded away the paper and carried on, 'your mum. The Social. My... well, you know I like a drink.'

Ruby hung awkwardly in the doorway, wishing she'd never come in.

'What I mean is, we're still here, aren't we? We do alright. It's a good thing, this baby. You might not think so now, but you wait, Ruby. You and Cal...' he trailed off, fighting the urge to cry. 'You and Cal,' he continued, shaking, 'you're the best thing that ever happened to me.

Having kids changes everything. I was young, stupid, when I was with your mum. I've been a shit dad. I know I have. I always thought I'd be better than my dad was. Never wanted to be like him,' he shook his head, blinking away tears, 'and I won't be with this one. Or with you, from now on. I promise.'

Ruby looked at the floor. She was desperate to believe him, but she couldn't. She couldn't bear to look at him, for him to see that she was crying too, that this meant something to her, and that he would break her heart when he failed.

*All this time you told yourself you didn't care about him, that you didn't need him, or anyone else.*

She breathed deeply. *You still don't.*

She told herself she had to stay strong, she had to keep her distance. Ruby couldn't let herself believe that he'd never hit her again, that he'd never throw her out on the street again, that he'd never again let her fend for herself for weeks on end while he drowned himself in drink - because she knew that he would.

'I know, dad,' finally, she managed to speak. It was a lie she had to tell. 'I know.'

'Thanks,' he said, opening his newspaper back up, pretending to read.

# CHAPTER 19

'I'm so proud of you, getting a job,' Madge said, 'and now I get free coffee!' She pointed to her cappuccino, nodding. 'Mondays are normally terrible - but today is a good day.'

Ruby smiled. *I'm not good at much, but I'm good at coffee.* She leaned on the counter with one hand and cleaned the steamer with her other.

'She's fantastic,' said Gio, appearing from the backroom with a crate of smoothies, 'just like her mother.'

Ruby looked at him and tried to stifle the emotion he'd stirred up.

He carried on talking as he stocked up the big fridge display.

'All those years Ruby was here, watching Lisa. Keeping busy in the holidays, after school. I think she learned how to make a pattern with the cocoa powder before she learned to tell the time.'

Ruby smiled, looking at the floor.

'When do you get your break, Ruby?' Madge asked, 'shall we have a catch-up?'

'Oh, I've had it...' she lied.

'You have another. No problem,' said Gio.

*Dammit.*

'So, what's new? How are things?' Madge said as they sat down.

'They're good,' Ruby said, smiling. *Please believe me. Please stop asking questions and leave me alone.*

'Really? I heard your dad's got a new girlfriend.'

'How did you know that?'

'It's a small world. Your dad's social worker is in my office. She says he's doing better?'

'I didn't know he still had one. Yeah, he is.'

It was true. Finally there was something she didn't have to lie about. Ruby scratched at a blob of chocolate that had stuck to the table top.

'I hate her, but she's good for him.'

'Kaz? You hate her?'

'No. I don't,' she laughed nervously, realising she needed to backpedal.

'I don't hate her. We just, don't really know each other yet. We don't get on that well right now, but I'm sure we will.' Ruby attempted a smile. 'Besides, like I say, she's good for him. He's stopped drinking. Not completely, obviously. They still go to the pub - but, you know, I haven't seen him drunk in ages.'

'Well that's great,' Madge smiled, 'and give it time with Kaz. It's always going to be hard when a new person moves in.'

Ruby nodded. *A lot harder when that person is Kaz.*

'She does some of the housework,' she said, sliding sugar crystals across the table with her finger, 'there's two lots of benefits coming in now. It's not all bad.'

Madge smiled, nodding.

'There was one thing I wanted to mention…' Ruby added, hesitating.

Madge stopped, mid-sip. 'What, what is it Ruby?'

'Tia. Have you heard from her?'

'Why?'

Madge wiped the foam from her upper lip with a napkin.

'I saw her again, on Friday. She asked me to come over.'

'Aw, that's nice.'

'She's pregnant,' Ruby blurted out.

'Oh,' Madge put down her mug. 'Right. Listen, Ruby, I can't discuss confidential things about her with you, but I didn't know that. Thank you for letting me know. What did she say about it?'

'It was an accident, her boyfriend doesn't want anything to do with it. Her auntie wants her to keep it... and I think she's really weird. Like, *really* weird. Did you know she's in a cult?'

Madge frowned. 'Like I said, I can't discuss confidential matters... but... carry on. Please.'

'I should have said something... but when I got back after that... well, it was a really busy weekend and... it slipped my mind. Plus, I thought she would tell you.'

'Did she say what she was going to do?'

'She didn't know. I've messaged her, since, but I've not heard anything back.'

'Okay. Leave it with me. It's not your problem, Ruby. But thank you for telling me.'

'Thanks, Madge.'

Ruby put her apron back on.

'Listen, Ruby,' Madge said, 'you need to sort yourself out before you try to sort everyone else out, remember. Are you still going to school?'

Ruby nodded, shifting awkwardly in her seat.

'Not skipped anything in the last week. I'm trying. I thought about what you said... well... what mum would want... and how I can do what would make her proud.'

She wasn't intending to be so earnest, but it was the truth. *Besides, it'll make Madge smile.*

163

'You're made of strong stuff Ruby. I knew you'd be okay,' she smiled.

\*\*\*

Message to Tia:

*Just let me know you're okay, Tia. I know it's none of my business, I just want to make sure nothing bad has happened. I hope you're okay xxx*

Ruby stopped and decided to ring her instead. The clipped, haughty voice said: *It has not been possible to connect your call,* over and over again.

She finished the message and sent it, hoping that Tia would get it, somehow. She rolled over in bed.

*Madge is right. You have to sort yourself out first.*

She lay awake, turning over the new responsibilities she had. *Something has happened to Tia. At least Madge knows, now. I'm going to be a big sister. Dad and Kaz will implode, and I'll have to pick up the pieces. Leo and Natalya might get deported. If Tony doesn't kill them first. And Dad works for him, now. Fuck.*

The prospect of seeing Leo in the morning was the only good thing she could think of. She remembered what Natalya had said about their visas and felt nauseous. *He can't go. Not now.*

*Natalya said she had a plan. I have to find out what it is.*

\*\*\*

Ruby met Leo at the bottom of the stairwell the next morning.

School seemed so distant in her memory. Just four days ago she was sat in Physics, texting Annabelle in a panic about what to wear the next day. *Then… then it all kicked off.*

Her phone buzzed. She looked at it then quickly turned the screen off. It was a snapchat of Annabelle grinning with both thumbs up and GOOD LUCK!!! scrawled across it in pink letters, decorated with hearts.

She laughed.

'What was that?' Leo asked.

'Oh, just my friend. She's a bit bonkers.'

They walked on.

'I love that word,' he said smiling. 'There are so many slang words here that sound so…I don't know. I can't translate.'

'I need to learn Ukrainian.'

'Ha. I'll teach you. So how did it go, when you got back? You said they just acted like nothing happened?'

Ruby told him everything. She realised she was rambling, after a while. *Wrap it up.*

'I don't know. It's all such a mess. I keep trying to get my head together and I can't –' she said, stepping out to cross the road. Leo grabbed her hand and pulled her back. She jumped at the blaring horn of a bus that flew past, inches from her.

'Shit, I just wasn't looking!' said Ruby, her heart thumping.

'You need to get some sleep!' Leo said, smiling.

He didn't let go of her hand. They walked on, continuing the conversation, hand-in-hand, a little voice inside Ruby's head squealing. His hand was warm. *We're holding hands. I love this.*

Finally, she mustered the courage to ask him the question.

'Why did you and your mum come here?'

'It's a long story,' he said, looking at the floor, 'we had problems with family, and business. I never knew my dad. Mum was young when she had me. She had to rely a lot on our family. They run a business and one of the people they did business with… well, he did a lot for us. Tony. Mum fell in love with him. He's the one who brought us to the UK. He's the reason we're here.'

*Fell in love with him?* Ruby couldn't see how Natalya could have ever loved him.

'This was a problem though. My family didn't like him, they didn't accept it. They told her he was a gangster, he was trouble,' he laughed, 'coming from them – it must have been bad. But she didn't listen. So they disowned her. *Us.* They disowned *us.*

'He told mum that he loved her, that we could start a new life in the UK. He owns a club near here. Owns a few places. I think they're all just covers, though. Has a lot of people working for him.'

*Shit. Dad.*

'Like what?' asked Ruby.

'Drugs,' Leo said, shrugging. 'I don't know. I don't want to know. Guns, maybe. Whatever it is, it's not legal,' Leo said, shaking his head.

'Leo…' Ruby started, not knowing how to finish.

'Hm?'

'My dad is one of those people. One of those people that works for him. He… found that card you gave me,' she lied, 'I thought I'd thrown it away, but…'

'Are you kidding?'

'No. I'm sorry. He knew him, anyway, from way back. I mean, you know he did, you heard him –'

'This is bad. Really bad,' Leo said, then exhaled loudly, looking up.

They were silent.

'It's okay,' Leo finally said, 'It's not your fault. You just need to be careful. So do I. It's alright,' he said.

*He's a terrible liar.*

'So Tony brought you both here?' she asked, desperate to fill the silence.

'Yeah. Tony got us visas, told mum he would marry her as soon as we got here. She'd be a UK citizen, we could stay here forever. He said he'd put me through school, university, that we'd live in a mansion...' he half-laughed, '...he's a charming man. Mum believed him. I think I did too, at one point.'

'So he lied? Why?' Ruby asked.

'I ask myself the same thing. It cost a lot to get us over here. I think...' his voice wavered, 'I think he did it so that she owed him everything. Not just the money, but the escape, too.'

'Escape from what?'

'My family don't forgive. It's a big family, they run a powerful business. They're not as bad as him, but they weren't exactly inside the law either. Whatever they are, you don't want to make enemies of them,' he shook his head. 'So we couldn't stay there...and now we can't go back. He did it for the power. I don't think he ever loved her. Not like she thought he did. I think he wanted something beautiful, to play with... to ruin, just because he can.'

'That's awful,' she said, not knowing what else to say. 'Your mum is the nicest person. I can't believe what's happened to her... to you.'

Leo looked at her. His eyes were glazed with tears, but they didn't fall. He smiled, but he couldn't hide what he was feeling. He didn't have his mum's talent. She could instantly make over her surface. Choose from a cabinet full of different masks, each perfectly portraying the required emotion, giving the desired impression, at her fingertips, in any situation.

'She is,' he nodded, smiling, 'but we'll be okay. We'll get out of his hands. Somehow. He won't win.'

They stood at the school gates.

Ruby desperately wanted to ask him how.

*How? What's the plan?*

They stood, still holding hands, both thinking. The bell rang, for a second time.

This time, Leo managed a more convincing attempt at pretending to be happy. He smiled, held her hand with both of his and turned to face her.

'I want to stay here. I will stay here, because now I have something to stay for,' he pulled her hand towards him and kissed it, then let go. He walked off.

Ruby stood, unable to make her way, just for a couple of minutes, letting the moment spread through her, warming, dizzying, like black tea with vodka.

# CHAPTER 20

Message to Annabelle:

*It went well xxx*

Annabelle:

*Eeeek I knew it would! Did he ask you out? Did you kiss? OMG this is SO EXCITING xxx*

Ruby: *No and no. But we held hands. And he kissed my hand. And he said I was worth staying in the UK for xxx*

Annabelle: *Are you living in a Jane Austin novel?*

Ruby: *Shut up. He's romantic. We're walking to school together from now on*

Annabelle: *Congratulations* – she added a crying laughing face – *sorry, I'll stop now. He sounds like a gent. I'm v excited for you. Just see if you can get to first base at some point before he proposes xxxx*

Ruby rolled over in bed and grinned to herself.

*School is going to be good from now on.*

***

'...and she was under the bed, in this pile of stinking clothes. Dad went mad, but not so much because of the dog. More because I grassed on his mate. I've not seen that guy since they evicted him.'

She watched the kids piling through the school gates

and thought about how lonely she would have been without Bella.

'She looks out for me. That night outside Park Hill - if she hadn't gone for that man... she's like my guardian angel...'

Leo suddenly turned, held her face in his hands and kissed her. She kissed him back, holding him closer. Ruby felt electric, as though she had lightning coursing through her viens.

'Sorry,' he said, eventually, 'I just needed to do that.'

They laughed.

'Are you busy on Saturday night?'

'You know I'm not,' Ruby laughed.

He smiled.

'Okay. Well, Mum's going to a Eurovision party at a friend's flat.'

Ruby looked surprised.

'She *does have friends*, you know!' Leo said, smiling. 'There are a lot of people like her, from all over, doing the same thing she does. Cleaning, au-pair, whatever they can. They know each other through the work. They understand each other.'

'And they like Eurovision?'

'Love it. I don't. But they're showing horror films all night on Film4. Like an antidote to Eurovision. Do you want to come over and watch with me?'

Ruby smiled.

'Sure. I can hold your hand when you get scared.'

'Good,' he said, smiling.

Ruby couldn't wait. As soon as she got back, she started searching through her wardrobe. *You're no good at this. Call Annabelle.*

Annabelle was there in half an hour.

'Okay. So. You've already kissed him, so it's not like a *first kiss* kind of outfit we're looking for,' her face was serious. She was concentrating on each item of clothing, holding it up to the light, checking the length, putting various items next to each other.

'We're looking for a *let's spend the night together* kind of outfit,' Annabelle concluded.

'Annabelle!'

'Come on. Don't tell me you hadn't thought about it…'

Ruby put her hands over her face, smiling, shaking her head.

'Oh god, Annabelle, don't, I'm already so nervous I feel like being sick everywhere.'

'Don't do that on Saturday,' Annabelle waved a finger, 'not attractive. Here we go, this one!'

She pulled out a dress. It was the wraparound one. Ruby's favourite.

'Really? Isn't it a bit…much? I was thinking of just - I don't know - jeans and a nice top?'

Annabelle raised one eyebrow and looked at Ruby.

'Jeans? Seriously? No. You live in your jeans. Always with the jeans. And the hoodies. There's nothing wrong with looking nice. Sorry. I mean, y'know, feminine.'

Ruby sighed.

'Now,' continued Annabelle, 'I came prepared, because I know you don't wear them…' she reached into a carrier bag she'd brought with her and produced a pair of heels. They were peacock blue, satin, stabbing stilettos. Ruby read the black and white label on the nude inner. *MANOLO BLAHNIK*

'These look…really expensive - Annabelle, I can't borrow them. Besides, I can't wear heels.'

'Yes you can.'

'It's too much. All of it, I can't- I'd really be happier in my jeans…'

Annabelle looked horrified.

171

'Okay,' said Ruby, 'okay I'll wear the dress. But at least let me wear leggings and flats with it. It'll look a bit less...over the top. I'm only going to watch a film in his flat, it's not like it's the premier in Hollywood.'

'Leggings? No. No, no, no. But flats – okay. I concede on that,' said Annabelle, putting the shoes away, 'but *one day* I'll get you in heels. One day.'

Ruby hugged her. 'Thank you.'

The next morning, she locked herself in the bathroom for a hair removal session. *Just in case.* Kaz knocked on the door every five minutes.

'What are you doing in there Ruby? Some of us need the shower, you know!'

Ruby finally emerged. 'It's all yours,' she said, wrapping a towel round her hair.

'At last! Jesus.'

Ruby was about to close her bedroom door when she heard Kaz calling her.

'Ruby! Come here.'

'What?' she walked back through.

*For god's sake. What now? Is she going to tell me off for not cleaning the mirror again?*

'What you doing tonight?' Kaz asked.

'I'm out. Why?'

'Out where?'

'Just at a friend's house.'

'Oh. Right. You sure you don't want to stop here? Keep me company? Your dad's working.'

Ruby did her best to hold in the incredulous laughter.

'Erm. I can't, really, it's my friend's birthday,' she lied.

'Fair enough,' Kaz said, disappearing into the bathroom. 'We should have a girls' night soon though, he's working nights a lot these days. I get bored.'

*Right. That's not happening.*

She took Bella for a long walk later that day. The time dragged. She willed every clock she caught sight of all day to say 7pm. Each hour felt like an entire day that wouldn't end.

Finally, it was time to go to Leo's.

She left Bella in her bedroom, tired out and happy to spend the night snoozing on Ruby's bed. On her way out, she passed the front room and saw Kaz watching TV with her Silk Cut and Smirnoff. She sneaked past, desperate not to be noticed and end up dragged into a conversation, or an argument. *Not this time.* As Ruby quietly closed the front door, she heard Kaz call through: 'have fun!'

She took a deep breath and knocked on Leo's door. As soon as he opened it, she grabbed him and kissed him. It seemed like forever since she'd seen him.

'Hello Ruby!' Natalya called through from the other room. Ruby pulled away, mortified. She thought Natalya would be out.

'Sorry!' she whispered to Leo.

He shook his head, smiling.

'You look beautiful,' he whispered back.

'I'm leaving you two alone, don't worry!' Natalya said, coming through to the hall to put her boots on.

*Wow. She looks stunning.* The hall filled with Natalya's perfume, exotic and warm. She was wearing a PVC black catsuit, with her peroxide hair tumbling over her shoulders and two black cat-ears peeking out from an Alice band on top of her head. She had drawn whiskers and a black nose on her face with eyeliner, which she'd also used to make her eyes appear even more feline. Her lipstick was the colour of blood, the same as her nails, filed into razor-sharp claws.

Ruby suddenly felt very much like a girl in her flat

shoes, with her mousey flat hair and bitten-down nails. Not much like a woman at all.

'Why are you dressed as a cat, for Eurovision?' Leo asked, frowning.

'Haven't you seen the Ukrainian act this year?' she asked, 'they –'

' – I don't want to know,' Leo said, shaking his head. 'I'll take your word for it.'

'Natalya, you look amazing!' Ruby said.

Leo looked irritated.

'Please, mum, wear your big coat,' he said, walking over to the peg and thrusting the huge parka into her hand, 'it's freezing outside. And... people round here... you don't want them seeing you like that.'

They continued the conversation in Ukrainian. Natalya put the coat on.

'He's embarrassed of his *old* mum, Ruby,' she said, rolling her eyes and smiling. 'When you get to my age, you'll realise, it's not old.'

Leo folded his arms and sighed impatiently.

'Alright, alright. I'm going. See you soon, Ruby.'

Natalya kissed them both on the cheek before leaving.

Leo shut the door and turned round. Ruby laughed.

'What?' he asked.

'You have lipstick all over your face.'

'Oh, god!' He wiped his cheek with his sleeve. 'She's right, I *am* embarrassed.'

Ruby took a deep breath as she followed Leo into the living area. *Calm down. It will be fine. You can do this. Why are you so nervous?*

The coffee table was covered with bowls of sweets and plates of cookies.

'Don't ask,' Leo said, grabbing a handful of Haribo. 'Mum got carried away.'

Ruby was too nervous to eat. She noticed one of the boxes on the table and smiled.

*Ptasie mleczko*

'Did the lady start serving you again, in that shop?' Ruby asked. The one who didn't like Ukrainians?'

'Oh, yeah. I forgot I told you that. That's not why she didn't want to serve me. It was because of Tony. Lots of people round here don't like him.'

'Oh…' she didn't know what to say.

They fell silent. She had so many questions. *It's not the time. Change the subject.*

'What films have we got lined up then?' she asked, reaching for a cookie in a bid to act normal.

Leo flicked through the menu and read out a list of titles. Ruby watched his side profile as she nibbled around the edges of the crumbling cookie.

'I'm so glad I've found you,' Ruby found herself saying. She was thinking out loud, but she meant it.

Leo turned and smiled. 'Really?'

She nodded.

'You're just… cool. And…fit.' she laughed, cringing at hearing herself. *Oh god. Don't ever say anything like that again.*

Leo smiled.

'I'll take that,' he said, brushing his hair out of his eyes, 'I'm really glad I found you too, Ruby. School is suddenly okay,' he laughed, 'I never used to see you there much before we… before we started hanging round.'

*Hanging round.* Ruby smiled.

'I wasn't there, much. I used to come back here for Bella at lunchtimes. I was new, didn't know anyone.'

'I live in the library room. I think I am what you would call a *geek*,' Leo said. 'I don't have any friends there, so being in the library was just better than standing on my own. And I love reading. I want to go to

175

university one day. How about you?'

Ruby shifted, suddenly uncomfortable.

'I don't think that's for me. I wouldn't get in,' she picked at her sleeve, 'I've hated school for ages. I fell behind with my work when mum was ill... and there's just been so much going on.'

'I don't know where I'll be in six months-' he said, 'but I know that I want an education. I want to be able to make something of myself.'

*Right. Good for you.* Ruby felt small. She turned away from him slightly and bit her nails.

'Well, I'm in a lower set than you...' she said, staring at the TV, '... so maybe I'm not supposed to change the world.'

'Ruby,' he said, grabbing her hand, 'you are smarter than anyone in my class. No question. You can do anything. You've been through so much but you're still here, holding everything together. Don't listen to anyone who says you can't change the world, Ruby. You can. What do you want to do?' he asked.

She smiled. She could tell that he meant it.

'I don't know... all I've been doing for so long is just getting through the day. The week. I mean, I did have this one idea. I was talking to Gio about it the other day. But it's a bit...'

'What?'

'I don't know. I just wonder if it's a bit...crap,' she laughed, apologetically.

'Crap?'

'Rubbish. Well, not exactly - I mean, Gio thinks it's a good idea. But then he's so nice to me. I think he'd tell me anything was a good idea, just to save my feelings.'

'He wouldn't,' said Leo, 'he owns his own business, he wouldn't bullshit you.'

'I - well. I had a tough time, when mum was ill. We

didn't get much help. It wasn't so much because it wasn't there. We just…didn't want it. Didn't want people interfering. I was worried about someone taking her away, and I think she was worried about someone taking *me* away. Looking back, I don't think that would've actually happened. But when you're young and you don't know anything, or when you're ill and you can't think straight… I don't know.

'Anyway, the point is…since then I've realised there are loads of other kids who have to look after parents, brothers and sisters. Madge told me how many kids at the care home there were who used to be carers. How many there were on her caseload. There's stuff for them, at the moment, but it's all being cut. Closed down. I wanted to start like a drop-in thing, at Gio's,' she put her hands over her face, 'so cringeworthy, but I was thinking of calling it the Carer Café…'

'That's a really good idea, Ruby, why are you embarrassed?' Leo smiled, 'It's a great idea.'

'Really?' Ruby turned to him and leaned her cheek on her hand. He nodded. She smiled.

'It'd take so much doing, though,' she said, smoothing the wrinkles in her dress. 'I'd have to figure out how to tell the right people, raise money to keep it going - Gio said he'd help me out. But I want to give them free drinks. Or at least, nearly free. That'd be the point, they could come for a couple of hours, I don't know, every month or whatever, and meet other young carers, get a free drink. I could invite people from the charities and stuff. Or have their leaflets or something. I could give them free barista training. Might help if they need to work, like I do. It'd be in Gio's café, but just for the drop-in session, it'd be the Carer Café.'

'I could help you,' he smiled, 'I'd love to.'

'I'm not paying you,' she said, laughing. 'What's your

grand plan for life, then?'

'I want to be a Human Rights Barrister,' he said, instantly. 'I want to help people who have no-one to defend them,' he looked at his hands, 'there are so many people who don't have a voice, who get taken advantage of, abused, who live in constant danger. People who live in fear…people like my mum.'

They fell silent again.

An old black and white classic horror film was on the TV, the volume low. She tried to look as though she was genuinely watching it, focussed on the long, creeping shadows and glinting eyes. The end-credits rolled up.

'So… I was going to ask…' he started fumbling with his watch.

Ruby waited.

'…do you want to go out? Like, be boyfriend and girlfriend, kind of thing?' he looked up at her.

She nodded, squealing inside.

He let out a sigh of relief.

'Thank god,' he laughed and she kissed him.

*Let The Right One In* was about to begin.

*Don't rush this. Enjoy being normal. Watching a scary film with your boyfriend. Boyfriend.*

She cuddled into him and they lay together, watching the scariest film Ruby had seen in her entire life. Ruby avoided horror films. She didn't need more nightmares, but it was a good excuse to hold him close. She listened to the noises of his body, his heart, his lungs, his mouth. Every time a scene made her wince, she squeezed her hand on his shoulder or buried her face in his side, so that he stroked her arm, or held her tighter.

As the final scene faded to black, she felt as though she should get up, but didn't want to move. She'd been lying down watching TV for hours. She should've felt relaxed, sleepy. But the adrenaline was coursing through her, the butterflies inside were caught in a tornado. She could feel he was the same - tense, waiting.

'Scary,' he murmured, breaking the silence.

She looked up at him and shifted to lean on her elbow, so that her face was directly in front of his. His dark brown eyes looked black in the low light.

'Yeah,' she said, holding his gaze, 'but cool.'

They kissed, sudden and intense.

They clamoured to feel each other all over as they kissed, each taking the other in, desperate and fierce, as though they were slipping through a net into darkness, as though they were only kept alive by each other's touch. They pulled at each other's clothes, undressing clumsily, blind, drunk on one another. *This is it*.

The sound of a key in the door cut through everything. They froze, then as they heard the door open, both scrambled to put their clothes back on and straighten up.

Natalya lingered in the hall, Ruby thought maybe to give them time. They both sat up straight, staring at the TV, trying to act natural. Ruby's heart was pounding. Still Natalya waited. Leo turned and looked at the empty doorway, confused. They heard a quiet sniff. They looked at each other. *Something's wrong*.

'Mum?' Leo said, softly.

She still didn't enter the room.

'I don't feel well, Leo. Too much to drink. I'm going to bed,' she said, her cracked, quiet voice disappearing into the bedroom as she quickly flashed by the door, face turned away. The bedroom door closed.

They stared after her, then Ruby watched Leo as he rubbed his eyes and combed his fringe away from his face with his fingers.

'She never drinks too much,' he said, looking at the floor, 'something's not right. It's him.'

179

Ruby silently nodded, eyes downcast. The moment had gone, and in its place was the same quiet, sad anger that always returned, whenever reality walked in.

# CHAPTER 21

'We need to start doing seasonal coffees, Gio,' Ruby
shouted through to the back room as she flipped the sign
on the door to say 'Closed'.

'Like one of the big chains? Nah,' he shouted back.

'It'd sell well though, people like stuff like that. St
Patricks' Day, Halloween, Christmas. People love
anything to do with Christmas. I don't, but most people
do,' she laughed.

'Like what though?' he asked, coming out of the
back room and rummaging in the cupboard under the till,
'have you seen my calculator?'

'Like with syrups. I don't know, like gingerbread
lattes or chocolate-orange mochas... something like that.'

'Hmm. I don't know. Doesn't sound very authentic
to me...' he frowned and squinted through his glasses at
the sums he was trying to add up.

'Smoothies aren't Italian. We sell them,' she said.

He laughed.

'Okay, okay. See what you can come up with. Look,'
he slid a piece of paper with scribbled sums and notes all
over it across the counter, 'I've been figuring out the
numbers. For your Carer Café.'

She held the paper and attempted to decipher it.
Ruby hadn't thought about it for weeks, since her date

night with Leo.

'That's how much we need, to run it,' he pointed at the bottom figure, 'how you want to run it, anyway.'

'Wow, that's a lot more than I thought.' Ruby said.

'That's with everything though - printing flyers, a website, how much the stock will cost to give it away for the average number through the doors each time, based on a six-month trial period...'

'Wow, Gio, thank you - I really appreciate it. I guess this just proves it's impossible though, really. I mean, where do I get that amount of money from? Thank you for looking into it though,' she said, half-smiling, defeated.

'Ah,' he held up his finger, pointing, 'hang on.'

He disappeared into the back again and emerged with another bit of paper.

'This is what you should do.'

He handed it over. It was an application form to the Prince's Trust.

'Thank you,' Ruby said, reading through the questions.

'I'll help you. You need a proper business plan. But it's worth it, if they liked it, you could get enough to start things off, then they'd help it keep itself going-'

She hugged him, nearly welling up.

'This is amazing, thank you so much!'

He laughed and adjusted his glasses.

'Hey, we don't have the money yet. Anyway. How are things going with your dad?'

'Alright. He's got more money now. Too much, if anything. Kaz is just spending it all the time. She loves it. But, I don't know. It's all dodgy. I'm not asking him about it. I don't want to know.

'The other day he just handed me £200 in cash and said *get yourself something nice*. I haven't spent any of it. I've never seen that much money. I don't want to use it for this,' she held up the application form, 'it's dirty money, I don't trust it.'

Gio nodded.

'You're right,' he said, 'just hang on to it. You don't know what could happen.'

His words hung in the air.

*No, I don't.*

'Are you doing anything next week?' he asked.

They both knew what he meant. It was her mum's birthday.

Ruby nodded.

'I was going to go to Park Hill. Where the ashes are. But...I don't know.' The last time she was there flashed through her mind. The man, Bella, the blood. 'It didn't feel right, somehow. So I'm going to go out to the Peak District, with Leo, instead. We said we were going to go ages ago but it never happened. He loves it. I thought it'd be nice to just do something happy. You know?'

'Very good idea,' he said, smiling, 'so it's serious with this boy then?'

Ruby blushed.

'Yeah, I think so. I don't know. I'm just making the most of the time I have with him.'

'What? Why? Is he ill?' Gio looked panicked.

'No, no. He's...' Ruby thought about whether she should tell him. *I trust Gio.* '...his visa is running out. You know about Tony, don't you?'

'Mmm, it depends what you're talking about. I know *of* him. And I know this boy's mother is involved with him, which is why I told you to be careful...'

'Okay. Well, they were supposed to get married, Tony and Natalya. When they got here. So they could stay forever. But it didn't happen. Now he's threatening to tell the Home Office...' Ruby suddenly started crying, out of nowhere. It surprised her.

She'd tried so hard to put it out of her mind, the thought of losing him weighed on her, terrified her. Gio held her in a big, warm, bear-hug.

'Shhhh,' he soothed, and muttered something in Italian. The only thing she could make out was *bastardo*. He patted her back.

'Are you sure this boy is worth it?'

She sobbed into his shirt, nodding.

'If I'd known…' he trailed off. 'Shhh. It's okay. You stay away from that man, though. And don't let Leo do anything stupid. He's in a mess, but it could be worse. Don't you get tangled up with him in it, Ruby.'

She pulled away, shaking her head, wiping the tears, 'I won't,' she managed. She knew that was a lie.

\*\*\*

It was nearly two months since she'd seen or heard from Tia. *Madge won't tell me anything. Other than her case is in the system. It's being looked into.*

Ruby rolled over in bed and took her phone from under her pillow. *Just in case. Just in case it's working again, or someone she knows has her phone. Or she's back.*

Message to Tia:

*Hey Ti. Just me again. I know I've messaged you a million times already but here's another, just in case you get it. I told Madge about you, I don't know if she's helping you, I hope she is. Let me know you're okay when you can xxx*

She put her phone back under her pillow and tried to sleep. What Gio said kept circling over her as she looked up at the ceiling in the dark. *Don't get tangled up with him in it.*

Eventually she fell into a fitful sleep, expecting to have her old nightmare again. To wake up sweating, shivering, crying.

It was a new one.

*'Tia. Tia!' Ruby tries to shout, but the words won't come out. Tia is standing there, right in front of her, on a cold, wintry beach. Ruby is stuck, her foot trapped between two rocks. It's bleeding, the skin grating away more and more as she struggles to free it.*

*The beach is long and flat. With the sky clouded over, the water looks grey-black, the sand is the colour of eggshells. It smells like a storm is coming. Tia turns and looks at Ruby. Her expression is calm, neutral. Ruby screams but nothing comes out of her mouth. Tia turns away and looks at the sea. She starts walking, slowly, into it. Darkness splashes up her jeans as she gets deeper.*

*'No, No!' Ruby can only watch as Tia disappears slowly under, lingering a little when the water is just above her lip, then she's gone. Tears are running down Ruby's face but she still can't make a sound. Something huge, grey, wide, appears on the horizon. It's growing. Advancing towards Ruby. It's a tidal wave, swelling towards the shore. Tia is gone, and Ruby will go the same way. She wrenches her foot free, snapping the bones to do so. The blood gushes everywhere but she's free, she can escape- but it's too late. The grey wall of water is right over her now, waiting to crash.*

Ruby woke to the sound of knocking. Bella barked, scratching to get out of the bedroom and investigate. It was a Saturday, so she'd slept in. She heard Kaz answer the door. The conversation sounded bad-tempered. She sat up and strained to hear.

'Oh. For Ruby? Right. What's she done?'

'If we could come in, Madam, we just need to ask her a few questions.'

'Ruby!' Kaz called through.

*Shit. What do they want? Is this something to do with Leo? Tony?*

She scrambled to pull some clothes on and emerged into the hall at the same time as her dad.

'What are you lot doing here?' he asked. 'I've done nothing. Search the place. You won't find anything, you bastards.'

'Mr Morton, we're here to speak to Ruby.'

Gaz glanced back at her. 'She's not done owt.'

He moved so he was between the police and Ruby. She couldn't help smiling.

'No, she's done nothing wrong, Mr Morton. She's not in trouble. It's concerning a friend of hers.'

*Leo.*

'What friend?' Gaz asked, not moving.

'Tia Williams.'

*Tia.* Her nightmare came back to her.

'Oh. Don't know her,' Gaz said, turning to Ruby. As she walked past him, he whispered *Remember, don't grass.*

'Is she okay?' Ruby asked, feeling knots start to tighten in her stomach.

'Can we sit down, to talk?'

Gaz stepped aside so they could go through to the living room.

'She's in the care of Social Services, at the moment,' the first officer said as they sat down.

'Oh, thank god. I was really worried about her.'

'Why were you worried?'

'Well... I don't know, it's not like I knew her really well, but the last time we spoke, she was in trouble, then she just disappeared.'

'Go back to the start – when did you see her?'

'A couple of months ago, on a Friday night. She asked me to come over, because she wanted to talk to someone.'

The officer nodded. The other one scribbled in a notebook.

'And when you got there?'

'She was really upset. I'm guessing she told you

186

about…well, she'd just found out she was pregnant, and her auntie was going to make her keep it, but she wasn't sure if she wanted to…'

'Make Tia keep it? Is that what she said?'

'Well, no, actually. She said her auntie wanted her to have it at the centre. Commune. Whatever it is. Have it there, then leave it with them… as though nothing had ever happened.'

'And how did Tia feel about that?'

'Well… confused, I think. I mean, I don't think she'd have ever actually let that happen. Nobody would.'

'Did she want to keep it?'

'No. Well, I don't know. She talked about getting an abortion, but she wasn't sure if she could, because of her age. I said I'd go with her.'

'How would you describe her relationship with her aunt?'

'I really don't know her – I'd only met her the week before. Our social worker introduced us.'

'Why?'

'She thought we'd get on. We had… similar circumstances,' she said, glancing sideways at her dad. 'I went back, later that night, but they said she was doing outreach.'

The officer with the notepad scribbled again. The other's radio started transmitting. She turned the volume down.

'What's happened to her?' Ruby asked.

'She was taken, against her will, to one of the communes, on the coast.'

Ruby thought of her nightmare again. *The wintry beach, the grey sea.*

'It's weird, I had this dream last night, about her – she was drowning, in the sea.'

'Did you have any idea of what was going to happen

to her?'

'No! Jesus, no. I told my social worker about her, because I was worried about her, but I never thought anything like this would happen.'

'You said you went back there, later that night. Why?'

Ruby shifted. She hesitated.

'Would you like to talk down at the station, Ruby?'

She could feel her dad's eyes on her.

'No, it's fine. I'd just... we'd had an argument, here,' she said, looking at Kaz, 'and I needed some space. That's all. But she wasn't there, when I went back. Geraldine's brother answered. He creeped me out a bit.'

'He's not her actual brother,' the officer said, 'it's just what they call each other, in the...' she trailed off, gesturing with her hands as though she was trying to find the right word.

'Cult?' Ruby offered.

'Bloody hell,' said Kaz, 'who is this friend of yours, anyway?'

'Sect, maybe,' the officer said.

'So how did you find her?' Ruby asked.

'She escaped. Called the police. You were the last person to see her, before she was taken. Thank you, for your time. We might have further questions for you. We'll be in touch, if we do.'

'So what's going to happen? Is Geraldine being charged with anything? Where is Tia? Can I see her?'

The officer held her hand up.

'I can't give out any confidential information, or information pertaining to the ongoing investigation. But thank you, you've been very helpful.'

They both stood up. The one with the notepad tucked it away into his top pocket. The other turned the dial on her radio back up to full volume.

Ruby watched them leave.

'Sound like a bunch of nutcases,' said Kaz.

'Poor girl,' said Gaz, lighting a cigarette.

Ruby walked to her room to get Bella's lead.

'Come on, Bella. We're going to Denby House.'

\*\*\*

She knew she couldn't just walk in. She waited outside, sitting on the bench in the smoking area. A couple of girls came out for a smoke.

'Either of you know Tia Williams?' Ruby asked.

'Who are you?'

'A friend. I was here, round Christmas.'

'She the one who ran away from Scarborough?'

'Must be. Is she here?'

The girls looked at each other, then back at Ruby.

'How do we know you're not one of them?' one asked.

'Could be trying to kidnap her again,' said the other.

Ruby exhaled. 'I swear, I'm just a kid who was here, I was friends with Kay Cooper.'

'Everyone knows Kay Cooper.'

'Okay. The Home Manager is called Frank. One of the care workers has pink hair... argh, what was her name... I can't remember. Erm... the TV room has a newspaper article from the Sheffield Telegraph on the wall – from when the mayor visited –'

'She's here,' one of them interrupted her. 'You want me to see if I can get her to come see you?'

'Yes. Thank you. I just want to know she's okay.'

They disappeared inside. Ruby waited. Bella yawned, then lay down on the grass next to the bench. Ruby flicked through different feeds on her phone. Five minutes went by. Ten more. She watched the automatic doors of the entrance. *Nothing.* Bella sat up and stretched, then shook herself from nose to tail. Ruby sighed.

'She's not coming, is she?' Ruby said.

The doors opened.

'Tia!' Ruby shouted.

Tia hung back, by the entrance. She was holding something. A book. Ruby stood up and walked over.

'Tia,' she repeated, hugging her.

Tia smiled, briefly. She looked behind Ruby, then to the street in front of the home.

'Did anyone follow you?' Tia asked.

'No, I don't think so – are you worried they're watching you?'

Tia nodded. 'I know, I'm paranoid. Maybe it's the hormones. I can't risk it, though. I really wasn't sure whether to come out to you. I can't stay. I have to get back inside. But I wanted to give you this. In case something happens to me.'

Tia handed over a notebook, watching the cars driving by, the woman walking past on her mobile phone.

'What is it?' Ruby asked.

'You'll see. They took my phone, on that first night, so I don't have your number, but mine's in there.'

'Are you going to a foster family?'

'My cousin and his wife are going to have me. They already foster. The social just have to make sure he doesn't have anything to do with… well, with my auntie, before I can go.' She pointed to the book in Ruby's hands. 'If anything happens to me, give this to the police.'

'What do you mean? Shouldn't you be giving it to them, now? If it's important?'

'Don't hand it in, Ruby. Please. I haven't told them everything. I need to have the baby, first. Make sure it's safe. Read the book, in case you lose it or it gets taken.

Someone needs to know. I have to go. You've got my number.'

She went back inside. Ruby looked around, then turned to the wall, putting the notepad under her hoodie.

'Let's get back home, Bella.'

# CHAPTER 22

*My name is Tia Williams. I'm 15 years old and I have been kidnapped. My details are at the back of this book. I was taken from Sheffield city centre by my Aunt, Geraldine Williams, and two other people. A man and a woman. I don't know their names. They were doing outreach with us in the town centre that night. She told me they were part of her branch. Of her religion, I mean. It's not really a religion. They don't believe in god, they believe in a man. The Followers of His Divine Light.*

*I thought we were getting a taxi home, but the car drove past Burnside and kept going. I don't know where we are. The coast, about two hours away, I think. It could be further. She said we were going on a retreat, to one of the communes on the coast. It would do me good to see the sea. She said she knew if she'd asked me, I'd have said no. So I was never asked. I was taken. She said a short break would be the best thing for my health, the health of the baby.*

*We're up on a hillside, overlooking the sea. I'm not sure what the building is. It's old. Grey stone. There's one big open room on the ground floor and separate, small rooms in the top. I think they're in the attic space maybe because all the ceilings slope. The toilet is outside. We all eat together at the long table. Or we did, to begin with. I broke the rules, on day one. Then I broke them again, and they locked me in my room. They gave me this book and a pen, to copy out the founding statement of His Divine Light, over and over again.*

*I have a bucket, to go to the toilet in. He only opens the door to give me food, or take the bucket. I tried to get past him, the first time, but it was pointless. He's huge. He just stood there and let me hit him, shove him, never reacting. Never moving, either. He tried to be nice about it, as though if it were up to him, he'd let me go. Brother Johannes, they call him. There are people from all over, here. He's German.*

*I have a window, but there are bars in front of it. On my side, not outside. It makes me think they must use this room for keeping people in. Why would you have bars, on the inside of a window, unless you wanted to keep someone in? I have a plan. I just need to figure out the timing, to give me the best chance.*

*Well, I have two plans. I keep working on Johannes. Trying to talk him round. If I could just make him see. It's so hard, though. They all think they're doing the right thing. They're convinced. I can't un-brainwash him. But if I could just convince him that His Divine Light wouldn't want a pregnant girl to be in distress — that he'd want her to get the medical treatment she needs — maybe he'd feel sorry for me. Agree he was doing the right thing by letting me go. I'm not hopeful for that, though. These people are so far gone. So my other plan is the bucket. It's disgusting. I keep being sick. I've got diarrhoea, too. Maybe because I'm pregnant, but it might be because I can't wash my hands, either. If I decide I can't get through to him, then the next time he comes, I'm going to wait behind the door, then throw the bucket over him. It might give me enough time to get past him. Get downstairs and out, especially if it's at night, when he comes last thing.*

*If you find this and I'm still missing, I think we're in Lincolnshire.*

193

*I saw the county road sign. I was stupid, though, and asked why we were there, so they blindfolded me then. Unless they turned back, or drove through to another county, we're there, somewhere on the coast. Along the stretch of cliffs, I can see a lighthouse. I think I can see a lifeboat station, too. That might help.*

*If someone finds this, and I'm still missing, you have to tell the police. Give this to them. Not just for me. I think stuff has happened here. I can't be sure, because I've been locked up, but on that first day, when I could walk around the place, I went down to the cellar. I was looking for the toilet. I didn't know there wasn't one in the house, then. I couldn't see much, because it was dark, but there was this smell. It was a wrong smell, a rotten smell. I called out, but there was no reply. Then I heard my name being screeched behind me, and it was my aunt, hurrying down the stairs to grab me. That was the first time I broke the rules. Do not enter the cellar.*

*I don't believe in His Divine Light, but I do believe in God. I pray that God will forgive me. If I escape, I'm not going to tell the police anything about the cellar. I'm not going to tell them that she told me I was in Scarborough, because I know it definitely wasn't there. I've been there, I know it. I don't want them to find them, or to search the place, until I've had my baby. I honestly believe that the only person who was in danger there was me, but I think something awful could have happened before I got there. I hope I'm wrong. I really do, because I don't know if I'll forgive myself for not saying anything if I'm right. I hope God does.*

*I hope nobody ever reads this. If you do, please find out what happened to me, and to my baby.*

*Fucking hell.* Ruby read it again. The handwriting was rushed, scruffy. Different to the other end of the book, where she'd written the same four lines again and again in neat, capital letters.

*HIS DIVINE LIGHT IS THE SECOND
COMING. HE WILL BRING US SALVATION.
MATERIAL POSSESSIONS ARE SURRENDERED.
OUR SPIRITS ARE SURRENDERED. OUR WILL IS
HIS. WE WILL BRING SALVATION TO THE
IGNORANT.*

She closed the book and held it, watching Bella. She
wished Bella could talk. *I'd tell you everything. You'd help me
figure out what to do. What could you do, even if you wanted? You
don't know where it is. Tia doesn't even know. She's scared for her.
Scared for the baby. But then…*

She started drafting a message to the new number.

*I read the book. I know you're scared to tell them everything –
but wouldn't you be safer if they were arrested? Disbanded? Is it
because you think they'll come after you and the baby, like a revenge
thing? Surely if there's something going on, they'll all be put away.
Plus… what if you're not the only one? I understand that if
someone's already dead then you can't save them but if someone has
died, someone will be missing them. If they can do that to you, they
can do it to another girl.*

She kept drafting and redrafting. She didn't know
what to say or how to say it. *It's easy for you to say that,
Ruby, you have nobody to look out for except yourself. You can't
say what you'd do, because it's not you it's happening to.* She took
a deep breath and put the book under her bed. Bella
woke with a start, then trotted over to investigate what
was being buried. She sniffed and wagged her tail, then
sat back and looked at Ruby, whining.

'Look,' Ruby said, dragging the book back out, 'it's
nothing interesting. Just a book. You can't eat it.'

Bella sniffed and barked.

'What's up with you?' Ruby asked. Bella barked at
her again.

'Shit. Okay. I'll do it. But I'm going to tell her I lost it, okay?'

Bella sprung up and walked over to the door, then clawed at the edge to get out.

# CHAPTER 23

The day of her mum's birthday was a clear, sunny day. It was cold, for Spring, but bright. Ruby and Leo stood outside the train station, looking up to town. She loved what people saw as they walked out.

To her right, a sweeping wall of steel curved up and across, water cascading down it like shimmering heat. In front, long ledges of stone, overflowing with water, made their way down to end in a fountain that separated into a fringe of streams, pooling into the reservoir that began the cycle all over again.

'Come on,' she said, 'I'll show you something.'

They walked up the sweeping path beside the wall of steel and when they got to the road, she turned around.

'Look,' she said, pointing to Park Hill. 'Mum grew up there. Before it was done up. Didn't used to look like that.'

Leo smiled. Bella yawned.

Park Hill stood directly behind the station, looking completely different in the daylight - as though it were the city walls, stretching wide, solid and secure.

'She said it was the happiest time of her life,' Ruby continued. 'It went through bad times. But she had a happy childhood in that flat. I want to get a memorial bench on that slope, there. That's where her ashes are scattered.'

She thought about her failed pilgrimage. Leo waited patiently, stroking Bella in the cold sunshine. *Time to move on.*

Inside, the station was full of students going home for reading week, weighed down with suitcases and rucksacks, staring up at the departures board, dragging everything up the stairs to the platforms, calling home.

On the platform, she sat on the bench with Bella in her lap, holding her close.

A girl next to them was on the phone.

'I know, I know. I will,' the girl said, impatiently. 'Alright. Well I'll see you soon. Love you mum, bye.'

Leo put his arm round Ruby and she leaned on his shoulder. *Don't cry* she told herself, over and over.

A lot of people on the train were dressed for hiking, rambling, cycling. All dressed in the right clothes. Waterproof thermal coats, hiking boots, huge rucksacks. Then there was Ruby, in her jeans, hoodie and pumps - with a Staffordshire Bull Terrier. Ruby knew what they all thought of her. *I don't care. I'm with Leo.* She saw a *welcome* sign at one of the stations they stopped at and thought of Tia, seeing *Welcome to Lincolnshire.* She wanted to tell Leo about it, but something stopped her. She didn't want him to tell her she'd done the wrong thing, handing the book in to the police. The thought that something might happen to Tia, to the baby, because of her, was too much. *You told them. You told them she needs protection. The reason she kept it from them. They have to look out for her. They have to.*

She stared out of the window at the unfolding countryside, still glistening with the dew of the morning. The sun was still climbing in the sky, casting long shadows over the fields and hillsides, like a vast, green-brown sea, rising, dipping, swelling, frozen in time millions of years ago. She'd never seen anything like it before, except for Leo's drawings.

'Your pictures were really good,' she said, finally smiling.

'Thanks.'

He grabbed her hand and kissed it.

When they got off the train, Leo led the way. She had no idea where they were going. Very quickly, civilisation seemed to disappear. In its place were trees, mud, stone and water. *The smell is incredible.* Ruby breathed it in - deep, sweet and pure. The air was so clear, as though it was an entirely different kind from the air in the city. She felt her lungs, clothes, hair, even Bella - all being cleansed of the cigarette smoke that had become as much a part of them as their skin.

They stood, breathing it in, surveying the trail stretching out in front of them. Under a canopy of a hundred shades of green, dappled sunshine spotted the scrabbling slopes, covered in mouldering brown leaves.

She bent down and let Bella off her lead. The dog immediately bolted off, tail wagging furiously, snuffling through the undergrowth, darting between interesting smells, bounding over and under everything in her way. Leo and Ruby laughed at her, and followed.

*So I've got the wrong clothes. Wrong shoes. Don't know where I am or what I'm doing. I love it, though. I love this.* It was a new feeling. Different. They emerged from the wooded area to a steep incline, the stony path winding through a three-dimensional jigsaw of black, brown and grey rocks. Some were smaller than Bella, others were up to Ruby's shoulder.

At the top, she felt giddy, breathless, invigorated. The world stretched out forever before them, in front, to either side, behind - every way she turned, the clear horizon never ended. The wind whipped round them, speeding in from hundreds of miles out to take their breath away and onto its next destination halfway round the world.

Ruby felt like screaming into it, shouting into the chasm all around her, just because she could. She did. Leo did the same. They stood shouting into the wind on the deserted peak, a craggy shard jutting out into the sky, like the crest of a giant wave, set in stone just before it crashed down to break.

They laughed, tears in their eyes teased out by the cold wind, holding each other, on top of the world. Ruby took out her phone and got a picture of them both, windswept and beaming. She wanted to remember this, the happiest moment of her life, forever.

# CHAPTER 24

Facetime with Annabelle:

'Ruby, you're revising? Seriously? I thought Burnside High was supposed to be shit?'

'It is.'

'Then why are you bothering?'

'You've answered your own question, Annabelle. It's shite, so I have to do it myself. Just because I'm there doesn't mean I've given up on getting decent grades.'

'Is this because of him? He's not some kind of genius, Ruby, he just likes reading books. It doesn't make him *better* than you. My grandad is always reading but it doesn't do him any good. He can't even remember when bin-day is.'

'It's not because of Leo,' Ruby lied, 'I just want to do something with my life, you know? Change the world.'

'Change the world. Realistic ambition. I like it.'

'Shut up.'

'And you need an A in Physics GCSE, for that?'

'To start off with, yep.'

'Well, just make sure you get a break. You've done nothing except see him and revise. You don't even have a desk. Don't you get cramp?'

Ruby panned the camera to show her set-up - sat on her bed, leaning against the wall, with two pillows across her legs, leaning her book and writing pad on them.

'This is fine, look!'

'Mmm. Well, you have that wild-tired look in your eyes. You know, like on a nature programme when they show an animal that's about to die of exhaustion because it's been desperately searching for water for like, days. That kind of look.'

'Brilliant, thanks Annabelle. Anyway, I have to go.'

'*Please* get some sleep. Don't open that book again tonight, yeah?'

Ruby nodded.

'What night are you working at Gio's? I'll come see you.'

'Tuesday.'

'See you then. Mwa!'

*The Bernoulli Effect. Come on Ruby. Focus.*

She thought about what Annabelle said and looked in her phone camera to examine the red blotches in the whites of her eyes and dark shadows under them. *It will be worth it.*

She liked to imagine her and Leo opening their results next year together, planning what they would do now that the world was theirs for the taking. *Don't. He might not even get to take his exams here.*

*Electromagnetic induction.* Ruby sighed. The words on the page swam, the diagrams and formulas blurred into each other. Nothing was making sense or sinking in. It just sat there on the page, incomprehensible as a foreign language.

She heard some commotion coming from the hall. *Here we go again. Dad's back from work. She's having a go about something or other.* She frowned. It sounded different. Frantic.

'Jesus, Gaz, it's not 'nothing' - look at it!' Kaz shouted.

'I said, leave it!'

Ruby stepped into the hall and saw him from behind, stumbling into the bathroom.

'What's happened?' she asked Kaz.

'Eurgh. Your dad's lost a bloody finger, that's what's happened!' Kaz said, screwing up her face in disgust. Ruby ran to the bathroom.

'Dad, let me see -'

'It was an accident!' he said, as soon as he heard her voice. Blood was pouring down the sink, as he held his hand under the tap. His face was white-grey, glistening with sweat. Ruby could see he was shaking all over, as though he was freezing cold. He stuffed up the wound with a flannel and grabbed a towel, trying to wrap it around with his one free hand.

'You have to go to A&E, dad-' Ruby said. She stopped as he turned and glared at her, slowly shaking his head. She'd never seen that look before. She backed away. *Leave it. Don't get involved. If he wants to bleed to death, let him.*

In her room, she listened to Kaz continuing to question him. Ruby knew it wouldn't end well. *Leave it, Kaz. There's no talking to him when he's like this. You should know that.*

'How was it an accident? How? You don't cut your own finger off, for Christ's sake!'

'I'm telling you Kaz, leave it. Fucking leave it!'

'He did this to you, didn't he? Or one of his boys - am I right? Or was it that other lot? Wouldn't you tell them what they wanted to know? Is that it? That Tony is fucking evil.'

'You don't know what you're talking about. Stupid whore.'

'Oh I'm a whore am I?'

'I pay you enough don't I? This-'

Ruby could heard Kaz struggling. *He's grabbed her.*

'This here - this is where my money goes. On you. All of it. So you don't ask questions, Kaz, because you don't have the right!'

Kaz made a sound, a sort of yelp.

*Please drop it. Please, Kaz.* Ruby was worried about the baby. She could hear Kaz's breathing. Angry, rapid. *Shit. She won't back down.*

'If I'm a stupid whore, then what does that make you?'

Ruby didn't know exactly what happened, but she heard running, a stumble, a thud, her dad shouting, Kaz screaming. Then silence. She heard her dad spit, then he walked out, slamming the front door.

Ruby stood, not knowing whether to face the situation or pretend it hadn't happened, but then she thought of the baby. She walked into the hall, quietly. She didn't know what to say.

In the living room, Kaz was sitting against the wall, holding her face on one side, mascara streaks down her cheek.

'Kaz…' Ruby said, gently.

'Fuck off,' Kaz spat, 'Fuck off Ruby. I fucking hate you. Don't make me have to look at your ugly fucking face!' she snarled.

Ruby backed off, shut herself in her room and buried herself under the bedding. She hoped that somehow, if she closed her eyes tight enough, wrapped herself deep enough, that when she emerged, everything would be fine.

\*\*\*

The next day she walked to school with Leo, shattered.

'Neither of them were there when I got up,' she

continued.

'Ruby, you shouldn't have come in today. You look so tired.'

*Great. So now I feel bad and look bad.* She knew he was right though. Annabelle was right. *That wild-tired look.*

'I'd rather go to school than deal with whatever's going to happen with them today, to be honest,' she said, shrugging. He nodded.

In History, Ruby stared out of the window over the school field. Even though she was so tired and distracted by what happened the night before, Ruby could tell something was wrong with Leo that morning.

She pictured his face. *He looked sad. Anxious. Maybe he knows it was Tony. He's worried about what else he'll do.*

Neither of them talked on the way home. Ruby had so much that she wanted to say, but didn't know where to start, or even if she should. She hadn't heard from Tia, since she told her she'd left the book on the bus. *The police promised me they'd protect her.* Leo was on her mind, too. Him and Natalya. Their visas. The fact they might disappear at any minute. *He's already a million miles away. Said nothing since we left school.* She worried that she was losing him, that she was just another concern he didn't need.

*He needs a normal girl who's always happy and smiling, with a lovely family that isn't up to their neck in shit. Someone who skips to school after a good night's sleep. Someone like Annabelle. Not me.*

'I need you to do something for me,' he said, as they reached Burnside. *He looks serious.*

'What?' Ruby shivered. She didn't want to hear whatever it was. *Get your dad to grass on Tony.* Or worse - *don't speak to me again, leave me alone.*

Leo took a deep breath.

'I need you to apply for a passport.'

'What? Why?'

It started to rain.

*Shit. They're being deported. I knew it. Fuck.*

'We need to leave soon. We don't know when it will be. But the plan is to stay in the UK.'

'So why do *I* need a passport?'

Leo looked around, as though someone might overhear, and lowered his voice.

'Mum has saved enough. She's buying the paperwork this week. We're moving up to Newcastle, starting again, with new identities. As citizens.'

'What? How can you... when?'

She couldn't process all the questions rushing through her head fast enough.

'As soon as we can. I want you to come with us,' he said, taking her hand, 'we can start a new life.'

He smiled. Ruby pulled her hand away.

'What about me? Where's *my* new identity? They'll come after me and they'll find you!'

'We have it taken care of. Trust me. You need a passport, maybe even a visa. If it all goes wrong and I get deported, I have to know you'd be able to come with me, or to follow me. I can't go back - knowing I won't see you again,' he paused, staring at her. 'I'd rather kill myself.'

Tears surfaced in Ruby's eyes. It was too much to take in. She hugged him, crying into his shoulder, the rain soaking them both. She had so many questions. It wasn't the time to ask, yet again. It never was.

She pulled away, her face soaked with tears and rain. She sniffed and wiped her eyes with her sleeve, nodding.

'I'll do it,' she said, fixing her eyes on his. 'I'll do whatever it takes.'

He grabbed her and pulled her close, kissing her so hard, she felt as though he took a part of her away when he left.

\*\*\*

'Ruby, how are you darling?' Annabelle's mum said, taking off her scarf as she stood on the other side of the counter.

'I'm good, thank you,' Ruby said, willing her to make an order and leave her alone.

'How's the new school treating you? Hmmm, what should I get, Belbel?'

Annabelle shrugged, rifling through the different types of biscotti.

'She's embarrassed,' Annabelle's mum said to Ruby, 'doesn't like me calling her that in public.'

Ruby saw Annabelle behind her mum, rolling her eyes and shaking her head.

'She'll have a tea and I'll have a chai tea latte, to take away please.'

'Oh, we don't do that… I can do a latte?' Ruby offered.

'Oh, it's not quite- no, of course. Yes. That's fine. So anyway, how's school?'

'Fine.'

'I bet you're glad it's nearly summer. Must be nicer in Burnside, when the weather's good. Anywhere's nice when it's sunny, isn't it?'

'Mum!' Annabelle interjected, 'just sit down and wait for me. I'll get the drinks.'

'Okay, okay, I'm going. Lovely to see you, Ruby. Pass on my best to your… to your family.'

Ruby tried to make her smile look sincere.

'Sorry,' said Annabelle, 'she means well. She's just a nightmare sometimes.'

'You want to meet a real nightmare? You should

207

come meet Kaz. She'd traumatise you.'

She steamed the milk, hearing Kaz's voice, *Don't make me have to look at your ugly fucking face!* in the screaming fizz. She swallowed and focussed on making a leaf pattern in the foam as she poured it out, for Annabelle's mum.

'I thought things were better, with her there? No?' Annabelle asked.

'Yeah, they are. She just does my head in. Anyway-' Ruby put their drinks on a tray and pushed them towards Annabelle, 'thanks for coming to see me.'

'I came to ask – what are you doing for half term? We always have a big family get-together in Spring half term and fall out over who should host it, and people always have to sleep on sofas or in camp beds, so this year dad put his foot down and said the only way to stop everyone murdering each other was to rent out this cottage that has enough bedrooms and bathrooms to mean we all have our own space. I was going to ask... I mean, I don't know what you're doing, but - if you wanted to come, you'd be saving me from having to deal with them all on my own...' she smiled, hopefully.

'Aw. Thanks, Annabelle. To be honest I don't know what I'm doing, but...thanks.'

'Think about it. I'll message you the address. Just in case you decide to take pity on me.'

Annabelle handed over a gift bag.

'What's this?'

'Just a little thing. Because I hardly see you, now. I see things and they remind me of you. I bought this one.'

'Thank you,' Ruby said, leaning over the counter and hugging her.

'I better get these drinks over to mum. She's always mortifying me by complaining that stuff's too cold. Hopefully see you next week.'

Ruby wiped the counter and thought about how much she'd miss Annabelle, if she had to leave. She checked her notifications, to see if she'd had a reply from the PDSA vet about getting a pet passport for Bella. *Nothing.*

***

As soon as Ruby opened the front door, she saw her dad standing in the hall, bottle in hand, glaring at her. She shut the door behind her and didn't move, bracing herself.

He thrust a piece of paper into her hand.

'Read it. Everything's gone,' he said. The smell of spirits was on his breath and seeping through his skin. *He's been drinking all day.* Her stomach knotted. She read the letter.

*Gaz,*

*I'm leaving you. That's the last time you'll raise your hand to me. I thought deep down, you were a good person. I thought you'd be a good dad. I was wrong.*

*I'm sorry it had to end this way, after all these years. I always thought you did the wrong thing marrying Lisa. Thought you should've been with me. But now I thank god I didn't waste my life with you. I feel sorry for her, that she did. I almost feel sorry for Ruby too. If she wasn't such a poisonous little bitch I would do. I'm sure she'd want me to stay, be her mum too, but she's turned out to be a nasty piece of work, just like her dad.*

*I've booked my appointment at the clinic. You're not fit to be a dad, and I don't want anything tying me to you. I'm not raising a kid on my own. It's not what I signed up for. My decision is final. Don't try to stop me.*

*I thought I could put up with you, for the money, but I can't. I don't want to see you again.*

*Kaz*

'Dad, I didn't-' Ruby stammered.

'You've lost me *both my sons*!' he shouted, right in her face. She backed up against the wall. Her legs suddenly felt fuzzy, weak.

'First you drove Cal away. Now you've driven off the mother of my *unborn son* and she's going to *kill him*. It's your fault I hit her. You drove me to it. Got me working for that fucking psycho...I always knew you had no respect for me, and here's the proof,' he shook his head, draining his glass of whiskey, 'my own daughter thinks I'm a fucking idiot. And you *attacked* her, Ruby. You made her life *hell!*'

'I didn't, dad-' she started.

'S*hut up*!' he hit her across the face with the back of his hand, one of his sovereign rings catching her cheekbone. She fell to the floor, conscious, but reeling.

While the impact smacked through her skull and the stinging burn throbbed through her cheek, he continued shouting at her. She barely heard any of it.

'She's taken everything. The plasma screen, surround sound, all that shit I bought her, the cash… everything! I suppose that was your idea too, eh? Rob him blind, Kaz, he doesn't deserve anything he's worked for! Just like when you said, 'I'll invite Cal round just to show Dad what he's missing, then cut him out of Dad's life forever!"

He knelt down so he was directly facing her. He pointed at her, his red face covered in pulsating veins, his yellow teeth bared.

'You see this?' he said, thrusting his bandaged hand in front of her eyes, pointing at the bloodstained stump where his finger used to be.

'*This* is loyalty. That stupid bitch thought Tony did

this to me? She's wrong. *I did this for him.* Someone tried to get me on their side. Against him. I wouldn't do it. I lost a fucking finger for him. *That's* loyalty. You don't know the meaning of the word. Supposed to be family. You side with anyone as long as it's not me!'

He shook his head again, narrowing his eyes on her.

'You know what? I'm not having this,' he continued, 'I don't want you here. I'm going to call up the social and have them come take you away. And that stinking dog. Get it put down. You're both fucking parasites and I want rid of you. You can both go live with that fucking foreign creep you're seeing, I don't care.'

The room spun. He got up, threw his bottle and it smashed on the floor next to her. She had to shield her eyes from the flying shards.

'I'd be gone by the time I get back if I were you,' he said as he walked out, then slammed the front door behind him.

Ruby got tunnel vision. She had to focus on sorting herself out before allowing herself to be upset in any way.

She went to the bathroom, shaking. Her face was red, but not yet swollen or bruised. The ring had split the skin slightly. *Just a graze. Okay. Nothing is broken, or bleeding much. I can still see. I'm fine.*

All she wanted to do was to call Leo, but she didn't let herself.

*He has enough to deal with. He doesn't need me running to him with all my problems. What could he do about it anyway? Nothing. It would just upset him, make him angrier. Or worse, he might try to have a go at dad. That would be horrific. No.* She decided to stay off school until her bruising had gone.

In her room, Ruby sat on her bed, numb. Bella came and sat in her lap, nuzzling her head into Ruby's stomach. Mechanically, Ruby stroked Bella with one hand and checked her phone messages with the other.

One from Leo:

*Come round sometime this week and I'll go through what you need to do for the passport. Thank you for being amazing xxx*

She sighed and looked at his face. Her phone background was the photo of the two of them in the Peak District, on top of the world. They looked so wildly happy. A glimmer of a smile crossed Ruby's face, but the pain of her cheek made sure it faded quickly.

She felt sick. All she could do was hope her dad drank enough to forget what he'd said about Social Services, and Bella. The thought of going back to Denby House made her want to vomit. The alternative was even worse - being placed with a foster family. At least at Denby House she could shut herself away, get out to see Leo whenever she wanted. She didn't have to answer to anyone as long as she kept to a few rules. A foster family would be completely different. *They could be anyone. Even if they were nice, they'd want to keep tabs on me, ask questions about Leo.* As for what he'd said about Bella, she couldn't even think about it.

*They'd have to kill me first.*

Ruby texted Leo back and prayed that he would buy her excuse.

*Not feeling well, think it's just a bad cold. Might skive the last few days of school. I'll come over when I'm better, don't want to spread it around. I love you. See you soon. Xxx*

She looked in her mirror. There in the reflection, she could see Leo's window and his bedroom. Just like she had when he saw her dancing, all that time ago. He wasn't there now. Ruby looked at her face, the blood on her cheekbone. Touching the swelling, she winced.

She wandered into the dark hallway on automatic pilot, to lock the front door. She heard a noise outside, a kind of moan. She knelt down and silently lifted the letterbox, letting the blue-white light of the walkway strip-lights in. Her dad was there, crumpled against the balcony wall, sobbing. He didn't see her.

She watched his wrinkled, blotched complexion twist and strain. He swore, hitting his head with the heel of his hand again and again. He got up and turned, looking over the balcony, staring at the ground, six floors below. Ruby could hear him crying. She imagined his tears, dripping off the end of his nose, glinting in the electric light against the darkness, falling over the edge. Suddenly he turned and looked at her. She dropped the letterbox flap, clattering shut, and stood back from the door, backing up the hall, her heart thudding. She waited, for a shout, banging, something. She could hear her own breath and tried to make it completely silent.

She sensed a shuffle, behind the door.

'Rubes?' the cracked voice came from behind it.

She swallowed and gripped the wooden doorframe of the kitchen.

'I'm sorry. Ruby,' he said, 'I'm so sorry. I need help. I know I do. I always...' she heard a breaking in his voice, a sniff, 'always said I wouldn't be like my dad. I don't want to be like this. You don't deserve this. I just - when I've been drinking... the red mist just comes down...'

Ruby shook her head. She stayed, facing the door, focusing on the letterbox.

'I'm going to stay with a friend,' he said, 'it's for the best. You should... you should call Madge.'

Ruby tried to keep the tears in as she spoke.

'I will,' she managed.

The footsteps shuffled away.

Ruby took a deep breath and looked up at the peeling wallpaper on the ceiling. *Breathe. Just breathe.* As she let her head fall back down, she caught sight of her rucksack.

She carried it back to her room and sat on her bed, opening up the gift bag from Annabelle. She untied the ribbon and pulled something out, wrapped in purple tissue paper. She pulled at the edge and it tore away.

She stopped, seeing the surface beneath. She stroked it, pulling the rest of the paper off. She had no idea where Annabelle had got it from. It was a framed photo of her mum, from before she was ill. There she was, in her little black dress, with her smoky eyes and her sleek hairstyle, her beautiful smile lighting up the room.

# CHAPTER 25

'Bella pulled me over, in the park,' she said. 'It looks worse than it is. She was chasing a squirrel.'

The bruises still weren't gone by the end of the week. She watched his face. *He doesn't believe me. Change the subject.*

'So like I said on the phone, Dad hasn't come home. He said he was staying at a friend's, but I don't know. He could be anywhere. Sleeping on a park bench, probably,' she said to Leo, trying to sound as though she didn't care.

'Ruby, did your dad do this?' he asked, pointing at her face.

*Shit.*

'No, no. Like I said, he hasn't been here. I don't know where he is. Honestly, it was an accident. Don't you think I'd have called you up in floods of tears if Dad had hit me? Believe me, I would've been straight over.'

She smiled and held his hand.

'I'll always tell you when I need help,' she said, and kissed his knuckles.

He smiled.

'Okay. Good. Now, let me go get those forms.'

He disappeared into the other room.

Ruby exhaled.

*Christ.* She never wanted to have to lie to him again.

It felt awful.

Natalya was out. Leo didn't say where, which meant she was probably with Tony. *I wonder if he's seen dad, since he left? Why hasn't Tony picked up all that stuff yet?*

'Dad's keeping a load of stuff in boxes for Tony in our flat. I opened one of them,' she said as Leo came back in. It just came out. She didn't realise how much it had weighed on her mind until she said it.

'Did you wear gloves? Can you tell it's been opened?' Leo looked panicked.

'I wore gloves,' she lied.

*Covering my hands with my sleeves is the same thing.*

'I used a small knife. I don't think you can tell.'

'You need to make sure. They're serious people. If they think anything has happened, they'll kill your dad. I'm not exaggerating.'

He stared at her.

Ruby swallowed.

'You can't tell, I promise.' she desperately tried to picture the box in her mind, and the packages inside. *I didn't leave a mark. I'm sure. I didn't.*

'Was it drugs?' he asked.

'I think so. It was covered with cling film but…there was a gun in there, too…' as soon as she said it, she wished she could take it back.

*Why did you tell him about the gun?*

'A *gun?*' he exclaimed, 'right. You stay here tonight. You can't go back there. I can't believe you've been there on your own with that stuff for days. Ruby, why didn't you come over sooner? How can I look after you when you don't tell me the truth?' his voice sounded despairing, as though he had gone through the argument in his head before, or had it with someone else. *Natalya.*

Ruby suddenly felt angry with him, for the first time.

'Look, Leo, I don't want you to have to look after

me. I'm not a kid. I had a lot of shit in my life before I met you and I dealt with it on my own. I don't need looking after. You and your mum have your own problems to deal with. Just let me deal with mine on my own,' she snapped.

A voice inside was screaming at her to stop, but the words carried on coming out.

'Things were easier before I knew you, Leo. I didn't care about school, or anyone except myself.'

'So I've made everything worse, have I?' Leo asked. 'You wish you'd never met me?'

'No, that's not what I meant. I'm sorry, look, I think maybe we just need some space.'

Ruby couldn't believe what she was saying. She needed to clear her head - that was all she meant, but it came out wrong.

'What? Really?' he asked, 'I might be leaving the country any day now and you want time apart?' he shook his head and let out a short, flat laugh, 'I get it. This is why you've been avoiding me this week. Suddenly it's all too real, with the passport and the plan... you want out, don't you? Well if you're trying to let me down gently, Ruby, this isn't working.'

He had tears in his eyes.

'God, Leo, I don't even know where to start with *how wrong* you are!'

Ruby was so frustrated. She wanted to shake him, to click her fingers and make him instantly understand how she felt. But it wasn't that easy.

They sat in awful silence, Ruby with her head in her hands, Leo biting his nails.

Finally, Ruby spoke. 'I'm sorry. I didn't mean what I said. It came out wrong. All I meant was that so much is happening to me, and I have no control over any of it. I don't like relying on people. Everyone in my life leaves,

217

or breaks promises, or isn't there when I need them. It's just hard for me, that's all.

'And I don't want any time apart from you. I'd spend every waking second with you if I could,' she said, searching his face. He looked at her, silent.

'As for this week,' she carried on, looking at her hands, 'it's been horrible not seeing you.' She realised she had an excuse to use. It was another lie, but it was plausible. 'I just didn't want you seeing me because I'm vain and I looked a mess with my cold and my face. I don't want you to stop liking me…' she gave him a sideways glance.

He reached over and wrapped her in a hug, smiling in spite of the tears in his eyes.

'You never need to worry about that,' he said, 'I'm sorry if I'm too much sometimes. I felt like a bit of a stalker over these last few days. I was just stressed out, I thought I was losing you,' he said, stroking her back.

'Maybe,' he carried on, holding her tighter, 'maybe everyone else who's made a promise to you has broken it, but I'm different. You might not want me looking after you, but I will, when you need me to. If I didn't, I couldn't live with myself. It's a selfish thing. I want to take care of you because I love you. If anything happened to you, my life wouldn't be worth living.'

She kissed him.

'I'll stay here,' she said, stroking his hair, 'I have to go get Bella and some of my things though, will you come with me?' she asked.

'Of course.'

\*\*\*

Ruby was surprised at just how little she owned that actually meant something to her. Other than Bella,

everything she cared about was now sat in a small holdall
on Leo's bedroom floor, and even that was mainly full of
essentials like clothes and toiletries. There were a few
things from the boxes Madge had saved, the ticket from
their trip to Edale and the framed photo of her mum,
from Annabelle.

The £200 cash her dad had given her was in there,
still untouched.

'We don't know when we'll have to move,' Leo said,
interrupting her thoughts, 'we've started packing, just in
case.'

Ruby hadn't taken any notice of the bags and boxes
all over the place. She looked around and realised most
of their belongings were gone - empty shelves and bare
surfaces everywhere. It put her on edge.

*This is real. He's really going. Soon.*

'Don't leave me behind,' she said, involuntarily.

He turned to her and walked over to where she sat
on the bed.

'I won't. I promise,' he said, and kissed her.

She kissed him back then stopped.

'Wait,' she said, pulling back. She started to get
undressed.

He watched her, hesitating.

She lifted his T-shirt. He took it off and kissed her,
harder.

Ruby knew it was what she wanted. In that moment,
it was all she could think about. She held him close, as
though he would stay forever, if she could just get under
his skin.

\*\*\*

'We have to get up,' Leo said, sighing.

They were lying in the bed, her head nestled in the

nook between his shoulder and chest, looking up at their entwined fingers.

'Mmmm,' Ruby said. It was a noncommittal sound. She didn't want to go anywhere.

'Mum's due back,' he said, kissing the palm of her hand.

'I thought she was with-' Ruby checked herself, 'I thought she was working.'

'She's at work now. She'll be seeing him tonight, probably.'

They got dressed and decided to watch TV in the main room until she got back. Ruby didn't want Natalya to come back and find them in his room, even though she knew she probably wouldn't mind. It just felt disrespectful.

She flicked through the channels, unable to settle on anything. Ruby felt weird. She wasn't sure how she was supposed to feel after sleeping with someone for the first time. She was glad it had been with Leo.

In a way, she felt weird precisely because she *didn't* feel any different to before. The way people talked about it, she'd expected to feel like a completely different person - to suddenly feel like a woman - older, wiser, fearless.

But everything was as it had been before - messy, uncertain, terrifying - and she felt exactly like she had done before - sick with fear. The rug was still going to be pulled from under her feet at any second, without warning.

She looked at Leo. He smiled at her.

*I do feel closer to him. But that just makes this harder. It makes it worse.*

They watched low-effort stuff on E4. Leo started to get restless. Natalya was late.

'Do you think she might have gone straight there,

from work?' Ruby asked, knowing the answer.

'No. She never does that. She has to come back, get changed, do her make-up.'

He checked the time on his phone again. He paced up and down, looking out of the window every now and then. Bella followed him. *His anxiety is rubbing off.*

'She'll be fine, Leo,' Ruby tried to soothe him. 'Doesn't she ever work late?'

'Sometimes,' he said, checking his phone again.

'Why don't you make a drink, take your mind off it,' she said, following him round the room with her eyes. She had to get him to do something. He was making her nervous, too.

He went over to the kitchen and filled up the kettle.

'You could make it a Ukrainian tea?' she suggested, smiling. He nodded.

He handed her the hot glass.

'You do know that Ukrainians don't always have vodka in their tea, right? In fact, I think most of us never do,' he smiled.

'Yeah. But my favourite one does.'

He laughed, then checked his phone again.

*Well, you managed to distract him for three minutes.* Ruby sighed and looked at her tea.

The smell took her right back to that first time in his flat, after the fight in the play area. The rain, the adrenaline, his eyes. She drank it down, savouring the scent, the warmth, the memories.

'She's two hours late. Why doesn't she answer her phone?' Leo interrupted her reverie. Ruby was helpless. There was nothing she could offer. She rubbed his shoulder – it was all she had.

There was nothing she could say that would make it better. She knew that he was right to be worried. Ruby was worried, too. She tried not to let herself consider the possibilities.

The longer it went on, the more convinced they became that something awful had happened.

'Should we call the police?' Ruby asked, after another half hour spent pacing, calling Natalya's mobile and biting their nails.

Leo shook his head.

'And say what? My mum is late home from work?'

Ruby looked at the floor.

'Sorry,' he said, sitting down, 'I just know something bad has happened. I know it.'

Ruby's stomach turned. She knew it, too.

'Could we go looking for her? Do you know where they'll be?'

Leo rubbed his face, thinking.

'She always meets him at the club. He's there every night. He runs everything from the back rooms. If something's happened though, they could be anywhere.'

'Where's the club?' Ruby asked, relieved they were at least talking, even if it got them nowhere.

'Turner Road. The Lace Lounge.'

He shook his head.

'How have I let this happen, Ruby? Why do I let this happen, every day?'

His fists were clenched.

'You have no choice, Leo, there's nothing you can do, except for what you *are* doing - you have a plan. You're getting out, both of you, remember?'

She could see him bristling. He looked at her.

'If she's alive,' he nodded, 'If she's alive.'

Ruby bit at a loose bit of torn cuticle at the edge of her nail, avoiding his gaze.

There was a knock at the door. Leo leapt to his feet, vaulting the sofa. He opened the door and exclaimed something in Ukrainian. Ruby ran after him.

'Natalya, oh my god, what's happened?' she cried.

Natalya was there, alone, barely standing. Leo put her arm round his neck, shouldering her weight as she struggled to walk in. He cried as he carried on talking in Ukrainian.

Her face was covered in blood, coming from a cut on her forehead. Her eye was swollen shut and her lip was split. She was trying to answer him, but was struggling to move her mouth. Her leg was lame, and she was cradling her arm as though there was something wrong with her elbow, or her wrist or shoulder - Ruby couldn't tell which.

'I'm calling an ambulance!' Ruby shouted, panicked.

'No!' Natalya managed.

Leo said something to her then looked at Ruby, shaking his head.

'No. We can't. Just make some salt water - and the basket under the sink,' he nodded towards the kitchen, 'there are dressings.'

Ruby ran over to the kitchen and did as she was told. She was shaking, with the shock of seeing the state of Natalya as much as the relief of seeing her alive.

They continued to talk, Ruby not understanding a single word. She knelt beside Natalya, dipped cotton wool into the salt water, gently wiped the blood stains away and dabbed at her wounds. Natalya winced. Ruby hesitated.

'Is okay, Ruby, I need it.'

The words were almost inaudible. She motioned with her good hand for Ruby to carry on.

Leo made a sling from his jumper. They struggled to get it over her head and put her arm through. Leo turned his attention to her foot. He pressed in different places and waited for her reactions. Everything hurt her. He put a cushion on the coffee table and motioned for her to rest it on there. She managed to lift it up, but cried out as she placed it down.

Natalya rested her head back on the sofa and breathed out. She murmured something to Leo, a tear escaping down her cheek. He stood shaking his head, his face twisting with the pain of seeing her.

He breathed deeply, in and out, angrier with each breath. He was almost bouncing on the balls of his feet, eyes full of fire. *Whatever Natalya is saying, it's not getting through. Shit. Don't.*

'Leo…' Ruby said. It was too late. He looked at her, then Natalya, then headed into his mum's room. He emerged, pausing in the doorway to say something to Natalya, then ran out of the front door, ignoring her reply. She tried to her feet, trying to get him back. She couldn't get up.

'Leo!' Ruby shouted. She got to her feet and ran out after him into the darkness.

He was at the end of the walkway, about to run down the steps.

'*Leo!*' she shouted again. He stopped. She caught up, breathless.

'Don't go,' she panted, 'please. Don't go.'

'She needs your help,' he said, pointing back to the flat, 'back to her. Go!'

Ruby stepped towards him. 'Leo, I can't let you-' she began. Leo backed away.

'Go back!' he said, pointing her back. 'Please. She needs you! She's suffering,' he shouted, his eyes desperate.

Ruby nodded, and watched him disappear down the stairs. *Fuck.*

She ran back to the flat. Natalya was still stuck on the sofa, craning to see out of the door.

'Ruby! Where is he?' she asked.

'He's gone, I couldn't stop him,' Ruby said, shaking her head.

'No, no-' Natalya said, hauling herself up with her one good arm, 'he can't-' the pain stopped her as she tried to put weight on her foot. She screamed, falling back down. Ruby noticed Natalya's ankle was bent in the wrong direction.

'You stay here. I'll go. Where is he going? Where is Tony?' Ruby asked. It was the first time his existence had been acknowledged between them.

Natalya was distraught, barely able to speak through her swelling and her sobbing.

'The club. His club,' she managed.

'Right.'

Ruby turned to leave.

'Wait!' Natalya stopped her.

'Don't go, Ruby. Too dangerous. Call police. Stay here.'

'But you *know* what will happen if I get the police involved - you'll both be deported!'

'And if we don't, he could die. Call them, Ruby, we'll be okay,' Natalya said.

'So if they arrest Tony, and have you deported - won't they still be looking for you after that? You could both be killed!'

Natalya let her head rest back on the sofa, exasperated. She had no answer.

'If I catch him before he gets there, nothing bad will happen. I'm going.'

She made for the door.

'Ruby! Take Bella!' shouted Natalya, 'he hates dogs.'

Ruby ran back through to Leo's bedroom, grabbed Bella's lead and clipped it to her collar.

'And money. Here…' Natalya struggled to reach her purse.

'It's okay,' said Ruby, grabbing her holdall with the £200 in. She stood for a second, Bella's lead in one hand, holdall in the other, taking in Natalya. Ruby hoped she would see her again.

She turned and ran. She was living her nightmare. Running through the night, over the pavements and the roads and the grass, her legs heavy, not keeping up with what her brain wanted from them - as though she was just running on the spot getting nowhere, her final destination never getting closer.

Ruby turned the corner and felt her legs start shaking, giving way. The feeling was overpowering. Suddenly she realised that the vibrations were coming from her phone, in her front pocket. Leo. She took it out, focusing on the caller ID. His name stared out from the screen. *He's alive.* She answered, slowing down, panting.

'Where are you? Are you okay? What's happened?' Ruby's questions spilled out as she walked along, scanning around in case he appeared.

'Ruby, listen to me. You have to listen to me and do exactly as I say, right now. Are you with mum?'

She stopped still.

'No, I'm on my way to the club. What's happened, Leo-'

'Right. I'll call her. Meet me at the bus stop outside the Red Lion. As soon as you can. We have to go, now. They're on their way.'

His voice was controlled on the surface, but underneath she could hear it shaking, trapped, desperate.

'Okay. I'm coming,' she said, as he hung up.

'This way, Bella,' she said, turning to run in the other direction.

*Fuck. Who's on their way? The police? Tony? His men? What have they done to him? Oh god. Please be okay. Please.* She pictured him, bleeding, swollen and broken like Natalya.

Bella was struggling to keep up, panting. Ruby scooped her up and carried on running, hold-all over one arm, Bella under the other. The sweat ran down her back and sides.

She ran towards the railings and clambered over them, hauling Bella under her arm. The blood thudded in her ears. The bus stop was in sight. *No sign of him yet.* Blue flashing lights and sirens blared past.

She stood in the shelter, panting. She tried to control her breathing, to stop herself shaking, to calm down. It was useless. Ruby felt each screech of the sirens sear through her whole body. *There!* She saw him.

She felt herself running towards him. His image flashed in and out of sight as he ran through the shadows, as though he was in her imagination. *No, he has to be real.*

# CHAPTER 26

At the bus stop they collapsed into each other. They clung together, panting, struggling to get their breath back. As the bus drew up, they let go.

'Station, please,' Leo asked the bus driver.

*We're getting the train. Shit.*

On the bus, Leo said nothing. *It doesn't matter. He's alive. No injuries. He's okay. That's all that matters.*

In the train station, Leo's eyes kept flicking between people, watching whoever was watching them. The station was nearly empty. The board only showed two trains left to depart.

'What did he do, Leo? Why did you call the police?' Ruby asked, as they made their way to the platform. The last train to Newcastle was the one he chose.

Leo forged ahead faster. Ruby picked up Bella again.

Finally, on the platform, he spoke.

'I'm okay. We just have to leave.'

'We're leaving. You can tell me what happened now,' Ruby said, searching his face.

'Someone could hear. We'll talk about it later,' he said, avoiding her gaze.

Ruby watched the train approaching and stood up, clinging to Bella. She suddenly felt like running. Her stomach tensed as the train came to a stop.

*What are you doing?*

Leo ran to the door and got into the carriage. Ruby couldn't get her legs to move. He turned round, realising she was still stood on the platform.

'Ruby! Come on, quick! The train is leaving!' he shouted.

She stood, stuck.

He jumped off the train and grabbed her hand.

'I love you, Ruby, please, come with me - now!' he begged, staring into her.

Finally, she managed to move and they ran, just managing to slip inside the bleeping doors, seconds before the train pulled away.

Ruby was shaking. Suddenly she felt as though her stomach was leaping up her throat.

'Here', she said, handing Bella over to Leo. She ran to the toilet cubicle and shut herself in, vomiting into the bowl, one hand on each plastic wall in an attempt to steady herself as the train rocked from side to side.

Her stomach muscles hurt with the effort and her throat felt as though it was bleeding by the end of it. She gripped the sink edge and sat back on her heels, panting, not daring to sit on the urine-soaked floor. She took some deep breaths and gathered the strength to stand up, her vision swimming. She rinsed her mouth with tap water and splashed her face, looking in the mirror.

'Come on,' she said to her reflection, 'pull yourself together.'

Leo was waiting for her in the gap between carriages, with Bella.

'Are you okay?' he asked, pale.

'I'm fine. Just felt sick. I think I need to sit down,' she said, feeling her legs giving way from underneath her. She was shivering.

'Come on,' he said, putting his arm round her, 'you

need to sleep. We have a couple of hours. Let's get some rest.'

She collapsed into her seat. Bella lay across both their laps. Ruby put her head on Leo's shoulder. All the questions she wanted to ask melted away as she concentrated on breathing and the beat of her heart, which seemed to kick her skull every time it thudded.

She kept her eyes closed and stayed still, scared that if she opened them, or moved, she'd vomit again. Eventually blackness enveloped her and she fell asleep, sweating and shivering at the same time, seeing Tony shooting bullets at them as they ran across train tracks, in the middle of nowhere.

\*\*\*

By the time they checked in to the Travelodge, Ruby was desperate for a shower and a bed. Her clothes were damp with sweat. The fever had been replaced by a crashing headache, and the nausea with fear, as reality began to sink in.

She clutched her holdall, which was now twice as heavy. It was hiding a stowaway, Bella. Just as she had done on the day she was rescued, hidden under Ruby's jumper, Bella kept still and quiet.

The receptionist narrowed her eyes at them, but took their money and handed them a key card.

In their room, Ruby unzipped the holdall and let Bella out. She sniffed around the room, wagging her tail. She did a wee on the carpet. Ruby would have laughed, if she'd not felt so hollow.

Leo exhaled, sitting on the edge of the bed, leaning his elbows on his knees, and his head in his hands.

'I'm having a shower,' Ruby said, 'then you can tell me what happened.'

She was exhausted, almost past caring. She just wanted to be clean, and to sleep.

Leo nodded, staring after her as she disappeared into the bathroom.

The steaming hot water soothed her mind. She washed the day away - the sex, the running, the fever sweat. Her pounding headache became a dull thud. The freshness of brushing her teeth felt so good after hours of acid vomit clinging to the inside of her mouth. She finally felt clean.

Now she had to help Leo. She had to hear what Tony had said, or what he had done, and help him get over it. She had to convince him that everything would be okay, even though she had no idea how. *Then you can sleep.*

In the bedroom, Leo was lying back on the bed, staring at the ceiling. Ruby sat next to him.

'Right,' she said, gently, 'tell me.'

Leo looked at her, swallowed, and sat up.

'You have to understand, Ruby, that I love you, and I would never do anything to hurt you.' he said, his eyes filling with tears.

*What?*

'What do you mean?' she asked, frowning.

'You were right-' he managed, before the tears took over and he broke off.

'About what?' she asked, terrified. 'Leo, Leo look at me,' she said, turning him towards her, 'what happened to you?'

His whole body was convulsing with the sobs as he looked at her, then put his hands to his face, blocking her out.

'Leo!' she shouted, trying to pull him back.

'I don't know what I was doing...what I thought would happen,' he said, his hands skittering back down

231

his face, 'I took mum's knife…I was just so angry… I wanted to kill him…' he shook his head. 'As if I could do that! I knew as soon as I got there, it was a mistake. It was busy. I went to the back, where I knew he'd be…there were men on the door,' he paused, rubbing his eyes, 'I should've ran away then. I should've just left. But I didn't. I told them I wanted to see him. One of them took me in…'

Ruby rubbed his back, saying, *shhhh* as he struggled to get the words out.

'He was there, with about four others,' Leo looked at her, 'one of them was- was your dad.'

'Shit. I knew he'd be there, up that dickhead's arse…'

Leo shook his head.

'No… listen to me. He was there, with the others. Tony knew why I was there. He was grinning…nearly laughing, and he said, *so she got home then?* and I just lost it. I went for him, but they stopped me. Of course they did…it was so fucking stupid of me.'

Ruby stayed silent, tense. She felt like shaking him, screaming at him. Instead, her hand rested on his back lightly and she tried to press the rage down inside herself, under her ribcage.

'Two of them had me, then Tony was there, with this knife… holding it to my face while they held me. Said he wanted to teach me a lesson –' Leo stopped as Ruby quickly stood, her hand over her mouth, running to the bathroom. She couldn't help it. There was nothing left to sick up, just bile. She came back out, pale and shaking. She stood, waiting to hear the rest.

'You see me here, Ruby, I'm fine,' he said, pointing his hands to his chest, 'please, this isn't about me. It's about-'

'Tony?' she interrupted, 'did –'

232

'No. Listen,' he looked at her, 'your dad told him to put the knife away. He was behind him. He said: *come on, he's just a kid, leave him be*.

'Tony doesn't like being told what to do. He turned on him, swearing, shouting. Waving the knife around. So angry. I was scared... we all were. Nobody could tell what he was going to do. Your dad tried to calm him, he could see he was just spiralling. He said, *turn them in, to the Home Office - let them deal with them*.'

Ruby shook her head, eyes full of tears.

'Don't you see, Ruby? He was trying to save my life! Better deported than dead,' he held her hand tight, 'the only reason he bothered, was because he knew you loved me, I'm sure. That's why he did it. For you, because he knows what I mean to you.'

Ruby didn't know how to deal with the emotion taking over her. It was anger, shock, fear, all at the same time. She sat down on the bed. Leo sat beside her, continuing.

'Tony just laughed. He said, *do you think I'm fucking stupid? I called them about this son of a bitch and his slut mother already*, then he looked back at me and said *they're coming for you, sweetheart. But that's not enough. Not now. What did you think you were going to do, coming down here? Were you going to come get me?*

'He laughed, turning away, then before I blinked, he lunged at me. It all happened too fast, all I saw was the blade, coming towards me, the men holding me either side, gripping - I tried to move but - then I realised the blade had stopped, inches away from me. Your dad was behind him. Tony was just still, staring, blinking. He dropped the knife. The men either side of me, they let go...and Tony just dropped, like a sheet, he just crumpled forwards...he nearly fell on his face but the men caught him... that's when I saw his back - there was just a handle, sticking out of it, on the left side, under his shoulder blade...your dad ran. One of them started after him, the other one was trying to stop the blood...I ran, too. I just ran.'

He looked at her, eyes flicking between hers, tears still falling.

Ruby looked through him, unable to process the information. He carried on talking, but his voice was just white noise in her ears.

He stopped saying whatever he was saying, and she saw him wipe away his tears. She felt his breathing slow.

'Ruby - say something...'

She stared at the gap under the door, frowning, still unable to speak, or even think.

'Ruby, listen to me. Your dad - he might have got away, okay, Ruby...' he put his hand on her shoulder, 'Ruby?'

Instinctively she shrugged off his hand, turning toward him finally, staring into him.

'You *think* he *might not* be dead. But they *might* have killed him. My dad. They might have killed him, because he killed one of the most dangerous men in the area...because he was defending...*you*,' she said, slowly, deliberately. She wanted each word to hurt him.

'Ruby, I'm sorry, please, believe me, I was a fucking idiot to go down there, I know I was, but I never thought-' he stopped as she shot up off the bed, diving into her holdall, pulling out the first clothes she got hold of, struggling to get out of her pyjamas and into them as quickly as possible.

'Don't leave, Ruby, please!' he begged her. She pulled her hoodie over her head and shoved her feet inside her shoes, reaching for Bella's lead. She couldn't look at him. She didn't want to see his face, hear a word he said, even be in the same room as his scent.

'Ruby-' he grabbed her arm as she bent down to put Bella's lead on.

'*Get off me!*' she shouted at him, pushing him with all her strength, so that he fell back on to the bed.

'You're just the same as everyone else. All of them. I thought you were different,' she said, the tears finally falling from her eyes. 'You told me you were different. You told me you'd never break a promise. Dad, Kaz, Cal - you're one of them. Horrible, vicious, lying fucking scumbags!'

'I loved you,' she continued, holding her head in her hands, turning away from him, 'I did. But I knew something was wrong. I didn't want to get on the train tonight and you made me. Remember? You *made* me do it.'

She turned to look at him. He looked at the floor, nodding.

'I got on the train and felt so sick, like I was making a mistake. I felt wrong. Why did you drag me all the way up here? Why did you wait until I was sat here in this fucking hotel room, stuck with you? Why wait until now to tell me?!'

Her heart was pounding, the fight-or-flight reaction was in full swing in her system. Her instinct was to run, but he'd started a fight, when he tried to stop her. Ruby wanted the fight now.

She stood, fists clenched, waiting for him to defend himself.

'You waited,' she said, 'until I was fifty miles away from him, to tell me my dad killed someone...and he might've *been killed*, minutes after. Or not. Maybe he's been hiding out and they've just found him, and now they're torturing him to death-' she felt dizzy, sick with the spiralling tornado in her head.

'Ruby! Don't...' he grabbed her, 'I waited because I

knew you wouldn't come with me if I'd told you the truth.'

She turned away, unable to look at him.

'Of course I fucking wouldn't!'

'I know, I know - but I thought, we'd be safer here, both of us... and - I love you, I had to try...I had to try, Ruby. I had to get you here, even if it's just to say goodbye to you properly.'

He stood up, taking a tentative step towards her.

She shook her head, closing her eyes.

'The police will be on their way,' he said, 'I'm sure of it. I witnessed a murder, I ran from the scene. I fled. Even without all that - immigration know about me. It's just a matter of time. At least, let me say goodbye.'

She stood, motionless.

She felt him behind her, looking at the back of her, still and silent.

She turned to face him, clinging to her mouth with her hand, shaking, breathing hard through the tears. A noise escaped her mouth, a moan, as she backed into the wall and slid down it to the floor, eyes still on him.

He rushed to her, holding her, repeating the words *I'm sorry* over and over. She struggled against him, pushing him away, weakly, through her sobs. He stayed, clinging to her. She stopped fighting and collapsed into his shoulder, one hand grasping to his arm, the other hit his chest with her open palm, before holding him.

They stayed, crumpled in a heap against the wall, holding each other in silence.

After a while, Leo spoke.

'They'll come for me soon.'

Ruby nodded.

'I thought,' he continued, 'I thought, when I called you, that maybe we could run away up here and start again. Like we were planning, all along.'

She looked up at him.

'We can try...' she said, her voice cracked.

He shook his head.

'Not now. Even if we could do it without my mum, without the documents – I stormed in there, then ran out just before the police came... so many people saw. The police will find me.'

'They might not...' she said, desperate to believe it.

'The CCTV - it will track the whole way to us getting on the train,' he said, putting his head in his hands.

Ruby bit her nails. It was 2:30am.

*How did we get here?*

She pictured Tony, falling to his knees, the knife still stuck in his back, eyes wide, unbelieving. She saw her dad dead, face down in an alley, a skip... beaten to death, unrecognisable. Ruby tried to erase the images, looking at Bella, who was lying in the corner of the room, watching them.

'What about your mum?' she asked, standing up, suddenly remembering the broken, swollen heap she left behind.

'She's okay. I called her when I was running to meet you. She's staying with a friend who's a nurse. I told her-' he broke off, holding back the tears, 'I told her to go ahead with our plan, on her own. Even though immigration are on to us, there's a chance for her, if she starts again without me, doesn't go to the police.'

'What did she say?'

'No,' Leo gave a half-laugh, looking at the floor, 'she won't leave me. She'll end up getting deported. And it's all my fault,' he said, staring out of the window. 'I told her if she won't run away, then she has to go to the police, for safety. I don't know who is above Tony, but someone will come after her. And us,' he said, looking at Ruby. She knew what he was about to say.

'I have to hand myself in. I have to tell them where they can find me. I need to make sure mum is safe. You need to know what's happened to your dad. We need to know what happened...after,' he said, nodding, his face crumpling with the effort of holding back the tears, 'you need to know. And I have to tell them...why it all happened. I have to tell them it was my fault.'

Ruby felt her world collapse all around her. She knew he was right, but it didn't make it any easier. She stood, limbs creaking in the silence, staring at him, taking him in.

'Either I do this,' he said, getting to his feet, 'or Tony's men come for us, and my mum, and-' he looked at his phone screen, 'I'd take the police over him, even deportation. At least you can come to visit me...' he began to dial.

'No!' Ruby shouted, suddenly lunging for the phone, throwing it across the room.

'I can't just give you up, Leo... I can't just let you go!' she kissed him, holding him tight to her body. She didn't want to let go. She clung on, tears soaking his T-shirt. She shut her eyes, breathing him in.

'I forgive you, for what's happened, you know?' she continued, 'I don't care. I don't care about it. It wasn't your fault... even if he's dead...Dad... it's not your fault. He's the one that stabbed someone!' she said, still holding him. She felt him nod, gripping her waist tighter.

'Are you sure we can't carry on, start again...like we said?' she asked, knowing the answer. He nodded again, letting out a sob that couldn't be held in any longer.

Finally she let him go, watching him dial the number.

As he spoke, the consequences of the last 24 hours flashed through her mind.

*Orphan. Care. No Leo.*

For the first time in her life, she seriously thought

about how she could kill herself. If the future played out as she was convinced it would, she knew that she didn't want to be in it.

She pictured throwing herself off a tall building. *Park Hill.* Hurtling towards the floor, free-falling, instant, hard death. *That's how I'd do it. Only after finding Bella a good home. I have to make sure she's okay.* She looked at the dog, who instantly skittered over, jumping up on her lap, nuzzling into her.

Leo ended the call, turning to her.

'It's done.'

Ruby lay on the bed, motioning for him to join her. Bella lay between them, at their feet. They huddled close, facing one another. They had no tears left. They stared into each other's eyes, taking them in, memorising the face in front of them. Ruby stroked his face. They stayed like that, each absorbing the other in silence, while time slipped through their fingers.

After minutes, hours had slipped by without her registering them, Ruby heard footsteps in the corridor, heavy, hurried.

*They're here.*

She gripped Leo. Bella's ears pricked up, eyes on the door.

The knock came. Bella barked.

Ruby and Leo sat up, looking at the door, then each other. They shared a last, desperate kiss and clasped tight, breathing each other in.

Another knock.

Leo patted Bella, who looked up at him, whining softly.

He opened the door.

Ruby looked at them. Standing there in black, with their heavy boots, they looked just like the men who came for her at Denby House in her nightmare. The hivis vests and radios were the only difference. The men looked at Leo, then glanced into the room at Ruby and Bella. A voice blared through one of their radios, crackling through the silence, incomprehensible.

'Leo Kovalenko?' one of them asked. Leo nodded.

The officer held Leo's gaze and turned his head slightly, holding the radio on his vest, speaking into it.

'Yep, we've got him.'

# CHAPTER 27

**Next summer**

'Come on, you're going to be okay, I promise,' Annabelle said, rubbing Ruby's arm.

Ruby hesitated, looking back the way they came. Annabelle took her hand.

'Honestly Ruby,' she dragged her through the school gates, 'we've done mine. Now we can do yours.'

'Oh god. I feel sick,' Ruby said, turning round and walking back out of the gates.

'Oi!' Annabelle pulled her back. 'Not allowed. Let's just get it over with,' Annabelle said, marching Ruby up to the entrance.

*Shit.*

The room was packed with teenagers. They stood in groups, swearing, crying, laughing, smiling with each other. She watched a couple open their results together. They looked pleased, hugging. The girl grabbed the boy and kissed him.

*What would Leo's results have been? Would we have picked them up together? Definitely.*

'Name?'

'Morton. Ruby Morton.'

She took the brown envelope and walked out quickly.

'Aren't you opening it?' Annabelle asked, catching up.

'Not here.'

She waited until they were outside, behind the hedge next to the main gate. Taking a deep breath, she ripped the seal and pulled the papers out.

She was too hot, sweating. The skin on her face tingled and her legs started to buckle. The letters swam in front of her. She followed them running down the page, melting off the edge down to the floor. She fell with them, their black ink encircling her.

'Ruby! Ruby!'

She felt as though she was underwater in a swimming pool. Annabelle was stood on the poolside, shouting. She reached into the water and hauled her up.

Her voice was suddenly clear and she finally saw her.

'Oh thank god, are you okay?' Annabelle was kneeling beside her, helping her sit up against the wall under the hedge.

'What did I get?' Ruby asked.

'Erm, hang on...' Annabelle scrambled to collect the papers Ruby had dropped on the pavement.

Ruby took off her hoodie. It was a warm day, but she had put it on anyway before she left, needing something familiar and reassuring. Everyone else had used the day as an excuse to dress in the coolest outfit they could muster, seeing as they were all adults that didn't need to wear school uniform any more. Ruby stuck to the hoodie and jeans.

'Shit, Ruby, you got way better than they predicted, look!'

She thrust the paper under her face.

'That's *amazing*, congratulations!' Annabelle squealed, making her stand up to hug her.

'Bloody hell,' Ruby said, smiling, shaking her head as

she examined the papers.

'I knew you'd do it. All you've done is study and revise. You deserve it. Remember when we went to that cottage during half term with my family? The haunted one?'

'It wasn't haunted.'

'Er —' Annabelle put her hand up, 'I *think* it was. Auntie Mel *saw* a grey woman at the window,'

'That was her reflection —'

'Anyway, what I was about to say was, that night we played Trivial Pursuits and there were loads of questions that nobody had a clue on, but you knew the answers! Do you remember?'

'Only the ones about coffee and dogs.'

'Bullshit, there were loads of them. You're so smart. Now you have the proof!' she said, waving the papers. 'Anyway, are you saying I'm stupid? Cos you got better results than me!' she laughed, giving Ruby a shove.

Ruby smiled, looking at the floor. She was stunned. She'd thrown herself into it, day and night, since that night, and it had paid off. She couldn't help but feel the twinge of something nagging, though, on the edge of all her thoughts.

'Hey,' said Annabelle, putting her arm round her, 'you should be proud. I know you wish he was here. But don't let that ruin your achievement. Think about this time last year. You were facing resits in everything. Remember? This is a *sensational* set of results. And it's all your work. Nobody else's.'

Ruby nodded, embarrassed that she'd let her eyes fill with tears and she was trying to blink them away, simply because Annabelle had mentioned him. She sniffed and wiped her eyes with the back of her wrist, nodding again.

A car horn startled them both into looking up.

'Come on,' said Annabelle, 'your lift's here.'

They got into the back of the car. A woman dressed head-to-toe in Per Una from Marks & Spencers turned around with a sympathetic smile, perching her sunglasses on her head. She turned the engine off.

'Is it bad news, sweetheart? Don't worry. You can re-sit anything you need to, and we can get tuition-'

'No!' Annabelle interrupted, 'she's done really well!' She reeled off the results, grinning.

Ruby smiled.

'Ruby! That is absolutely *fantastic* I'm *so proud* of you!'

'Thank you,' Ruby said, then, pulling a thread off the ripped knee of her jeans, carried on, 'this last - well - since last year... you've done so much for me, I couldn't have done it without you,' she said, finally looking up.

The woman reached over from the driver's seat to offer her hand to Ruby, who took it, and watched her eyes glaze with tears.

'That means so much,' she said, 'none of my fosters have ever said anything like that. It means the world.'

'Don't, Rosie,' Ruby said, thumbing her eye, 'you'll start me off again.'

She heard a sniffing sound, next to her. She turned to see Annabelle, her face screwed up, tears rolling down her cheek.

'It's just so sweet,' she squeaked.

They laughed, sniffing, wiping eyes.

'Right. Come on, pull yourselves together girls,' Rosie said, 'Ruby's got to get to work. I'm taking us for a meal to celebrate tonight though, no excuses.'

\*\*\*

'Fantastico!' Gio exclaimed.

'I know. She's done herself so proud,' Rosie beamed.

Ruby felt herself blush as she tied the apron strings

behind her back. She busied herself, collecting empty mugs and taking them to the sink in the back.

'I'll see you later!' Rosie shouted through.

'Yep!' Ruby replied.

Gio was serving, behind the counter. Ruby stayed in the back to do the dishes. She watched the water spill down from the taps into the big, square sink, frothing the detergent in a steadily rising puddle over the plug. Once there was enough, she turned the taps off and plunged her hands in, before anything else. She looked at the difference above and below the water line. Above her arms were fresh, pink. Below, her hands and wrists were green-grey, translucent.

'So, have you rung your dad?'

Ruby jumped, turning.

'Jesus, Gio,' she put her hand to her chest, 'don't sneak up on me!'

She turned back and tossed all the mugs and saucers into the water.

'No...I can't ring him, he has to ring me. But they've only just decided he's allowed to do that. He's still getting used to everything. Since the transfer.'

'Can you visit him yet?'

'Yeah. Madge doesn't know whether it's a good idea...but I might do.'

She scrubbed at the congealed chocolate sprinkles and lipstick stains. Gio picked up a tea towel and dried as she washed.

'I can see why she thinks that. You've given him a lot of second chances. He let you down, a lot. But I remember your mum telling me about him, you know?

'Some days she loved him. Some days she hated him. But she always believed that deep down, he was a good person. I found it hard to see that, sometimes. But then other times, I got it. Little things. He used to call in, on his lunch break, he'd drop off bits and pieces for her. A magazine, something to eat on her break.'

Gio smiled.

'On her birthday, I remember him coming in. He'd got the day off. He announced that he would do the rest of her shift for her, so she could go home and get ready. He'd sorted a night out with all her friends. He stayed in with you and your brother, so she could go. It was all a surprise. She was so happy. Your dad really, really can't make coffee though,' he laughed, 'you don't get that from him, I can tell you.'

Gio started folding and unfolding the tea towel. 'Anyway, I'm rambling. All I mean is he had a tough start in life. Very tough. Considering what he came from, he did alright. I'm not making excuses for him, though. Some things are just wrong, whatever way you look at them. But -' Gio turned his head in the direction of the till. Ruby could see someone was waiting to be served, '- but - that was a long way of me trying to say, I think he'd be very proud to hear about your exams. Write him a letter, maybe?'

Ruby smiled and nodded.

'You go serve,' he said, 'I'll finish those.'

***

'Rosie... do you mind if we do the meal tomorrow, instead?' Ruby called as she got through the door. Bella bolted down the stairs, tail blurry with wagging. Ruby knelt down and fussed her.

'Why?' Rosie shouted down the stairs.

Ruby could smell her perfume. *She's already got ready to go out.*

'I'm so sorry, I just completely forgot, today's Thursday.'

'What's wrong with Thursdays?' Rosie appeared at the top of the stairs, fastening an earring.

'I babysit for Tia, remember? It's her night class.'

'Oh, of course, I forgot–'

'I just know she's got an assessment coming up, and –'

'Honestly, Ruby, don't worry about it. We'll do it tomorrow. Every where's probably booked up tonight already anyway.' She smiled. 'This means I get to put pyjamas on. It's not a bad thing. We can have a sofa night, can't we Bella? *Yes we can!*' Rosie said, putting on her babying voice to the dog.

'Thank you.'

'What time do you need dropping off and picking up?'

'Oh no, don't worry about that, I can get the bus.'

'To that side of town? And back again? *After dark*?' Rosie raised an eyebrow, 'no, Ruby. No way.'

'Well, if you're sure…'

'Don't be daft.'

Tia's house reminded Ruby of both her old homes. It was a terraced house, like Marlborough, but on the inside it looked like a Burnside flat. Damp, peeling, cold. Faulty wiring, a couple of boarded-up windows. But Tia had made the best of it. She'd decorated it with all the things she was never allowed at her auntie's house. Posters, photos, flowers. Charlie's toys were strewn about, bright splashes of colour here and there.

'He should be down. For a few hours, at least,' Tia said, putting her coat on, 'he's not done a poo yet today though, so…just watch out!'

'Great, I'll look forward to it,' Ruby said, laughing.

'How did you get on today?' Tia asked.

Ruby hesitated. She knew Tia would have done well, if she'd been able to take them. *She was the one that wanted top go to Uni.*

'Good. I did okay,' she replied, nodding.

'Did you get what you need for college?'

'Yep.'

'Aw I'm so happy for you, well done!' Tia hugged her.

'Thanks, Ti.'

'You wait, next year I'll be there with you,' Tia said, pointing her finger at Ruby.

'You will.'

'Right, I'm off,' said Tia, stepping out the door, 'See you round 10.'

Ruby waved her off.

She sat on the old sofa and looked at the framed photos on the mantelpiece and the windowsill. Tia's mum. Her dad. Charlie. She stood up and scanned the book case. She knew what she was looking for. She read it a lot. Not every week, but once a month, maybe. *There.* A black ring-binder, full of papers in plastic wallets. Tia had told her everything, but she still liked to pore through it. Letters from solicitors. Police. Court. Newspaper cuttings.

*Three found guilty of abducting pregnant girl*
*Cult held victims against their will*
*Case uncovers abuse of vulnerable*
*Group defrauded thousands from brainwashed victims*

She understood, now, why Leo wanted to be a lawyer. She loved reading all the details, cross-referencing events, analysing the evidence. She wasn't satisfied with the outcome, but she could see there was nothing more to be done. *At least they've disbanded. They're bankrupt. Three custodial sentences.*

She sighed, closing the file. Her thigh vibrated. It was her phone. She took it out and saw Gio's name across the Facetime background. **She'd never had a video** call from Gio before.

She answered. She could see a book case, but no Gio.

'Ruby? Can you see me? I can't see you...'

'Turn it round, Gio.'

'Oh, there you are! Can you see me?'

'I can see the top of your head.'

'Is that better?'

His face filled the whole screen. Ruby laughed.

'Yep.'

'Look what was waiting for me when I got back home,' he said, the image blurring as he spun the phone round. Ruby could see the edge of a table.

'What is it? I can just see a table...'

'What? Hang on.'

The camera spun again, settling on some curtains, then hovering over some paper.

'I can't read it, it's too shaky. Just tell me what it says.'

'It says, hang on,' he twirled the camera back on to him, squinting into the phone behind his glasses. They reflected the screen so that all Ruby could see was the rest of his face and two glaring white rectangles where his eyes should be. She laughed.

'It says,' he continued, 'that we have been successful in our application to the Prince's Trust Enterprise Project!' he started reading the bit of paper, meaning that the camera once again span away, to focus on the carpet this time.

'They liked our proposal and thought it showed real promise... it was much improved from the last time we submitted it...they thought we showed a great combination of business experience and impressive personal motivation for making it a success...they think we can be a valuable force for positive change in our community! Ruby!' he shouted, spinning the phone back to him.

'Oh my god, are you kidding me?'

'No! Look! It's here!' he said, attempting to show her a close up of the reply. She could make out *inspirational* then the phone spun round again.

'They're giving us a grant to do it Ruby, and do it properly - it includes money to make the cafe properly accessible, much better than it is now. And we get a mentor to help with the marketing-'

'Gio, I can't believe it!' Ruby realised she was squealing. She stopped to listen out for Charlie. *Nothing.* She carried on, quieter.

'Sorry, I need to shut up, I'm babysitting,' she whispered. 'This is amazing!'

'Yes it is. Sorry Ruby, I didn't know you were looking after Charlie. I'll leave you to it. I'm going to celebrate with Dante. Open a bottle of red!' he grinned.

'See you next week,' Ruby said, ending the call.

*Yes. Yes yes yes.* Leo's voice came into her head: *It's a great idea. I could help you.*

# CHAPTER 28

## Two months later

*It's really happening. Oh god.*

She pictured who would be there. She knew Rosie, Annabelle, Tia and Charlie were all coming, to show their support. *There'll be friendly faces. There'll be new faces. Hopefully. God, I hope we get the people who are supposed to come!*

The one face she wanted to see more than any other wouldn't be there.

*Let it go. Let him go.*

'The Sheffield Star are here!' Gio announced, putting his head round the kitchen door, 'come on!'

*Breathe. Breathe.*

She walked out into the cafe. Half an hour till opening time.

'Hi, I'm Ellen. Do you have time for a chat now?' a woman in a grey leopard print blouse and black chinos said, stepping forward.

'She does, yes she does,' said Gio, busying himself behind the counter.

Ruby swallowed and tied her apron.

'I'm Ruby,' she shook Ellen's hand and indicated a table where they could sit, 'please, take a seat.'

'Would you like a drink?' Gio called over.

'I'm fine, thank you,' Ellen said, then, turning to

Ruby, 'I've already had a lot of caffeine today!'

Ruby smiled.

'So, let's just start off by telling me a bit about yourself and the idea of the Carer Café,' Ellen said, pen hovering over her notepad.

'Okay, well, my name is Ruby Morton, I'm sixteen years old, and I - well, Gio,' she pointed over to the counter, 'Gio suggested that I apply to the Prince's Trust, for a grant, to help us start this up.'

'Great. Let's start at the beginning. Where are you from originally?'

'Hillsborough.'

'And you lived with your mum?'

'Yes.'

'She was ill, wasn't she?'

Ruby nodded. 'She had Motor Neuron Disease.'

'And you had a lot of caring responsibilities, didn't you?'

'Yes. Like lots of people do. Which is why I wanted to set this up-'

'Your mum sadly passed away, nearly two years ago. Since then things have been hard...'

Ruby hesitated.

'I interviewed Gio already, by the way. He showed me the application you sent off,' she smiled, 'you're incredibly brave.'

'Oh, erm - thank you.'

'Do you think there should be more support, for people like you?'

'Yes. Well, I don't know, I mean, there were things out there, but I didn't really know about them. Or I did, but I didn't want to...sorry, I'm not really making sense-'

Ellen shook her head.

'Don't be daft, you're doing really well. Carry on. Just take your time.'

'We had a health visitor, who told me about help we could get, but we didn't want...I think, well, I was worried about mum going into hospital, or even a hospice... and I think she was worried about me going into care...so we just shut people out.'

'I see what you mean,' Ellen nodded her head, scribbling, 'were you quite isolated, then?'

'I suppose so, yeah.'

'Tell me about what you did for your mum.'

'Erm...I suppose, most things, really. To begin with, she was just a bit clumsy. It was the fiddly things she couldn't do, like... I don't know...using a can opener. Tying laces. That kind of thing. But it got worse. She couldn't walk very far, then she couldn't walk at all without a frame, then she had to have a wheelchair. We had a stair-lift put in. It barely fit. The stairs were only,' she indicated with her hands, 'about this wide.'

'So when she could do less, what were you having to do?'

'Housework. The tidying, washing, ironing, cleaning, shopping, cooking...the pots... I helped her with things like dressing, bathing...I didn't mind, though-'

'Did you have any time for friends? Or your schoolwork?'

'Not really. I sort of drifted from most of my friends because I couldn't ever go out. There's only so many times someone can say no before you give up on them, I suppose...but I had one friend who put up with it all. Still wanted to hang out with me, when I could. Went around at break times at school, that kind of thing.'

Ellen smiled, scribbling. Ruby waited for her to ask more, but she kept writing.

'Annabelle. Her name was - is - Annabelle,' Ruby added, peering over the top of Ellen's notepad, but she couldn't make anything out from the shorthand.

'And school?' Ellen asked.

'It just wasn't important. I used to be good at a few subjects, quite liked them...till mum got ill. Then I just had less and less time. I stopped caring about it.'

'Did you know any other young carers at the time?'

Ruby shook her head.

'Is that one of the things you're trying to do here?' Ellen pointed to the *Carer Café* poster on the wall.

'I suppose so. I never used the support, but I know now that the stuff there is, is so good - but it all depends on donations or it's part of stuff that's getting cut and scrapped. I also know I was scared to get help, and I thought maybe something like this might be good for people like me...less intimidating.'

'So, why do you think that is?'

Ruby's mind went blank. She felt her cheeks heat up and the sweat starting to soak under her arms.

'Sorry?' she asked, stalling for time.

'Well, don't get me wrong, I think this is great, but I'm just wondering about how you're going to reach out to people who are like you were - reluctant to engage, y'know?'

Ruby nodded vigorously, as though she had a great answer lined up, but she was still trying to piece it together. She looked over at a girl, cradling a mug, listening to music on her headphones, with her eyes closed.

'It's relaxed,' Ruby said. 'I think the whole point of it is that there's no obligation. You don't have to sign-up, give your details, anything like that. There's no commitment to come to more than one time. It's just a drop-in. You can talk to other people who are in the same situation as you. Or you can just come and get a free drink, and enjoy a bit of time to yourself. Or you can bring the person you care for, and they can do the same.

We can signpost, but we're not *part of the system*, we're just… something else. It's just…easy.'

*That sounded good.* Ruby sat up straighter.

'I think that will help people who are scared of it being a big effort,' she carried on, 'or are worried that it might lead to people interfering. And as for reaching them,' she glanced over at Gio, who was stood grinning at her behind the counter, both thumbs up, 'er, sorry. Reaching them,' she looked back at Ellen, 'the grant that we got was based on our business plan…' she continued, talking her through the marketing campaign. She realised she was talking too fast, going into too much detail.

*Exhale. Remember to breathe.*

'Fantastic,' Ellen interrupted her, 'so what do you hope visitors will get out of it? Other than the free drink?'

'It's just a couple of hours a week…where they know they can come and relax. Talk to people. Make friends. Sit and think. Do their homework…whatever-'

'Is it just for *young* carers?'

'No. I mean, that's who it's aimed at, but anyone can come. It's for the people they care for, too. The money we got paid for these.' She pointed at the new disabled toilet and accessible cafe entrance.

'Great. How are you going to make money? I know it's a not-for-profit, but it has running costs, right? The grant just sets you up, but then you need to stand alone…'

Ruby glanced over to Gio again. *Help.*

'Well…Gio worked out…he…' *shit.*

'I suppose it's good publicity for his business, and might bring new people through the doors?' Ellen offered.

'Yes,' Ruby said, nodding again, 'and it's normally a really quiet slot, this, so…'

'So she's doing me a favour,' Gio said, appearing with brownies.

'For every free drink I give away, one more person knows about the cafe. They might buy a cake, or stay for lunch. They might come back for a coffee in normal hours, tell their friends and families. And my regular customers are helping to pay for it too, aren't they Ruby? Have you told her about your drink?'

'Oh, No-'

'All her idea,' Gio said to Ellen, nodding towards Ruby.

'Your drink?' Ellen asked, looking at her.

'I made a new drink, for our regular customers. All the profits go towards keeping the Carer Café going.'

'Can I try one?'

'Sure!' Ruby jumped up, grateful to get out of the hot-seat.

'Then I promise I'll get out of your hair. I'll just hang around and take some photos, talk to a few customers when you open, if that's okay?'

'Of course,' said Gio.

Ruby was already tamping the coffee.

'Do you like sweet things or spicy things best?' Ruby asked.

'Mmm, spicy.'

'Okay.' Ruby carried on while Ellen took some photos.

'Here.'

Ruby put a small glass on the counter. It was dark brown, nearly black, with a small white foam heart on top.

'Oooh. Is this an espresso?' Ellen said, picking it up.

'Nearly. More like a Cortado. Or a macchiato. With something extra...'

She took a sip. Her eyebrows sprang up.

'Bloody hell! What's in it?'

'It's chilli chocolate espresso, with a dash of foam,' Ruby said, 'sorry, I should've given you the sweet option…'

'No, it's good - I like spice. And I like espresso. Just as well! That'll wake you up no problem! Wow. What's the other one?'

'Well, I thought that was maybe a bit much for some people, so I made another that's the same except instead of chilli you have mint, and instead of chocolate you have white chocolate. So, mint, white chocolate and espresso, with a dash of foam.'

'That sounds lovely.'

'Yeah, it's a bit sweet but I think it'll sell well. The important thing is because of the mint, it's still a really bold flavour. It's super minty.'

'They both pack a punch!' Gio said, pointing at the mini blackboard on the counter.

*Try our NEW coffees! All profits support the CARER CAFÉ 'STRONG STUFF' available in sweet or spicy!*

'I like the name,' said Ellen, looking at Ruby.

'Thanks,' she smiled, 'I'm proud of it.'

\*\*\*

'Look, that's your mummy, Bella. Your mummy!' Rosie said, pointing to the photograph under the headline *Special coffee break for brave young carers.* The photo showed Ruby and Gio stood outside the cafe under the 'Carer Café' poster. In front of them, sat at the table was one of their first young carer customers, with his dad. They all held up mugs in a *cheers* pose.

Bella nosed the page.

257

'We're so proud of you.' Rosie said, looking up at Ruby across the kitchen table.

Ruby smiled and carried on texting Annabelle.

'Listen, I know that this means a lot to you, and it's brilliant, but make sure you leave time for college, yeah?' Rosie said, gently, 'and yourself. You've been a bit quiet these past few days… is everything okay?'

Ruby put her phone down.

*Do I tell her the truth?*

'You can tell me anything, you know, Ruby. I won't judge you. Is it about your dad?'

Ruby shook her head.

'Is it the boy they found you with, in Newcastle?'

As soon as she heard the words, Ruby felt her body crumple in on itself, nodding, her face contorting with tears. Rosie pulled her chair up close and hugged her, rubbing her back.

'Hey, hey. Shhh. It's okay. You miss him still, after all this time?'

Ruby nodded into Rosie's shoulder, letting out a sob.

She felt Rosie sigh. She could tell she was trying to think of something reassuring to say, but Ruby knew there was nothing to be said.

'He meant a lot to you. I know that,' Rosie said, stroking Ruby's hair.

Ruby pulled away and wiped her face, sniffing, looking at the floor, nodding.

'I can't imagine how hard it must be for you, not knowing where he is, or how he's doing. But you know he's safe, don't you?'

Ruby stared out of the window, her sleeve pulled over her knuckle, resting under her nose.

'He did the right thing, Ruby. He told the police the truth. He gave evidence that helped to reduce your dad's sentencing. But-' she hesitated,'…that evidence put them in danger. Him and his mum. They had to accept the help that was offered, Ruby, they had no choice.'

'I know all that,' Ruby managed, 'it's just...it's not fair. Why do you get punished for doing the right thing? Why should they have to leave their lives and go back to the place they ran from in the first place? I remember him saying...it wasn't safe.'

'Ukraine?'

'And it's not,' Ruby added. 'Even without all the shit they were in before they left, with their family... have you seen the news recently?' Ruby shook her head, 'it's like a warzone!' She bit her nails, her face screwing up again. 'And I can't even just get a line, a word from someone- anyone - that he's okay-' Ruby accepted Rosie's embrace again, unable to do anything else.

She swayed her gently, back and forth, stroking her hair. Rosie answered her.

'You have so much to live for, so much to look forward to, right here. It hurts, but there's nothing you or I or anyone can do. You just have to trust that he's safe, and you have to move on with your own life,' she made Ruby look at her, holding her in her line of vision. Rosie's hazel eyes and the lines around them fixed Ruby's.

'You're clever, you have your whole life ahead of you, you've come through so much yet you're still here, doing amazing things. Part of life is loss. You know that. But the most important part is *living*. Because you never know when you'll be the one that's lost. You know? Your mum would want you to make the most of your life.'

'I know,' Ruby said, 'I know.'

She took some deep breaths and wiped her face with her sleeve.

'Come on. Let's go and get some escapism at the cinema, yeah?' said Rosie, rubbing Ruby's arm, 'I think there's a new film with that actor you like in it...'

Ruby agreed, managing a half-smile.

# CHAPTER 29

Message from Annabelle:

*Are you coming to Jade's party on Saturday? You never RSVP'd the Facebook invite. Pleeeeaaaaase come otherwise it's just me and all the posh kids xxx*

Ruby: *Annabelle, you're posh*

Annabelle: *No I'm not! Come on, you'll have fun…*

Ruby: *Don't know if I have time. Working this aft, college all day 2moro. Sat = work 8-4 & I have tons to do on my coursework plus that assessment Monday*

Annabelle: *What if I promise to help with your prep allll day Sunday?*

Ruby: *Go on then xxx*

Annabelle: *Yesss! I love you xxxxxxx*

Ruby put her phone away, already dreading Saturday night. She pushed the door of Gio's to get in, wondering what she would wear.

*Hang on.* She stopped. The door didn't move, it was locked and the sign turned to CLOSED. She peered through. Empty.

She knocked on the glass, 'Gio?' she called, cupping her hands round her eyes against the glass, trying to see through to the back. The door to the kitchen was closed.

*That door is always wedged open. Always. What's going on?* She decided to ring him.

As she took her phone out, she saw the door to the kitchen open, slightly.

'Gio? It's Ruby,' she said, squinting through the glass. He emerged, closing the door behind him, scanning the street behind her. He hurried to the front door, unlocking it, motioning her inside.

'Gio, what the hell is-'

'Shh!' he said, locking up behind her, 'now, I'm going upstairs, just shout up if you need anything, okay? Come with me.'

He ushered her through to the back, closing the door behind them.

'I'm just up here,' he said, pointing to the doorway that led to the stairs.

Ruby looked around, frowning. 'Gio-'

He smiled at her, pointing again, this time through to the off-shot prep room. He started up the stairs.

Ruby peered at the doorway to the prep room. It was slightly ajar. She stepped towards it. She knew the contents of the room. Fridges. Freezers. A sink, cupboards. Chopping boards. She started most shifts in there- rinsing tomatoes, grating carrots, shredding lettuce.

She smelled something familiar, like cinnamon, bittersweet, warmth.

Her stomach felt like it was twisting, her hands started to tremble.

*What the hell?*

She pushed the door.

'Leo!' she shouted.

'Shhh!' he ran over, grabbed her, kissed her. She kissed him back, tears already creeping out of the corners of her eyes, down her face and onto his hands as they held it.

'What are you doing here?' she searched his face, incredulous, 'you are here, aren't you? I'm not dreaming?'

He shook his head, smiling. She took in his face properly, for the first time since they were lying, facing each other on the Travelodge bed in Newcastle. The dark rings under his eyes and slightly sharper cheekbones were the only alterations. His hair was shorter, no longer skimming his eyelashes.

'I'm really here,' he said, wiping the back of his hand over his eyes to get rid of his tears.

'I'm so sorry,' he continued, 'for everything. They took my phone...we were held in limbo for so long before we went back.'

'To Odessa?'

He nodded.

'They offered us protection, but it would've meant living life on their terms, forever. It was either that or they would let us take our chances, in Ukraine....so that's what we chose.'

'Then why - how are you-'

'We're not going back to Ukraine. We got British citizenship. Not legally, obviously. But we got the paperwork. Listen, I have to go. Give me your number. I'm on pay-as-you-go, so-'

'So you're staying?' she asked, suddenly feeling her heart race.

He nodded.

*Oh my god.*

'In the UK, yes. But we have to start again, somewhere else. Another city, as different people.'

*Okay. Breathe. At least you got to say goodbye. You know he's okay. Just breathe. Say goodbye.*

She took in his face one more time, then kissed him.

'We have to...' he carried on, 'but I can't. Not without you. I've tried, but I just-'

She interrupted him, kissing him again, holding him so tight she knew he'd have fingerprint bruises on his

263

back and neck.

'Neither can I,' she said, finally loosening her hold, 'everyone keeps telling me to forget you and move on with my life...' she held him close, her cheek against his chest, eyes closed.

'Come with me.'

He said the words quietly, resolutely.

'What? Where? Do you even know where you're going?'

'We don't know yet,' he shrugged, 'Glasgow, maybe. We only came to Sheffield to - well, so I could see you. Look. I know you have a new life now. I know it's a big ask. But I love you, and I want to be with you –' his phone started buzzing. 'Shit. I really have to go,' he cancelled the call. 'Put your number in-' he passed her the phone. She took it and keyed in her number, fingers shaking. He called her phone, to check it worked.

Her phone buzzed and she felt the vibrations go right through her to the ground under her feet.

'My number will keep changing, but I'll never lose yours. I have Gio's, too.'

She nodded.

'We're here for one more day,' he said, holding her, 'then we have to move on.'

His phone buzzed again.

'Think about it. I have to go now, I'll wait for you to call.'

He held her face, kissing her. She breathed him in and held his hand as he stepped away, keeping his eyes on her, until their fingers separated, and he disappeared out of the back door.

\*\*\*

264

That night in her room at Rosie's, Ruby lay on the bed and stared up at the ceiling. She remembered doing the same, the night before her mum went into hospital, at Marlborough Road. The pink quilt, the candy floss curtains, the fluffy rug. The daisies on the walls. Here, she had the bedroom she'd always wanted then: mature, neutral, stylish.

Bella curled up next to her side, grizzling. She stroked her ears.

Her thoughts were like a hive of bees. Loud, clambering all over each other, flying in and out, round and round.

There were so many reasons to stay. So many things she couldn't leave. *But then...*

She closed her eyes and emptied everything from her mind, focusing on her breathing. *The happiest moment of your life. Think. When was it?* In, out. She was on top of the crags in the Peak District shouting out into the abyss, breathing the clarity in.

She opened her eyes.

'Come on, Bella. Time to go.'

More from the author:

The Raven Wheel,  SRL Publishing,
ISBN: 978-191633735-0

Author proceeds from this book will go towards
supporting the work of
Roundabout: www.roundabouthomeless.org

Roundabout is South Yorkshire's local youth housing
charity providing shelter, support and life skills to young
people like Ruby, aged 16-25 who are homeless or at risk
of homelessness.

In addition to helping young people source appropriate
accommodation, they offer wraparound care including
practical and emotional support from dedicated key
workers. Their key services deliver comprehensive
programmes of training, involvement and empowerment
which help young people break the cycle of homelessness
and develop long term independent living skills.

*Thanks to Amy for choosing to support this critical work.*

To find your local youth housing charity
visit: www.eyh.org.uk/en/